"I wish to hell I knew for sure who you are."

"I'm sorry," Jessie said. "I have no way of proving to you that I'm not my sister. We left my identification at her house. Do you suppose you could just *assume* that I'm not lying?"

Ben eyed her assessingly. "Cops don't assume, princess, not if they want to last on the streets. There *is* something you can do, though, if you're really willing to prove it."

"I am."

"Good," Ben said. "In that case, you won't get all bent out of shape when you hear what I want you to do."

She raised her eyebrows questioningly, and he dropped his gaze to her mouth.

"I want you to give me the hottest kiss you can come up with."

Dear Reader,

Once again, we're proud to bring you a lineup of irresistible books, something we seem to specialize in here at Intimate Moments. Start off your month with award-winning author Kathleen Eagle's newest American Hero title, *Defender*. In Gideon Defender you'll find a hero you'll never forget. This is one of those books that is bound to end up on "keeper" shelves all across the country.

Linda Turner completes her miniseries "The Wild West" with sister Kat's story, a sensuous treat for readers everywhere. Award-winner Dee Holmes once again demonstrates her skill at weaving together suspense and romance in *Watched*, while Amanda Stevens puts a clever twist on the ever-popular amnesia plotline in *Fade to Black*. We have another Spellbound title for you this month, a time-travel romance from Merline Lovelace called *Somewhere in Time*. Finally, welcome new writer Lydia Burke, who debuts with *The Devil and Jessie Webster*.

Coming soon—more great reading from some of the best authors in the business, including Linda Howard, whose long-awaited *Loving Evangeline* will be coming your way in December.

As always—enjoy!

Leslie J. Wainger
Senior Editor and Editorial Coordinator

Please address questions and book requests to:
Silhouette Reader Service
U.S.: 3010 Walden Ave., P.O. Box 1325, Buffalo, NY 14269
Canadian: P.O. Box 609, Fort Erie, Ont. L2A 5X3

THE DEVIL AND
JESSIE WEBSTER

Lydia
Burke

Silhouette®
INTIMATE™MOMENTS®
Published by Silhouette Books
America's Publisher of Contemporary Romance

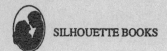 SILHOUETTE BOOKS

ISBN 0-373-07594-4

THE DEVIL AND JESSIE WEBSTER

Copyright © 1994 by Carolyn Flint

All rights reserved. Except for use in any review, the reproduction
or utilization of this work in whole or in part in any form by any
electronic, mechanical or other means, now known or hereafter
invented, including xerography, photocopying and recording, or in
any information storage or retrieval system, is forbidden without
the written permission of the editorial office, Silhouette Books,
300 East 42nd Street, New York, NY 10017 U.S.A.

All characters in this book have no existence outside the imagination of
the author and have no relation whatsoever to anyone bearing the same
name or names. They are not even distantly inspired by any individual
known or unknown to the author, and all incidents are pure invention.

This edition published by arrangement with Harlequin Enterprises B. V.

® and TM are trademarks of Harlequin Enterprises B. V., used under
license. Trademarks indicated with ® are registered in the United States
Patent and Trademark Office, the Canadian Trade Marks Office and in
other countries.

Printed in U.S.A.

LYDIA BURKE

was born in Michigan and comes from proud German stock. She grew up with her parents' marriage as a model of commitment and family values, a heritage she likes to think she and Glenn, her husband of three decades, have passed on to their own four children.

Lydia has taught high school English, operated her own word-processing business, worked as an executive assistant for a large corporation and traveled wherever her army-officer husband was sent in twenty years of military service. Today she lives in San Antonio, Texas, and is finally doing on a full-time basis what she likes best—writing.

In loving memory of my mother,
Lydia Burke Strefling
(1918-1978)

And for Glenn—thanks, honey.

Chapter 1

Jessie Webster came awake with a jerk. *What—?*

A hand clapped over her mouth. It was large, strong.

Male.

My God! Assault!

Fear froze her body, but her mind raced. Should she fight? Run? Surrender?

The man leaned close. Warm, moist breath filled her ear and Jessie trembled. He spoke in a low, quiet voice.

"Don't panic. It's me—Ben. I don't have time to explain, but there are people watching your house. You've got to get out of here."

His words were meaningless. She didn't know any Ben, and she could think of no reason for anyone to spy on her house.

Then she remembered. She was in Allie's house, Allie's bed. Alone.

As though confident his confusing explanation had calmed her, the man lifted his hand off her face."

Jessie took a shaky breath. "I don't—"

Hard fingers pressed even more tightly against her lips than before, muffling her words. "Quiet, dammit!" he whispered fiercely. "I'm trying to save your neck. Understand?"

No, she didn't understand, but Jessie nodded her head anyway. The pressure over her mouth slackened a little, and she breathed easier. The small consideration allayed some of her fear and enabled her to think more clearly.

The man—Ben—had identified himself. Rapists didn't do that, did they? Never having been in a situation like this before, Jessie didn't know.

"Okay," Ben said. "I'm going to take my hand away, but you've got to keep your mouth shut. Got it?"

Again Jessie nodded. True to his word, Ben withdrew his hand, taking with it the fragrance of spring-scented soap.

The moment she was free, Jessie clutched the covers to her throat and sat up, scooting as far away from him as possible. Even as her eyes grew accustomed to the darkness, she could see little more than a squat shadow next to the bed. Either the man was kneeling on the floor or he was a midget.

A low chuckle rumbled from the shadow's direction. "You weren't so standoffish a few nights ago."

His deep voice sent shivers across Jessie's skin, a reaction she ignored. Clearly he had mistaken her for her flamboyant twin. Evidently he didn't know any more about where Allie was tonight than Jessie herself.

Ben's first cryptic words came back to her. Why would someone be watching her sister's house?

"What's going on?" she demanded in a loud whisper.

"Shh! Keep it down! I told you, there's no *time* for explanations."

"Oh, I see. But there *is* time for you to make suggestive remarks, isn't there?" Jessie countered, though not so loudly as before. "I repeat, *what's going on?*"

"Oh, for—" Ben exhaled impatiently and leaned on the bed, crossing his arms on the exposed bottom sheet. The bed dipped, and Jessie saw the stark outline of his elbows against the white background. She could feel his eyes peering at her across the mattress and for a split second wondered whether she should try to make a run for it. But, no—if he intended to harm her, he wouldn't have released her in the first place.

"Listen," he said. "I'm only pretending to be a bouncer at the club. I'm really a cop, okay? And my partner just found out Mai thinks you're a reporter and doesn't much like the idea that you've been snooping around Club Duan. She or somebody worse has a couple of enforcer types posted outside in a Chevy. God only knows what their orders are. You're better off not finding out. *That's* why you've got to leave with me—now, before they make their move."

Caught in the low, compelling tone of his voice, Jessie was hardly aware of what the man was saying until he stopped talking. Then, his warning—a warning meant for Allie—penetrated.

Allie should have been here to greet Jessie after her long drive from Chicago to Port Mangus, Wisconsin. They'd planned to spend Thanksgiving together. But when her sister hadn't answered the door, Jessie had simply clicked her tongue and dug out the key Allie had given her the day they'd moved her into this place. Her twin had a history of ignoring prior arrangements if something "more important" came up.

Now it occurred to Jessie that maybe Allie's no-show wasn't due to her typical impulsiveness.

Nothing Ben had said made any sense to her, except the part about Allie being a reporter. The rest of it didn't jibe with the breezy news she'd heard from her sister during their weekly phone calls. Allie certainly hadn't mentioned a "Ben." Or any other man in particular, other than her boss and a few coworkers at the newspaper office. Since taking the new job in Sheboygan two months ago, she had been preoccupied with pursuing professional success, not dating. And she'd said nothing at all about a nightclub.

Ben's warning shaded Allie's absence with ominous overtones. Could the "enforcers" outside have already made their move? If they had, they wouldn't still be outside, would they? Of course, Jessie only had Ben's word for it that they *were* out there.

"How do I know you're a cop?" she asked suspiciously.

"I was afraid of this," he muttered. "Look, Angela, this isn't a trap, believe me. I really *don't* work for Mai. I'd show you my badge if I had it, but a cop under cover can't chance—"

"Did you say *Angela?*" Giddy relief poured through Jessie's body. "You've made a mistake, Ben. There's no Angela living here. You've come to the wrong house. How *did* you get in here, anyway? I'm sure I locked the doors.''

In the darkness, Jessie sensed Ben's sudden stillness, brought on, she guessed, by the realization he'd sneaked into the bedroom of the wrong woman. No point now explaining that she didn't live here. Why bother informing him that he didn't even have the right wrong woman? He had enough troubles.

''Maybe you should try next door,'' she suggested kindly. ''I'm sure there's still time—''

''Shut up!'' Ben hissed. ''Let me think a minute!''

''I only thought—''

''Shut up!''

Jessie closed her lips tightly. This man had been barking orders—okay, whispering, but the effect was the same—ever since he'd appeared, uninvited, in her sister's bedroom. He sounded altogether too much like her *mucho macho* ex-husband Antonio. Jessie had squirmed out from under that thumb years ago, and she'd vowed to never again become entangled with a dictatorial man.

Of course, he was on a mission to save some luckless woman named Angela—not Allie, thank God—and he'd obviously screwed up. Jessie had found herself in that position often enough to feel some kinship. She supposed she could tolerate his high-handedness while he figured out what he should do next.

She'd probably never see him again, anyway. Not that she'd recognize him if she did, given that in the middle of a moonless night in an unlit room, she couldn't make out so much as the color of his hair. Though maybe, if he talked softly in that sexy voice, she might know who he was....

''Is there a window in the bathroom?''

Jessie jumped. ''What?''

''I said, is there a window in the bathroom?''

''Oh,'' she said, believing he meant to find an escape route. ''No, I don't think so, but why don't you—''

''You don't *think* so! For crying out loud, woman, it's your bathroom, isn't it?''

Jessie had just about reached the end of her patience. ''As I was about to say, why don't you leave the same way you came in? You obviously weren't seen, so it should be safe.''

"I don't...want...to leave...yet." The terse way Ben spaced the whispered words made her think his teeth must be pressed tightly together.

"Then what—"

"Look, I can't see in the dark. I need you to lead me to the bathroom."

"Why? Are you sick or something?" Jessie left her protective covers behind and moved closer to where he knelt beside the bed. "No, I'm not sick, you little— Give me your hand!"

Ben made a grab toward her in the dark. His fingers missed her hand entirely and took a firm hold of her left breast, which was covered with loose flannel. And nothing else.

She gasped at the intimate contact, and Ben froze.

Jessie managed to recover first.

"Here." She grasped his hand and moved it away from her body. Her breast tingled, the imprint of his fingers leaving a heated memory on her skin.

Disconcerted, she swung her legs over the edge of the bed and got to her feet. Then the shadow that was Ben untucked itself from its crouching position and stood up.

And up...and up.

Jessie stared and swallowed when he had finally unfolded to his full height. Compared to her measly five-four, Ben was a giant.

He turned his hand so they were connected palm to palm. "The bathroom?" he reminded her.

"Um, over here." She had to feel her way, since she wasn't that familiar with Allie's house herself. Ben followed silently.

"There. Straight ahead," she said when she'd located the doorway. But instead of going in alone, he hauled her inside behind him and closed the door.

"Stay here," he said, still whispering.

She heard him fumbling around in a darkness more engulfing than that in the bedroom. He moved the shower curtain slightly and seemed to be patting the walls. Then he ran into something—the toilet, Jessie guessed—and cursed under his breath. The medicine chest opened and clicked closed again.

"What are you doing?" she finally asked.

"Checking for a window," was the brief response. "Okay, there isn't one. Turn on the light so I can see who you are."

With constrained patience, Jessie ignored the fact that she'd just received another order. At least now he'd know he'd made a mistake. She groped on the wall for the switch, closed her eyes and braced herself for the sudden white glare behind her eyelids. Then she blinked, and the man in front of her came into focus.

He was big, all right, several inches over six feet. But it wasn't his size that caught her attention. For some reason, maybe because of the earlier reminder of her ex-husband, Jessie had expected Ben to look more like Antonio, darkly handsome and full of arrogance. She saw immediately that there was no resemblance at all.

Ben's face was ruggedly masculine, the crooked nose and wide mouth decrying conventional good looks. His gold-flecked green eyes were compelling, well spaced and tipped slightly downward at the outside corners. Their gentle tilt balanced his stubborn, beard-roughened jaw and kept him from looking too tough, as did the fine lines etched around his eyes and mouth. Thick hair the rich, lustrous brown of coffee beans fell carelessly across his brow, gleaming under the overhead light.

But the biggest surprise of all was his complexion, abundantly awash with pale freckles from his forehead to the open vee of his collar. *And beyond?* Jessie wondered.

How odd that she'd always associated freckles with youth and immaturity. There was nothing boyish about Ben's face. Jessie found his craggy features and speckled skin appealing, far more attractive than Antonio's dark perfection.

"I never would have figured you for flannel."

His husky observation brought with it the realization that Ben's interested eyes were riveted on her body—in particular, on the conspicuous swell of her breasts under the granny gown she wore. She fought the impulse to cross her arms over her chest. She was decently covered from throat to toes, after all. *And you know that he knows how naked you are under there,* a little voice mocked.

Ben loomed over her in the confining space, reminding her of his formidable dimensions. His shoulders, garbed in a worn brown leather jacket, stretched from wall to wall. Or maybe it just seemed that way because he stood with his hands in his back pockets, pulling the jacket open over an impressive chest. The rest of him was narrow by contrast—flat stomach, trim hips and slim, long-legged jeans that subtly delineated the masculine bulge slightly to the right of his zipper.

He reached out and caught a lock of her hair between his fingers. The action startled Jessie, and she stepped back, abruptly conscious of the inappropriate drift of her thoughts. Sternly she ordered her mind back to her potential peril.

"You've cut your hair," Ben said.

Jessie's hope that the light would show him his error disintegrated with those words. He hadn't come to the wrong house, after all. He recognized her, or thought he did. Otherwise, he wouldn't have zeroed in on the hairdo. Allie wore her hair long, loose and sexily tousled, a style for which Jessie had neither the time nor the inclination. Her own unruly locks were cut short, the curls tamed each morning in five minutes with a blow dryer. The result wasn't glamorous, but it suited her.

"I'm not who you think I am," she told Ben, thinking it was time she set him straight.

Ben's eyes narrowed. "So you really *are* a reporter."

"No, *Allie's* the reporter. I'm a novelist."

"Allie?"

"My sister. We're identical twins. It's not often anymore that we're mistaken for each other, but—"

"You have a sister."

"Yes, I just said that."

Ben stared at her suspiciously. "And her name is Allie."

"Yes. Short for Alicia. I'm Jessie."

"And you're twins."

"Yes."

"Bull."

Jessie stiffened. "I beg your pardon."

"Oh, you're good, I'll grant you that. A real chameleon. I would never have guessed there was a hotshot reporter behind that wide-eyed come-on. But you're not as dumb as you pretend to be, are you, *Angela?*"

"Now wait a minute—"

Ben planted his nose two inches from hers and whispered vehemently. "No, *you* wait a minute. I've already wasted too much time trying to talk sense to you. Maybe you don't think it means anything that there are two damned shifty-looking characters outside watching this place. Believe me, they aren't there to check out the nice neighborhood. They're after *you.*''

Jessie tried again. "No, they're not. I don't know why, but it must be Allie they're after. If you'd just listen—''

Ben grabbed her shoulders and gave them a slight shake. "Look, it's *over,* sweetheart. It doesn't matter anymore if you're a reporter or a waitress in a strip joint or twins or even triplets. Now, unless you want to stick around to find out whether you're marked for just a friendly warning or for something more permanent, you'll get the hell out of here.''

"Ooh!" Jessie squeezed her eyes shut, her voice hushed but furious. Bringing her fists up between his arms, she knocked his hands from her shoulders and glared at him. "You are the most exasperating, thickheaded man! If you would only listen—''

Ben *wasn't* listening, she realized, at least not to her. Suddenly his body was taut with attention as he focused on the door behind her.

"What?" she demanded.

He touched a cautioning finger to his lips. "Shh.''

Jessie sensed his urgency and was instantly silent. Ben cocked his head intently. She held her breath, forgetting her irritation.

He must have heard something else then, because the next thing she knew, he had switched places with her, his ear was pressed to the door and, poised in his hand—barrel up, as though it were perfectly at home there—was an ugly snub-nosed pistol!

She gasped, and Ben turned his head just enough to look at her. He pursed his lips and said "shh" again, very softly. With his free hand, he reached over and turned out the light.

The darkness was sudden and blacker than before. What—whom—had he heard? Jessie listened, straining hard. At length the silence became a roar inside her head and it felt almost as though her ears were getting bigger. The palpable, throbbing tension in the small bathroom stretched at her nerves until she thought they might snap like an overstressed rubber band. For a crazy minute, she was tempted to shout, "Here we are!" just to put an end to the horror of not knowing what was happening on the other side of that closed door.

But Ben's solid presence gave her control. He was a police officer, or so he'd said, and the existence of the gun he held was distinct evidence. Not that policemen were the only people to carry guns, of course. But Ben hadn't hurt her when she was sleeping and vulnerable, and Jessie preferred to believe he was one of the good guys.

In fact, she told herself, being an officer of the law, he was probably used to situations like this. When it was over and good had triumphed over evil, he'd probably just blow the smoke from the barrel of his pistol, shrug and say, "Piece of cake," or some such. She was silly to be afraid.

Even so, she couldn't forget what he had implied might happen if those men got hold of her, thinking she was her twin sister.

Now if she were the heroine in one of her books, she wouldn't be standing here depending on the hero to get her out of trouble. She would be self-sufficient, assertive and extremely resourceful. By now she would have come up with a brilliant plan that would have trapped the hoodlums and left both the admiring hero *and* her unscathed, or, in extreme cases, with one or the other of them sustaining a minor injury that wouldn't interfere too much with the love scene to follow.

Jessie was far more suited to choreographing love scenes than contemplating impending doom, and she latched onto the welcome distraction of her thoughts. She could easily visualize a muscular, Ben-like hero with a stab wound in his shoulder—or thigh?—receiving, as he lay back against the pillows, the erotic attentions of his tenderly passionate lover. Who, coincidentally, bore a striking resemblance to Jessie herself. But the vision faded when she heard a muffled curse. A gravelly voice, muted by the barrier of the bathroom door, said, "She ain't here."

Someone was in the bedroom!

The fear Jessie had pushed aside with her fantasy rolled over her again in double measure. Automatically she groped for Ben in the dark, found the smooth leather of his jacket and, trembling, moved closer to his big, warm body. His arm stole around her, pulling her tightly against him. The gesture heartened her and she burrowed in gratefully, conscious of the reassuring bulk of his muscles. His was a strength to be reckoned with.

Then, in a surprise move, Ben hooked his wrist around her neck and clamped his hand firmly over her mouth again, pressing her head to his chest. Jessie struggled briefly, but he tightened his arm against her shoulders.

Why, he wasn't comforting her at all! In a typical show of male dominance, he was using his superior physical strength to prevent her from making noise and alerting whoever was in the next room! As though she didn't have enough sense to keep her mouth shut without his help, she thought indignantly.

The rumble of a second voice in the bedroom made her forget her disenchantment with Ben. Gooseflesh slithered over her skin. The two men out there must be the pair Ben had warned her about earlier. What they planned for the occupant of the now-empty bed didn't bear considering, and their loud voices made the prospects seem all the more threatening. Didn't they care that they might be overheard and later identified?

On the other hand, maybe that was a good sign. It could mean they thought no one else was here. Jessie strained to hear their conversation. Unfortunately, she couldn't make out the words over the pounding of Ben's heart; only the definite distinction between the two separate voices was clear.

She wished she knew what were they saying. If she and Ben were about to be discovered, if one of the men even touched the bathroom doorknob, she didn't know what she would do.

Pa-pum, pa-pum, pa-pum, went Ben's heart, and Jessie suddenly realized it was racing almost as fast as her own. Which could only mean that he was no more composed about their desperate situation than she was, in spite of his formidable height and brawn, not to mention that gun in his hand. His whole body, in fact, was stiff with tension.

Maybe, Jessie thought, she was foolish to place her confidence in him. After all, she'd only known him for what, thirty minutes? Three hours? How long *had* it been, anyway, since she'd first been awakened by the hand that was once again half smothering her?

Then again, what difference did it make? She ought to be applying her mental energy to finding a way out of this mess. Her last heroine, Sydney, hadn't wasted precious time wondering how long she'd been trapped in her father's warehouse. No, she'd reasoned calmly and constructively and then saved the day by coming up with a couple of gas masks and a canister of tear gas from a long-forgotten storage compartment.

Jessie gathered her wits and tried to reason calmly and constructively, mentally surveying the contents of the tiny bathroom. It was no good. All she could think of was razor blades, and it wasn't likely that Allie's, outfitted as they were with pink plastic handles, would be of much use.

Where was a handy bit of tear gas when you needed it?

Just when Jessie was beginning to feel the ordeal would never be over, Ben took a deep breath and his body relaxed. He moved his hand to the back of her neck and said, "I think they're gone."

Jessie sagged against him in relief. "Oh, thank God."

"Are you okay?"

She nodded her head where it still lay on his chest. She should move, she knew, now that the danger seemed to be over, but suddenly she felt exhausted. She hadn't realized that terror took so much energy. And Ben felt solid and warm, like a protective haven.

He smelled nice, too. Jessie thought he must have showered not long ago, because the same fragrance of soap she'd noticed earlier on his fingers teased her nose through the fabric of his shirt. It blended subtly with another, more earthy smell, musky and masculine, no doubt the result of him so recently sweating out their harrowing experience. It wasn't at all unpleasant. In fact, she found it almost . . . arousing.

"You sure you're all right?" Ben's fingers moved gently on the sensitive skin at the side of her neck.

It was then she realized her arms were twined around his waist under his jacket. She felt the heat of his body permeating her unbound breasts, which at the moment were pillowed against his rib cage. In a nearly imperceptible move, his hips nudged her abdomen.

Jessie raised her head in alarm. Good Lord! She was clinging to him like a baby chimpanzee!

Quickly she disentangled herself. It was a good thing the light was still out; at least Ben couldn't see how flustered she was.

Instinctively she attempted to hide behind a mask of irritation.

"Yes, I'm fine, now that I can move again and my jaw is no longer in traction. What was the big idea, anyway?"

"You were scared," Ben answered evenly. "For all I knew, you were about to have a fit of the screaming meemies. I had to be sure you wouldn't give us away."

"I assure you, I've never had a *fit* of anything in my life. I'm not a child, nor am I stupid." Anger felt good after the unsettling chagrin of moments ago.

"Well, la-di-da, little princess. Pardon me for saving your rear end. Maybe you'd have preferred it if those two bozos had found you in your bed, snoring sweetly on your lacy feather pillow."

"I don't snore!" she replied, stung by his scorn. She supposed she *was* being ungracious, but for now the emotional buffer she'd erected seemed more important than good manners. "Anyway, what happened? Did you hear what they were saying? *I* couldn't hear a thing, thanks to you. Why did they leave?"

"*Thanks to me,* they saw the open window in the other room where I came in and thought you had sneaked out. They were afraid you might have gone to a neighbor's and called the cops. So they took a quick look around the bedroom to be sure you weren't under the bed or hiding in the closet, and then took off. We're just lucky they were in too much of a hurry to check out the bathroom. Where, *thanks to me* again, you were safely tucked away."

His sarcasm banished any gratitude Jessie might have felt. "You had a gun, and you said you're a policeman," she shot back. "Why did you let them go? Why didn't you arrest them?"

Ben swore so bracingly in response to that, Jessie cringed.

"Look, *princess,*" he snarled. "While I'd love to hang around and soak up all this appreciation, there isn't time. For all we know, those guys are hiding in the bushes outside, waiting for you. And even if they're not, eventually they're going to make a return trip to take care of whatever business they came for in the first place. Which means you can't stay here. Though why in hell I should give a damn, I don't know."

His derision smarted. Still, Jessie conceded he had a point. It was unreasonable to stand around arguing when her very life could be at stake. What in the world had Allie gotten her into? Why did it have to be *this* man she was dependent upon to get her out of it?

"Okay, you're right," she said grudgingly.

"Well, glory be! She admits I'm right!" Ben declared to an imaginary third person. Then, to Jessie, he said, "Angela, baby, that's worthy of a headline in your precious newspaper."

Jessie heaved an exasperated sigh. "Look, you big ignoramus, try to get it through your head that my name is *Jessie.* Now I agree we need to get out of this house, so why don't we quit sniping at each other and just leave, okay?"

"At last!" came the sneering response.

Jessie managed to squelch the impulse to have the last word. "How are we going to do this? I assume we can't just walk out the front door."

Ben didn't answer right away, and she wondered whether he would accept the belligerent truce she was offering.

"Maybe we can," he said finally. His voice, while not exactly friendly, was at least neutral. "First I'll have to sneak outside to see if their car's still there. While I'm gone, you get dressed. We'll decide what to do after that."

He was still uttering peremptory commands, but Jessie settled for making a face at him, knowing he wouldn't see the small rebellion in the surrounding darkness. It wouldn't do any good to antagonize him again. Besides, he'd said *"we'll* decide." That placated her in a small measure. They were in this together, after all. So rather than objecting to his arrogant assumption that she would do exactly as she was ordered, she told him, "Be careful."

But all she received for her expression of concern was a brisk, "Don't turn on any lights."

She heard a rustle of clothing and the soft slide of metal as he opened the bathroom door. In the next moment, she was alone.

Mai Duan drummed long, elegant red nails on the desk blotter in the secret room behind the marina. For the moment unmindful of the incongruity of her exotic, well-tended beauty in these dingy surroundings, she waited impatiently for word from her men that their errand had been successful.

Never before had she had occasion to give them an assignment such as the one she'd given them tonight. Neither of the men had killed before, and they had been less than enthusiastic at the prospect. But in the end, their greed had won over their dubious ethics.

As distasteful as she would have found the task, Mai would have done the deed herself if they had refused. Angela West's removal was necessary. Everything, all that Mai had gained in the years since she'd escaped Vietnam with nothing but a will to survive, hung in the balance. She could not—*would* not—start over again.

Rage battled with desperation in Mai's almond-shaped eyes as she thought of the viper who had crept into her very bosom and betrayed her. Angela West.

No, not Angela West. The deceiver's true name was Alicia Webster. Only hours ago Mai had learned that the managing editor of the Sheboygan daily newspaper employed the impostor as a staff reporter. The editor himself, a frequent patron of Club Duan, who enjoyed all the services Mai offered, had recognized the cocktail waitress three days ago in the club. Unfortunately, he had been so anxious not to be recognized in return, he had fled.

Damn the man. Not until tonight had he sneaked into Mai's office with his suspicions that the woman was not merely moonlighting but was, in fact, investigating Mai in hopes of getting a newspaper story. The warning had come too late to prevent the theft that could ruin Mai's life.

"Bitch," Mai muttered, her red lips twisting in distaste. Alicia Webster had charmed everyone, Mai most of all, with her false simplicity. She had made a fool of Mai, caused her to lose face.

Tonight the conniver would pay for her treachery.

Even then it would not be over. Mai had told her men only that the woman was a reporter; she hadn't mentioned the missing journal. Nor had she mentioned it to the powerful man in Chicago whom she'd awakened with her call earlier tonight. She hadn't dared.

But once the Webster witch was out of the way, there would be time for Mai to locate the journal herself. She *must* locate it, before her ruthless associate discovered its existence. If she did not, the meticulous records she had kept for her own protection against him would become her death warrant.

Chapter 2

Jessie groped her way into the bedroom and followed the wall to her suitcase, where she'd left the underwear, jeans and fisherman's sweater she'd worn the day before. She slipped out of her nightgown, recalling her belief when she'd dressed for bed last night that her sister would be home in the morning. Now she didn't know what to think.

Where could her reckless twin be? Allie couldn't have known about the danger that would come creeping in the night, or she would have warned Jessie somehow. Of course, it was possible she'd tried and failed. Tired from the trip and the accumulation of too many late-night hours finishing her book, Jessie supposed she might have slept through a ringing phone.

She shuddered when she considered what could have happened if Ben hadn't come. She was grateful to him, maddening though he was.

Jessie dressed hurriedly. Thank goodness she hadn't unpacked anything but her nightgown and toiletries. Her getaway would be effected that much quicker.

Getaway. She could hardly believe she was thinking in such terms. This whole situation was preposterous, like something out of one of her novels. Except Jessie was finding that she preferred dreaming up danger and intrigue to living it. Whatever she was made of, it was not the quick-thinking, gutsy stuff of her heroines.

Now Ben as a hero, on the other hand—well, she hadn't made up her mind about that yet. She liked her leading men to have sensitivity, as well as strength, and Ben was about as sensitive as a water buffalo.

Jessie crossed the dark room carefully, and when she bumped into the bed, she dropped to her knees to find her shoes and socks. After a good bit of fumbling around, she located both socks, but only one of her high-top leather shoes. Great. With all the traffic in here tonight, its mate could be anywhere. Jessie began searching the carpet with sweeping hands, her brain drifting back to the book-worthy aspects of her current predicament.

Mystery, mistaken identity, unknown, sinister attackers—it had all the ingredients of a gripping adventure. Her writer's mind began probing it for weaknesses. There were always some. A writer had to be careful not to overlook the obvious but uninteresting solutions to her characters' dilemmas. If she didn't root them out and dispose of them, she could find herself with an unbelievable story or even no story at all.

Jessie wished she could come up with such a solution right now. This was one plot she wouldn't mind relegating to the scrap heap.

Her search for the elusive shoe was interrupted by Ben's low-pitched summons at the bedroom door. She scrambled to her feet to let him in.

"They're out in their car, still watching," he said without preamble.

"Oh, no. Why didn't they leave?"

"Probably because they didn't hear any sirens. And since it's not likely they're going to, we'll have to hurry, before they decide to come back in. Are you dressed?"

"All but shoes. I can't find one of them. Can you help me look?"

"We don't have time. It'll be daylight soon. Get a different pair."

Jessie thought about the meager contents of her suitcase. "The only other ones I have are dress shoes with heels."

"You've got to be kidding."

"I wouldn't kid at a time like this. Help me look, will you? This isn't easy in the dark, you know."

"Jeez, what *else* can go wrong? You are a damned troublesome female, you know that?"

"Me. It's not *my* fault. I put both shoes side by side, very neatly, right by the bed. If you and those other guys hadn't been tromping around in here, they'd still be there."

Ben breathed a long-suffering martyr's sigh. "Did you look *under* the bed?"

"Of course I did. But my arms couldn't reach very far."

He moved away, grumbling, and Jessie heard him rummaging around in the vicinity of the bed. "If it's not under here," he said to her, "you'll have to go in your socks. You *do* have socks on?"

"Not yet, but it'll only take a minute."

"If she hasn't lost them, too," he muttered.

"I heard that. I have them right here," Jessie retorted, thankful she'd had the presence of mind to hang on to each item as she'd located it.

She sat down on the floor and quickly slipped on both socks and the single shoe she'd found. She had already tied the lace and was fastening the ankle buckle when Ben said, "Here it is."

Good, Jessie thought. She wasn't relishing walking around with only one shoe. She'd be darned, however, if she would thank him.

"Where are you?" he groused.

"Over here, Mr. Sunshine."

She heard him moving toward her. "Where, dammit?"

"Right here!"

His hand brushed, then grasped, her shoulder, and the shoe dropped into her lap.

"Thank you," Jessie said before she could catch herself.

"Hurry up. I don't know how much time we have before those turkeys decide to try again."

She gritted her teeth and summoned her by now frazzled patience. "You know, Ben, I've been thinking—"

"Don't think, princess. Just get that shoe on so we can get moving."

"I'm *getting* it on, and I'm not your *princess*. I just wanted to—"

"Is it on?"

"I'm *tying* it!" If he interrupted her one more time, Jessie thought, she wouldn't be responsible. "Listen to me, will you? I think you should call for backup or whatever you police guys do, since that's what those men were afraid of in the first place. One way or another, it could solve all our problems."

Not the least of which, she added mentally, was getting this aggravating man out of her life.

"Good idea. Too bad it won't work. The phone's dead. I suspect our friends outside cut the line before coming in. Aren't you ready yet?"

"*Yes,*" she snapped, getting to her feet. "What are we going to do, if we can't call the police? How are we supposed to get out of here without those men seeing us?"

"If you can move your butt before the sun comes up, we can leave through the window where I came in. You'll need a coat. It's freezing out there."

"I left it in the hall closet. Is it okay if I move my butt out there to get it?" Jessie could be sarcastic, too, when the situation called for it.

"Get the damned coat."

She left the bedroom with Ben right behind her. Without light, she had to walk carefully, but she made her way through the living room to Allie's tiny foyer without tripping over anything. She opened the closet door and retrieved her heavy parka.

"Got it," she whispered.

"Put it on," Ben whispered back.

Jessie grimaced but followed his instructions. If it hadn't been so important to keep quiet, she would have let him know precisely how she felt about overbearing men. As soon as they were out of this, Ben's ears would peel like a bad sunburn from the blistering she would mete out. She zipped the parka viciously.

"Let's go," Ben said. "Stay close to me."

"Wait." Jessie found his leather-covered arm and restrained him. "What about my purse and clothes? My car?"

The muscles in Ben's forearm bunched under her hand. "God Almighty. Your purse. To *hell* with that and your clothes and your car, too. You'll be lucky to get out of here with your damned skin. Hell, I might murder you myself before this is over. Now, are you coming, or not?"

"Okay, okay." Jessie realized she had pushed him far enough. She'd worry about her belongings later.

"Come on." Ben took her elbow and guided her across the room to the open window, where she could feel the penetrating chill of the cold winter wind through the denim of her jeans. Her sister's house was on a street without lights, but Jessie could just make out the lines of the roof next door against the sky. It would soon be dawn. Ben had been right to worry.

He climbed out the window and reached up to help her. It was probably not deliberate that the hands he slipped under her arms pressed the sides of her breasts as he pulled her out of the house; most likely he hadn't even noticed through her thick parka. But Jessie felt it. And her nipples, oblivious to the danger of the moment, tightened in response. She shivered, not entirely because of the cold. Apparently her mind's rejection of Ben's imperious treatment mattered not a whit to her traitorous body.

When she was standing on the frozen ground, Ben took her hand and, keeping low, headed for the blackness of a row of bushes at the edge of the yard. Visibility was better out here, not only because of the advancing daylight, but because several homes on the street had outdoor lights. Which made their flight all the more precarious. At least there was no snow on the ground to further illuminate their escape. Thank God for this year's mild winter.

Ben led her through the yard behind Allie's to the sidewalk lining the street beyond. There he straightened and broke into a run, pulling Jessie after him. They ran for a couple of blocks, then cut back across unfenced lawns until they came out on what had to be her sister's street again.

Breathless from the run, Jessie was about to ask Ben to slow down, when she saw they were headed toward a car parked by the curb. There, finally, he stopped and dropped her hand. While she leaned against a fender to press a palm to her heart, he pulled keys out of his pocket and unlocked the passenger door, scanning the area as his hands worked. His breath pierced the frosty air in long, dragonlike puffs. His grim features, Jessie realized, were nearly discernible in the cold, gray light of the approaching dawn.

Ben opened the door for her and hurried around the hood of the car. Jessie scooted inside, closed the door and leaned across the seat to pull up the lock on the driver's side before he could insert the key, thinking she'd save him some time. But she found the inside locking mechanism in this car was located somewhere other than on the window panel. Then his door opened, and Ben was carping at her again.

"What are you doing, taking a nap? Move over, dammit."

"Well, excuse me for trying to help!" she fired back, sitting up straight and reaching for the shoulder harness.

It was remarkable how much scorn the man could dish out without raising his voice. If she were the type to be intimidated, by now she would have been beaten flat under his pulverizing onslaught.

But Jessie Webster was no man's whipping post. Not anymore.

Ben made no answering salvo as he settled behind the wheel and started the engine. Jessie sat back, and with the danger less immediate now, looked around. The road curved a block or so ahead, and Allie's house could not be seen. Neither was there any sign of the Chevy or its villainous occupants. Except for herself and Ben, this portion of the street was reassuringly deserted. Even so, Ben backed into a driveway and pointed the car in the opposite direction before turning on the headlights.

"Where are we going?"

He looked at her briefly and ran a hand through his hair. It was a tired, vulnerable gesture, curiously at odds with the confident, take-charge behavior he'd demonstrated so far.

"Now we find a safe place with a phone." For the first time he spoke without whispering. His voice was deep and mellow, perfectly suited to his large frame. "Then," he went on, "since I haven't had any sleep in thirty-six hours, a cup of coffee. After that, you tell me."

She frowned. "Tell you what?"

"Have you got someplace you can stay till this blows over? I don't think I can offer you police protection. The Port Mangus P.D. isn't that big."

Jessie was confused by the enigmatic words. Stay? Until *what* blows over? Police—? *Police protection!*

She gasped as a horrifying thought struck her. "My God! What about Allie?"

Either the woman was a hell of an actress, Ben thought as he headed the car out of town, or the unlikely story that she was Angela's—Allie's—twin was the truth. He was nearly convinced that the worry in those dark blue eyes was real. Then again, maybe she had just remembered that the role she was playing called for some sisterly concern for her fictitious clone.

Either way, he could no longer doubt that the woman he knew as Angela was a reporter. Which was all he needed. It wasn't bad enough that he'd run into one roadblock after another on this tedious assignment. Now there was the risk that a reporter who might have sniffed out Mai's connection to prostitution, drugs and organized crime could blow the whole operation by going to print too soon. If the operation was even salvageable anymore, that is. And if said reporter didn't get both herself and Ben killed first.

He was wary of the woman's story. He knew newshounds who placed more importance on the public's right to know than the critical confidentiality of a police investigation. This woman could be hiding her real identity, either to protect her story until it got into print or to trick Ben into giving her more information. Hell, she'd already succeeded in fooling him for more than three weeks. Ben wasn't about to be reeled in any further.

It was embarrassing to think how thoroughly he'd been duped. He hadn't suspected "Angela's" real occupation, because she fit the role of heart-of-gold cocktail waitress to a tee. She'd come off as friendly, flirtatious and a little bit dumb. Put that together with wild auburn hair, bedroom eyes and an overly endowed chest quivering like firm Jell-O over the top of her scanty uniform, and the last thing you'd imagine was that the woman was an investigative reporter.

Ben thought back to the last time he'd seen her as Angela. Several nights ago she had claimed car trouble and he'd given her a lift home. Though he'd declined her offer to come in for a drink, he hadn't objected when she'd kissed him good-night at her door. At the time he'd thought she was a sexy armful but not really his type, so he'd tried to let her down easy. Now he realized she'd probably been hoping to grill him about the club. It was no small feat to so completely deceive a master deceiver like Ben.

"What if she comes home and those men are waiting for her?" Angela/Allie/Jessie was saying. "We've got to warn her!"

Ben glanced over and found his skepticism faltering at the anxious look on her face. Maybe she was who she alleged, and her fears that something might happen to her sister were honest.

Still, the sting of having bought Angela's previous deception wouldn't let him give up his doubts.

"There's nothing we can do about it right now," he told her gruffly. "Anyway, I have the feeling that Allie, if she exists at all, will manage to find a way out of any trouble she may get into."

"*She exists,* I'm telling you. God, you're infuriating!" She slumped back in the seat and started chewing on her lower lip, apparently unwilling to talk further. That was okay with Ben. He wasn't in the mood for more arguments, either.

He took the southern lake route out of town, avoiding the well-traveled expressway he normally used to reach Sheboygan, which was less than ten miles from Port Mangus. On his left, Lake Michigan stretched to the horizon, calm and majestically beautiful with the sun rising over the water. But Ben gave the splendorous scenery only passing notice.

Instead he appraised his passenger as he drove, making comparisons. The hair was shorter, of course, but people got haircuts all the time, so that didn't prove a thing. Ben liked the new style better. It was still mussed from her pillow. Rather than detracting from her features, the unruly reddish brown strands highlighted the delicacy of her face.

That face. Though he'd caught her in the middle of the night with no makeup, it was clear she had the same high cheekbones, straight, finely etched nose and luscious mouth as "Angela." But somehow, without the feminine war paint, the effect was sensually elegant rather than blatantly seductive. He couldn't help noticing that even without mascara, her lashes were long and slightly curved, forming a thick, feathery fringe around her eyes. They'd probably feel soft against a man's lips, were he to brush kisses across her closed eyelids. Unbidden, the fantasy crept into Ben's brain, in seconds embellished to include naked bodies and the memory of his hand reaching out to encounter a soft, warm breast.

He kept his face impassive and pinned his eyes on the road so the woman riding next to him couldn't guess his wayward thoughts.

Hell, the lady *could* be telling the truth. God knows he'd never reacted this way to the scheming "Angela." Even in the middle of a hot kiss designed to burn him all the way to his toenails, his mind had been less on the woman in his arms than on forming an excuse to stay out of her bed.

No, the chemistry he felt pulling at him now hadn't kicked in until this morning. Being so close to her back there in the bathroom, with her sweet female smell filling his head and her opulent curves pressing against him—well, she had been damned distracting. At least, until she'd opened her mouth. Then she'd been just plain aggravating.

Come to think of it, the aggravation, too, was new. "Angela" hadn't annoyed him before; beyond amusement at her air-headedness, she hadn't made enough of an impact on him to arouse *any* significant emotions.

On the outskirts of Sheboygan, Ben pulled into an unpaved parking lot. He glanced at his passenger when he stopped and saw that she was still gnawing on that lip, bundled to her chin in her bulky blue jacket, apparently deep in thought. Familiar, he reflected, yet different.

She sat up straight when he turned off the engine and unfastened his seat belt. "The Piney Woods Motel? What are we doing here?"

He ignored her question, determined to clear up the issue of her identity once and for all. "So how come, princess, if you never saw me before today," he asked, casually propping his hand against her headrest, "you're not scared right now?"

"What?" Her dark blue eyes widened.

"I mean, I'm a stranger to you, right?"

"Oh, no." She shrank into the corner of her seat. "You mean you're *not* a cop?"

Ben saw the flash of fear in her face and cursed. "Stop looking at me as though I have *Hit Man* tattooed on my forehead."

He took back the hand he'd placed by her head and rubbed it wearily over his face. God, he was tired. "If I were a crook, don't you think I would have done something to you already? I'm a cop, believe me. And right now you're fouling up my assignment big time. I wish to hell I knew for sure who you are."

She was apparently reassured by his frustration. "I'm sorry," she said quietly. "I have no way of proving to you that I'm not my sister, at least not now. We left my purse with my ID back at Allie's house, remember? But I've been thinking about things. I don't know what Allie's been up to, or what she's involved in, but she's obviously in trouble. I'd like to help if I can. Do you suppose you could just *assume* that I'm her sister Jessie, and proceed from there?"

Whoever she was, Ben had never seen that particular expression on those features before. Her eyes were wide and earnest. With those tousled curls brushing her smooth cheeks and forehead, she looked young and hopeful and altogether too tempting. He eyed her assessingly.

"Assume? Cops don't assume, princess, not if they want to last on the streets. There *is* something you can do, though, if you're really willing to help."

"I am," Jessie said.

Ben leaned back against his door. "Do you trust me enough to believe I wouldn't hurt you? A minute ago you panicked, and I'd rather not see that look in your eyes again."

"Oh, that," she said. "I did feel threatened for a second. Do you blame me?" A glint of humor sparkled in her eyes. "But then I decided you were too cranky about having to rescue me to be anything but what you say you are. So in a backhanded way, I guess I do trust you."

"Good," Ben said. "In that case, you won't get all bent out of shape when you hear what I want you to do."

She raised her eyebrows questioningly, and he dropped his gaze to her mouth.

"I want you to give me the hottest, juiciest, tongue-in-my-mouth kiss you can come up with. Your very best."

Chapter 3

Jessie's mouth fell open and she stared at Ben speechlessly. She couldn't have heard him right.

"You don't need to worry that I'll grab you, or anything like that," he went on as though he hadn't requested anything more outrageous than passing the salt. "I won't even touch you while you're doing it, you have my word. Except with my mouth, of course."

Jessie's gaze zeroed in on his moist, slightly parted lips. Her own lips felt suddenly dry. For good reason, she realized with a start—her mouth was still hanging open. Hastily she snapped it shut and turned to stare blankly out the windshield.

"No?" Ben sighed and tapped his fingers on the steering wheel. "Oh, well. It was just an idea. A dim-witted one, maybe, but for a minute there, it seemed like a quick and dirty way to tell for sure whether you and your sister are the same woman."

Jessie's head whipped back around. "Quick and dirty! You're unbelievable!"

He shot her a quelling glance. "Okay, not the best choice of words, I admit. But give me some slack here, will you? I'm a guy who doesn't get home from work until three in the morning, and today I'd barely gotten out of the shower when my partner called with the bad news that I couldn't go to bed yet. Some screwball reporter, he says, has been poking her nose where she doesn't have any business. Even worse, she's been found out by the wrong people. So, tired though I am, I have to go chasing after her to warn her that she could be in danger, and sure enough, when I get there, it turns out I'm right."

Ben's words took on a snarl. "Only, after I've gone to considerable trouble to save her hide, I find out maybe I've got the right woman and maybe I don't. If I don't have her, I've got to figure out a way to find her and keep her from getting killed, instead of working on the case I'm *really* assigned to. But first I have to decide whether the woman I *have* got is jerking me around to suit her own plans. So pardon me all to hell, princess, if I'm lacking in finesse at the moment."

Jessie let both the "princess" and the patently insincere apology slide. Right now all that concerned her was Ben's reference to Allie getting killed. It sobered her, brought her attention back where it belonged.

"All right," she said.

"What?"

"I said, *all right.* If my kissing you will show you I'm telling the truth, I'll do it, so we can get on with helping Allie. Sit up."

Ben's eyes flickered, but he didn't say a word. He moved his big body away from the door where he'd been casually slumped. Without expression, he twisted his torso to face her, resting his left arm on the steering wheel. Then he waited.

Jessie watched her hands unbuckle her seat belt, while she feigned a nonchalance she was far from feeling. *This is for Allie,* she told herself.

Slowly she leaned toward Ben, her heart hammering, her eyes fixed on his mouth. When their faces were inches apart, she stopped and raised her palms to gingerly cradle his morning-stubbly cheeks. Though she was hardly touching him, his skin seemed hot under the tiny prickles.

"Remember, no hands," she reminded him. Then she brought her lips to his.

The kiss was a gentle moving of lips on lips that, once started, was difficult to stop. Jessie ended it with a series of delicate little lingering sips.

"That was nice, princess," Ben said hoarsely when she drew back, "but hardly a basis for comparison."

She dropped her hands into her lap and straightened her spine. She hadn't expected criticism, not for a kiss that had sent her own blood thundering through her veins. She could still feel the pulse pounding at her throat.

But she should have known he'd be Antonio all over again. She'd heard it before. She was too slow to arousal, too inhibited. A prude inside a sexy body.

She pulled herself up short. This was stupid. She was trying to prove to Ben that she wasn't her sister, not auditioning as his bed partner.

"Jessie," she said crossly. "My name is *Jessie*. What was wrong with it, anyway? If that kiss was different from Allie's, I've proved my point, haven't I?"

Ben shook his head, his goldish green eyes gleaming down at her. "Uh-uh. For me to be sure, you'll have to do it again. Open your mouth this time and come after me a little."

Jessie felt a blush heat up her whole face at the low, coaxing tone in which those words were uttered. What a voice the man had when he wasn't bristling with ill humor! She could almost forget what was going on here, if she wasn't careful.

Had he spoken to Allie in just that tone? So far Jessie hadn't let herself dwell on the obvious implications of Ben's dubious method for distinguishing one twin from the other.

"Have you and Allie . . . been intimate?"

Ben's eyes narrowed distrustfully. Then he snorted, effectively breaking the mood. "How delicate. You almost have me convinced you don't know the answer to that question. *Almost*. Come on, *Jessie*, you aren't home free yet. Get on with it. Plant one on me like you mean it."

Jessie flushed again, this time in anger. She'd like to plant one on him, all right! He was making fun of her, daring her, as though he thought she wouldn't—couldn't—pick up the gauntlet he'd thrown down.

Something she didn't recognize rose inside her. As a child she had left the risk taking to her twin, who had been more than willing to accept all challenges on behalf of the two Webster sisters. It was understood that Allie, the older by seventeen minutes, would be the one to preserve their standing in the Oak

Park neighborhood where they'd grown up. Jessie had always
stood by with her insides shaking while Allie climbed to the
highest limb or stood up to the bully on the block or snitched
petunias from mean old Mrs. Shrader's flower beds. The pattern had continued into their teenage years.

But the once-inseparable twins were grown now, thrill-
seeking Allie was in who-knows-what kind of danger, and Jessie was on her own.

"Well?"

She'd never known a man before who could pack such a
wealth of condescension into a single taunting word. Jessie had
had enough. So he was looking for a hot kiss, was he? By gum,
if Allie could do it, so could she, and then some! She'd *sizzle*
that detestable smirk right off his freckled face!

She reached for him again, putting her hands behind his neck
this time. Instead of drawing him down to meet her, she propelled herself upward and fused her mouth to his. Ben fell back
against the door with a startled grunt, and Jessie went with him,
hardly conscious that she came to rest sprawled on his chest, her
legs spanning the console between the seats.

Relentlessly she worked his lips open with hers and plunged
her tongue into the warm cavern of his mouth. Immediately she
noted his faintly minty taste and the already familiar clean,
manly smell of him as she plied his tongue with her own. He
moaned deep in his throat, and a tiny quiver of triumph rip-
pled through her. She was doing it!

Then his tongue moved against hers and Jessie forgot all
about his dare. She forgot about Allie, too. Ben's mouth became mobile, his tongue questing. Urgently he nudged her lips
wider apart and moved his head to adjust the fit. Jessie's own
head tilted in counterpoint, accommodating him, until—ah,
there. Wetly, deliciously, their mouths mingled. Heat swirled
down her body and collected in her breasts and between her
legs.

It wasn't until Ben's pelvis prodded gently against her hips
that Jessie began to pull herself out of the haze of desire. He
was aroused. She'd have to stop it soon, before things got out
of hand, but, oh, Lord—the man could kiss!

When the prodding became more insistent, she broke away
and lifted her head. Ben's color was high, his hot eyes heavy

lidded, his lips damp and glistening. His chest rose and fell with his labored breathing. He looked needy, ready for more.

Before she could be tempted to give it to him, Jessie braced her hands on his shoulders and awkwardly maneuvered her body back into her seat. Primly she folded her hands in her lap and pressed her legs together to keep from squirming under the aftershocks vibrating through her body. Whew! She'd never been so stimulated in her life before from just a kiss!

"Okay, I believe you," he rasped.

"You do?" Jessie's voice squeaked. She barely glanced in his direction, not knowing whether she could trust herself not to jump him again. Which was really astounding, since she could hardly believe she'd done it the first time.

"Yeah," Ben said. "You finally convinced me. And just for the record, I've never slept with your sister."

He sat up behind the wheel and stretched his right leg into Jessie's field of vision. His bottom hiked off the seat, and she caught a glimpse of his blunt-fingered hand reaching down to adjust his jeans.

Cheeks flaming, she said quickly, "What are we going to do now? To find Allie, I mean."

Ben opened his door. "I need coffee. How do you take it?"

The cold November air rushed in and Jessie shivered. Because the windows were fogged, no doubt from the heat their kiss had generated, the world outside the open door was sharply defined under the overcast morning sky, almost startling in its clarity. She saw a couple of cars parked at the end units of the small motel and, beyond them, a stand of stark, leafless trees.

"Where will you get coffee?" As far as she could see, it was still too early for anyone to be stirring. *Anyone who hadn't just narrowly escaped being murdered, that is,* she thought grimly, and shivered again.

"Cold?" Ben started the motor and flipped a lever on the dash. "There's a coffee machine inside the lobby. Do you want some, or not?"

The familiar trace of impatience in his voice, more than the warm air pouring through the vents, restored Jessie's equilibrium. "If you don't mind," she said, her tone matching his for testiness. "Black, please."

Silence filled the interior of the car after Ben left. Jessie felt
strangely deflated without his vital presence. She was relieved
that he and Allie weren't lovers. Not that it should matter, since
Jessie had no intentions of getting involved with him herself.
Still—

Boy, that kiss really got to you, Jess, old girl, she told herself when she realized what she was thinking. *You hardly know
the guy.*

Forcing her thoughts into more mundane channels, Jessie
took advantage of Ben's absence to peek at herself in the visor
mirror. Her hair was a mess, but without a comb she could do
no more than pull halfheartedly at a few wayward curls. Not
much improvement. With a sigh she flipped the visor up and sat
back to watch the condensation on the windshield slowly give
way to the warm gust of the defroster.

The windows were almost clear again when Ben returned
with a steaming disposable cup in each hand. Jessie accepted
the one he handed her with a murmur of thanks and immediately took a grateful sip. Ben did the same, then passed her his
cup.

"Hold this," he said.

Jessie clicked her tongue in annoyance. "So we're back to
master and slave, are we?"

He spared a moment in the middle of backing out of their
parking space to look at her with his leonine eyes. "Don't I
wish," he murmured before turning back to his driving.

Judiciously Jessie chose not to respond. Instead she turned
her attention to keeping the coffee from spilling. The next time
she looked up, she saw that Ben had driven around the back of
the motel to a row of small cabins nestled at the edge of a dense
evergreen woods.

"Where are we going now?"

"Right here." He pulled into a short driveway beside the last
cabin.

Jessie's feminine radar hummed a warning. "*Wait* a minute—"

"Now, don't get all excited," he said as he cut the engine.
"This is the rendezvous point for my investigative team, not
some sleazy bachelor pad. We rent it by the week, so it's always available. There's a phone inside where I can call my

partner, and after that, you and I need to talk. *Talk,*" he repeated. "Okay?"

"Oh." Jessie felt flustered that, while she had misread *his* motives, he had read *her* mind perfectly. "Then you don't live here?"

A look of mild alarm passed over his features. "Good God, no. I have a house in Chicago, though I don't get to spend much time there. Right now I'm hanging my hat in a run-down duplex in Port Mangus—part of my cover."

He retrieved his coffee, got out of the car and started toward the cabin. Jessie followed, catching up to him at the door just as he selected a key from his ring.

"I live in Chicago, too," she told him, "in Oak Park. I came to Wisconsin to spend Thanksgiving with Allie. We were going to cook a big feast today—turkey and the whole works." Jessie shook her head as she thought of how she'd looked forward to being with her sister for the four-day weekend. "So much for our plans, huh?"

Ben paused briefly in the act of twisting the key in the lock. "That's right, today's Thanksgiving Day, isn't it? Happy Thanksgiving, Jessie."

His softly spoken holiday greeting threw her off balance—again. "Uh, thanks," she faltered. "Same to you."

"Wait here a second while I check the place out."

He disappeared inside and left Jessie standing at the door, her heart fluttering from the impact of hearing her name on his lips without sarcasm for the first time.

In a minute or two he was back. "All clear. Come on in."

Jessie stepped over the threshold into a clean but very small and inexpensively furnished living room. The temperature inside was warmer than outdoors, but too chilly for cozy habitation.

"Welcome to the Ritz," Ben said, gesturing grandly.

"You can give me the grand tour later," she returned. "Where's the bathroom?"

His grin stretched over even white teeth, carving long dimples on either side of his curving lips. Amusement sparkled in his eyes, making him look rakish and sexy.

"Over there." He indicated a door to her immediate right. "You go ahead and . . . whatever. I'm going to turn up the heat and then make that call."

Suddenly aware she was gawking at him like a star-struck teenager, Jessie set her coffee on a nearby table, hastily made her way to the bathroom and closed the door.

You're falling for him, dummy, she berated herself. *Have you forgotten how many times he's behaved just like Antonio? Get hold of yourself. He's not for you.*

A few minutes later, feeling considerably better from the dual accomplishments of emptying her bladder and sternly reining in her runaway attraction to a man too much like her ex-husband for comfort, Jessie emerged from the bathroom. Her eyes went immediately to her rescuer, who was perched on the arm of a sickly green vinyl couch, talking on the phone. He covered the mouthpiece with his hand.

"Did you have a suitcase at your sister's house?" he asked her.

"Yes, why?"

"I'm arranging to have your clothes and car brought here."

"Oh, good," Jessie said, pleased that at least one problem was going to be solved. "The suitcase is in the bedroom. My keys and purse are in there, too, on the dresser. My car is the red Toyota parked in the street out front. Oh, and I left a cosmetics tote in the bathroom."

Ben repeated the information into the receiver, and, after cautioning his listener to be careful, he hung up and gestured to an easy chair against the wall.

"Make yourself comfortable." He reached for his coffee and drained the cup, tossing back the liquid as he would a shot of whiskey.

Jessie walked to the decidedly uncomfortable-looking chair, which faced the ugly couch at an angle and was upholstered in the same bilious shade of green. She unzipped her parka before she sat down.

"Was that your partner?" she asked.

Ben nodded. "You could call him that—my temporary partner, anyway. His name's Ed Brock. FBI."

"Are you FBI, too?"

"Nah. I'm a cop in the Chicago P.D."

"Isn't it kind of unusual for a city policeman and a federal agent to be partners?"

"We're not exactly partners, at least not in the classic sense. It's just that Ed and I are the only team members for this case who are based in Port Mangus. The investigation is being run from the bureau office in Chicago. It's a federal case, and the only reason I got tagged for it is because of my undercover experience."

Jessie wondered whether Ben had noticed they were having a normal conversation instead of exchanging barbs. It was a refreshing change.

"You've worked undercover a lot?"

"Enough," he said brusquely. He crumpled the cup in his hand and pitched it into a metal wastebasket near his feet. It thunked with ringing finality.

And that's that, Jessie thought. She was sure she'd seen a flash of emotion in his eyes when he'd discarded the mangled cup, but his terse answer showed her the topic was off-limits. Jessie had had plenty of experience with another male who refused to talk about himself. It was time to change the subject.

"So what happens now?" She settled back into the hard chair. Immediately she shifted in an unsuccessful attempt to find an accommodating position for her spine.

"Ed is sending a marked car and a couple of uniformed cops to your sister's to see whether those two goons are still hanging around. The patrolmen will pick up your stuff while they're there so Ed can bring it down here with your car."

"Are they doing anything about finding Allie?"

"Ed's going to see if he can get a man stationed outside the house to watch for her to come home, but that's the best he can do. Even that might not be feasible if the Port Mangus force is shorthanded because of the holiday."

Jessie dropped her head into her hand, her stomach churning as she considered the possibilities. "Where could she be?"

"Take it easy, Jessie. She's probably fine."

"Do you really believe that?"

"It doesn't help any to expect the worst. There's just as good a chance that she got wind of what's going on and is lying low for a while."

"What *is* going on, Ben? Tell me about this case you're working on and what Allie has to do with it."

Ben's face turned grim. "Your sister is an uninvited participant, so I'm not sure how she got involved. As for the investigation, a few months ago in Chicago, one of Ed's informers, a guy named Donno Carr, tipped him to a strip joint in Port Mangus that Donno said was a front for a major prostitution and drug ring run by some big bosses in Chicago."

Jessie thought about the sleepy town Allie had chosen to live in over the more urban Sheboygan, where she worked. "How could they hide something like that? Port Mangus is so small."

"Easy. It's a vacation resort for big spenders with big boats and miles and miles of Lake Michigan at their disposal. But we need evidence to prove it. I've been on the inside for almost two months, and so far we don't have much. The strip joint is a legitimate operation, but it's only a front. We know that Mai Duan, the Vietnamese woman who supposedly owns the place, also runs a stable of very upscale prostitutes to service an elite clientele. And along with sex, they provide drugs—anything the client wants and can pay for. What we *don't* know is where the drugs are coming from or who's calling the shots. All we've got is Donno's word that it's somebody in the Chicago mob and a hunch that he's right."

Ben stood up and slipped off his jacket, tossing it carelessly to the far end of the couch. Jessie's eyes went immediately to the shoulder holster he uncovered, reminding her of the terrifying scene in her bathroom. It brought home to her the unavoidable threat of violence that naturally followed a man in his profession. Rather than adding menace to his appearance, however, the sight of the gun nestled close to his armpit reassured her.

"It's finally warming up in here," he said. "Do you want to take off your coat?"

Jessie realized she did feel a little sweaty in both her parka and heavy sweater. "Good idea," she said, and began to work her arms out of the sleeves of the bulky cover-up.

After watching her struggle for a minute, Ben walked over to her chair. "Stand up."

Jessie looked up at him, vexation flaring once again. "Stand up," she mimicked. "Sit down. Hold this. Come with me.

Hurry up. Don't you know how to say *anything* without making an order out of it?"

Ben's lips twitched. "You want me to beg for the privilege of helping you out of your coat?"

"Oh, never mind." She got to her feet but stepped away when he reached for the cumbersome jacket. "I said, *never mind!*"

His eyes danced with amusement. The slick fabric slid off her arms easily, now that she was standing. "Here," she said curtly.

Ben took the offending garment she'd shoved into his stomach and walked with loose, masculine grace back to the couch. Jessie couldn't help admiring the breadth of his shoulders, accented by the straps of the holster over his chambray shirt, and the clean vee of torso to hips. His buns weren't bad, either, blast him. He looked as good from behind as he did face-to-face.

Jessie returned to the cold solace of the torturous vinyl chair and watched as Ben threw her coat on top of his and sprawled on the couch. He stretched out his long legs and crossed them casually at the ankles, causing the denim of his jeans to snugly outline his muscular thighs and emphasize the undoubtedly male endowments at their apex. She hurriedly averted her eyes.

"Anyway, as I was saying," he continued, "it's been slow going, but I've been working at Club Duan long enough for Mai to start to trust me. Soon, if things go the way we plan, I may be included in some of the meetings she has with a select few at the club and we can start building our case."

Jessie scolded herself. How could she be so easily distracted when Allie was in trouble?

"That's assuming," Ben went on, "that your sister's shenanigans haven't screwed up my chances. Mai is likely to be more wary than ever now."

Mentally she backtracked over what Ben had told her so far, and suddenly she straightened. "Did you say the mob is involved? Organized crime?"

"Unfortunately, yes."

"My God! Allie, what have you done?" Jessie knew that terrible things went on in the world, but to her they were the topics of books and movies and news reports. Never had she dreamed anything like what Ben had been telling her would ever touch her or someone she loved.

Ben's expression hardened. "Has Allie told you why she took a job at Mai's place, or what she knew about what's going on there?"

"No, nothing. All she's been talking about since she moved to Port Mangus is her job at the *Sheboygan Sentinel*. She hasn't mentioned this Club Duan at all, let alone that she worked there. Is it really a strip joint?"

"Yes, it really is."

"She didn't— She wasn't a stripper, was she?"

He smiled slightly. "No, a cocktail waitress. But Mai was trying to persuade her to give dancing a shot. She's built for it, you know."

His eyes strayed to Jessie's bosom, which matched Allie's in fullness. Quickly she asked, "What do *you* think she was doing there?"

Ben shot her a knowing look but answered, "I think she got a tip-off, just like we did, and thought she had the makings for a Pulitzer prize story. Only I doubt she knew what she was getting into."

Jessie didn't think it would have made any difference to Allie if she *had* known. Her twin was too determined to succeed. She was nothing if not tenacious; neither was she known for playing by the rules.

"How did you find out Allie is a reporter?" she asked.

"From Mai," Ben said. "We have a tap on her phone at the club, and during my shift last night, Ed heard her tell someone—we don't know who yet—that she wasn't getting the protection she was paying for. She said she'd just found out that one of the waitresses, Angela West, was a reporter, and though she'd handle the problem, she expected better screening from now on. That was the first time we had any clue that Allie was anything other than a ditzy female who knew how to rake in big tips."

"Who do you think told Mai about her?"

Ben shook his head. "I don't know, and Mai didn't say. She must have considered her source reliable, though, because she sounded certain that her information was good."

Jessie considered that and asked hopefully, "Was that all the information she had—that Angela West was a reporter? Did she mention Allie's real name? Maybe they don't know—"

"We have to assume they know exactly who your sister is," Ben said gently. "Even if they don't, Ed heard enough to know she's in trouble. That's why he called me as soon as he could reach me, and I rushed over to warn her. You know the rest."

What Jessie knew frightened her. More than once he had alluded to the possibility that Allie could get killed. "Ben? Do you really think they want to *murder* Allie?"

"I shouldn't have said that, Jessie, and you shouldn't think it." His voice was harsh. "It doesn't do any good."

She swallowed. "I'm trying not to worry, but under the circumstances—"

"I know. But there are good reasons to be optimistic."

"It's just that Allie and I have always been so close. Twins *are*, you know. There have even been times when one or the other of us just knew what the other was feeling, even when we weren't together."

"It would be helpful if you had one of those feelings now."

Jessie brightened. "I *don't*. That's good, isn't it? Surely I would know if something had happened to her." A great weight seemed to leave her shoulders, making her feel almost lightheaded. "Thank you, Ben. I needed that reminder."

For a minute Ben looked doubtful. Maybe he didn't want to get her hopes up on so flimsy a basis. But Jessie didn't care. For the moment she could relax.

"Do you have a family, Ben?"

She was thinking of brothers and sisters when she asked the question, but the greater implications struck her an instant after the words left her mouth, especially when Ben didn't answer immediately. Until now, she hadn't considered that he might have a wife, or even children.

To her relief, he shook his head. "Just my parents. They're retired and living in Arizona."

"So far away," she mused. "My mother moved, too, a year after my dad died. She couldn't take the hard winters anymore. Now she lives in Florida."

"That's why my parents chose the Southwest."

"I tried to get Allie to stay in Chicago with me, but she wouldn't listen. Her new job and everything..." Without warning, the worry hit her again. Jessie wondered how much she could rely on her intuition to be sure Allie was all right.

"Don't, Jessie."

She looked at Ben helplessly. "I feel as though I should be doing something."

He sat quietly for several seconds, his eyes brooding. "I'm not good at this. I don't know any words to make things easier for you."

Jessie saw a shadow of private pain in his face, pain that she felt intuitively had been triggered by her fears for Allie. Could he be remembering a similar experience from his past? She almost asked, but decided she hadn't known him long enough to pry into his background. He probably wouldn't allow it, anyway.

Responding to an unexplainable need to comfort him, she said, "I'm just grateful you're here. I don't think I could stand this if I were alone."

Ben caught her gaze and held it. "I'll have to get back to the job soon, but I'll stay with you as long as I can."

"Thank you," she whispered.

Neither of them looked away. Imprudently, perhaps, Jessie wished she was sitting closer to him. She wanted to touch him, to connect with more than just words. The moment stretched between them, charged with emotion. Tension swirled and grew in the space separating them, the memories of all they had shared in the past hours outlining its intensity with sexual overtones.

Finally Ben tore his eyes away and raked his fingers through his hair. Jessie watched him, feeling oddly limp, as though a current had been turned off, releasing her body from a powerful magnetic force. He glanced at his watch and then back at Jessie. Suddenly shy, she dropped her eyes and began to fiddle with a loose nub on her sweater.

"Don't take this wrong, Jessie, but I'm going to make a suggestion."

Jessie raised her head.

"We both need sleep, and Ed won't be here for a couple of hours, at least. Why don't you take a nap in the bedroom, and I'll sack out here on the couch until he comes?"

She saw signs of fatigue in his rugged features and remembered he'd said he hadn't gotten any sleep for more than a day.

"You need the rest more than I do, and you're bigger than me, too. *You* take the bed and I'll stay out here."

"No."

"Really," she insisted. "You'll be more comfortable. The couch looks too short for—"

"Jessie."

She stopped at his soft, warning utterance of her name. Oh, brother. He was back to being difficult again. In a way it was a relief to find familiar ground after the intense awareness of the past few minutes. Jessie was tempted to argue with him some more, but decided it wasn't worth it. If the furniture in here was any indication, the bed wouldn't be much improvement over the couch, anyway.

"All right, if that's the way you want it." She pointed to a partially open door across the room. "There?"

Ben nodded. Jessie rose and felt his gaze follow her to the bedroom. She paused at the door. "Is Ben your real name?"

"Yeah. Ben Sutton."

"Ben Sutton," she murmured as she pushed the door wide. She took a step inside the bedroom, glanced around and stepped back into the open doorway. "Hey, there are two beds in here. We can each have one."

There was an electric moment of absolute stillness.

"You're playing with fire, princess," Ben said. "My self-control is a chancy thing right now, and you're looking damned good to me standing there in that cuddly sweater and skinny jeans. So I'd advise you to get your sweet self inside that bedroom and close the door behind you."

The quietly spoken threat sent a thrill of excitement flirting along Jessie's nerve endings. For a heart-stopping moment she let herself imagine how it would be if he joined her on the other side of this door.

But he was right. A safe distance between them was the best thing right now. She should be grateful that he was keeping a rein on their attraction—she *was* grateful. Really.

Slowly Jessie turned and walked into the bedroom. And closed the door behind her.

Chapter 4

Ben didn't relax until he heard the latch click into place. He released the breath he'd been holding and dropped his head back against the couch to stare at the ceiling. Exhaustion burned his eyes. Even so, he had a feeling it was going to take some time before he could sleep.

If only all he had to worry about was this possibly shot-to-hell investigation. That would be routine, even with the complications Allie had introduced. After all, no case he'd ever worked had gone totally as outlined. He didn't even expect that anymore, no matter how sound the plan.

Ben was a strategist by nature who achieved his greatest satisfaction when people and events fell in line with what he'd mapped out for them. But it was an imperfect world, and he was used to having to switch gears any number of times before reaching his goal. It wasn't the process of getting there that was important; it was the goal itself.

His goal was a simple one: Get the bastards.

It was his personal crusade and had been for eleven years, ever since his little sister, Maddie, had become a casualty of drug traffickers. The names and faces changed, but the goal remained. *Get the bastards.* Ben would not be deterred, nothing could distract him from his purpose.

Until now.

On the phone earlier, he and Ed had plotted their next steps in the case, taking into consideration the possible ramifications of Allie's blundering. In some measure, devising a strategy had settled Ben's need for control of the situation. They had a plan. He should feel focused now, on top of things, in charge.

But he didn't. And the reason was right here in this cabin. The one wild card he and Ed hadn't factored in was Jessie.

Oh, Ben had mentioned her, but he'd necessarily left out a few details. He hadn't said that he already knew the sweet weight of her breast in his hand or that her kiss damned near turned him inside out. He could just imagine what Ed would say to that.

If Jessie were another kind of woman, he thought, he might be tempted to take her to bed and be done with it. But he sensed her caution and respected it. After all, despite their uncommon attraction, they'd met only hours ago.

That wasn't the only thing holding him back. For some reason, she made him feel uneasy. If it were only her physical assets that drew him, then Allie, her look-alike, would have turned him on. But there was something special about Jessie that set her apart from her twin and called to Ben's most elemental urges. Even when she was giving him a hard time, it was there, humming between them.

Jessie was aware of it, too, he was sure. A minute ago she'd actually considered inviting him into the bedroom for more than a nap. Ben grimaced as he put his hand over the nagging ache behind his zipper and pressed hard. His groin had tightened while he watched her think it over and hadn't relaxed yet.

Hell, this was ridiculous. He should lie down; maybe then sleep would come. He started to push the two jackets beside him off the couch, then reconsidered and let only his own fall to the floor. Jessie's down-filled parka he bundled into a makeshift pillow. Wearily he stretched out on his back, with his feet propped on the hard arm of the sofa, and shoved the parka under his head. Immediately traces of Jessie's perfume tugged at his nostrils. He turned his head and breathed in deeply.

The truth was, Ben hadn't been so tempted by a woman in a long time, maybe never before. And that was the hell of it. Because his job came first, and the last thing he needed right now was a woman who could mess up his concentration. Somehow he had to keep his hands off her until he could send her home. In Oak Park, she'd be out of reach of his hands and all his other randy body parts, as well.

Maybe when this operation was over and he returned to Chicago, he could call her up and see whether the attraction was still as potent. Maybe he'd even take some of the vacation time he'd been accruing so he could give her his undivided attention for awhile. Two weeks or so with nothing to concentrate on but Jessie was an appealing prospect. Especially if he seduced her quickly and kept her in bed.

He had no doubt he could do just that. Oh, she might try to take things slow, but that wouldn't last long if he pressed her. Their kiss back there in the car had begun in spitting challenge but had ended with sweet, acquiescent female oozing like honey on a pancake all over the top of him. He'd never gotten so hard so fast in all his life.

No, any resistance she put up would be token. And the next time he got that close to her, he wouldn't be bound by a promise not to touch. If he'd been free to put his hands on her the first time, she would have been his for the taking already. Not that he could do anything about it, with this case hanging over his head. But when it was over . . .

Yeah, two weeks in bed with her—three at the outside—and this itch would be thoroughly scratched. In return, he'd see to it that she had the best time between the sheets she'd ever had. They'd both be smiling when it was over.

Then Ben could get back to work.

Oh, yes, he would definitely look her up when he got back to the city.

Ben smiled and carried that pleasurable expectation into his dreams.

It was midmorning when Mai's lover unlocked the door to her apartment over Club Duan with his own key. He knew where to find her. He strode to the bedroom and woke her.

With a cry of welcome, Mai pulled him down and embraced him tearfully. She didn't ask why he was here in Port Mangus instead of vacationing in Pennsylvania with his wife and family. All she cared about was that now she wouldn't have to face her terrible trouble alone.

Immediately she began pouring out in her careful English all that had happened since she'd last seen him. From him there was no need to hide anything, and she told it all—that Angela West was a reporter; that the journal was gone, almost certainly stolen; that her men had failed to get rid of the bitch who had taken it.

"When they entered her bedroom, she had already left through a window, probably to contact the police. So they had to leave."

Masculine lips curled in a sneer. "Likely they didn't have the stomach for the job. Those two are small-time punks, not killers."

Mai saw the coldness in his eyes. Uncertainly she said, "You are right, of course. Tell me what to do."

"Your problems are bigger than you think, baby. You've not only got a reporter on your payroll—you've got a cop. He's one of your bouncers. I don't know what he's calling himself these days, but his name is Ben Sutton. Chances are your Angela West has already passed the journal over to him. It may already be too late to keep anyone else from seeing it."

"What? But how . . . who—?"

"It doesn't matter anymore, at least to you, Mai."

"What do you mean? Of course, it matters. We must do something to protect my business."

"You've already done too much by writing everything down in that journal. The man in Chicago isn't going to be pleased when he finds out about it."

"But . . . it was you who told me to keep it. It was our 'ace in the hole,' you said, in case he one day decided we were expendable."

The hard gaze he fixed on her grew colder. "I also told you to keep it in a safe place. Now, because of your carelessness, it's fallen into the wrong hands. If the feds in Chicago don't already know about it, they soon will." He shook his head slowly from side to side. "The man was already upset over having a reporter and now a cop snooping around at the club. When I tell him about this..."

Mai gasped. "You would not tell him. He will kill us!"

"Us? You've got that wrong, Mai. I had nothing to do with that journal."

"You did. It was your idea."

"Nobody knows that but you, sweetheart."

Mai stared at the gun in his hand, first in disbelief, then in resignation.

"It's a shame, too. We've had some good times together." He got to his feet, keeping the gun trained steadily between her eyes. "Get up. We've got to go now."

"Where are you taking me?" Her voice was dull with the knowledge of his treason.

"Well, let's see. How about a nice boat ride? We can pretend I'm a client and you're one of the hookers. It'll be cold out there on the open water today, but you Saigon sweeties know how to warm up a man, don't you? I think I'd like that, Mai. Once more for old times' sake."

All the boats were dry-docked for the winter, but Mai didn't argue. Rising from the bed without protest, she preceded him out to his light-colored rental car in the back lot. He was right. It did not matter what he did to her; nothing mattered anymore. She had already withdrawn to that place inside where nothing—not rape, not the screams of bleeding, dying children, not even the betrayal of a lover—could touch her.

"Wake up, Jessie. Ed's here."

Jessie opened her eyes and frowned at the door. For a moment she felt disoriented in her unfamiliar surroundings, but memory came seeping in with Ben's second knock.

"Come on, Jess. Up and at 'em. We need you out here."

She yawned, stretched sumptuously on the unexpectedly comfortable bed and sat up, feeling fuzzy with sleep.

"Jess!"

"I'm awake," she called back.

"Shake a leg, will you? There's something I want you to hear."

"*Mein Führer*," she muttered under her breath. Ben was obviously back to his normal autocratic self after his nap.

"What?"

"I'm awake, I said!"

She yawned again and stood up, surprised that she'd been able to sleep. She felt hot and grubby from lying in the warm sweater and snug jeans. Reaching under the sweater, she adjusted the band of her bra, which had bitten cruelly into her flesh.

Vaguely wondering what time it was, she rubbed the sleep out of her eyes and ran her fingers through her disheveled curls. When she kept getting caught on snarls, she gave it up as a lost cause. Certain now that she resembled a well-used mop at best, Jessie made a conscious decision to ignore the mirror over the dresser. There was nothing she could do about her appearance, anyway, so why make herself feel worse?

When she came out of the bedroom she noticed Ben had shaved and combed his hair. He was sitting on the edge of the couch fiddling with what appeared to be a small portable tape recorder, looking wide-awake and refreshed.

Figures, she thought. *He's the one who sleeps on the bed of nails, and I'm the one who feels like a flat tire.*

Beside Ben was a slender, middle-aged man with receding gray hair who could only be Ed. Both men looked up at her entrance, and Ed came to his feet. It was Ben's eye that Jessie sought, however.

"Jessie, this is Ed Brock," Ben said. "Ed, this is Jessie . . . is it Webster, like your sister?" Jessie searched his gaze. His eyes were those of a polite stranger with a faintly questioning look on his face. She sighed inwardly. All right. It was disappointing, but if he wanted to pretend those few moments of emotional susceptibility earlier hadn't happened, she'd oblige him.

"Yes. Didn't I mention that?" She turned to Ed and held out her hand. "Please call me Jessie, Mr. Brock. Or is it *Agent* Brock?"

"For you I answer to Ed," he replied with a smile that barely turned up the corners of his mouth. Perhaps he didn't smile often, Jessie thought. He seemed a little rusty.

Everything on Ed's face seemed to sag downward, from the bags under his eyes to his prominent earlobes to the lines around his nose and mouth. Even his eyelids drooped, though the eyes under them were bright and alert. He was less muscular than Ben, but still looked lean and fit in his neatly tucked striped shirt and belted corduroy pants.

"Hell of a way to spend Thanksgiving, isn't it?" he added conversationally. "Welcome to the world of law enforcement."

Jessie came to attention, remembering Allie. "What did you find at my sister's house, Ed? Were those men still there?"

He shook his head. "There was no sign of them by the time the cops got there."

"Don't worry, Jessie," Ben said. "The police are keeping an eye on the place. If Allie comes home, they'll see that nothing happens to her."

Jessie turned. Ben cleared his throat when their eyes met and said almost curtly, "Come over here a minute and sit down. I want you to listen to this. It's the tape from your sister's answering machine."

He placed the recorder on the spindly legged coffee table in front of the sofa while Jessie came around and took a seat next to him. She was careful to leave plenty of space between them. Ben helped by inching away a little when she sat down. He pressed a button, and she heard a long beep. A man's irate voice came out of the recorder.

"Webster? I want your butt in my office the minute you hear this, or else! You got that? Now!" There was a click, and a mechanical voice said, "Tuesday, 7:32 a.m."

Another beep sounded. "Where the hell are you, Webster? You were supposed to be at work two hours ago! Get the lead out and get over here! I want to talk to you!" It was the same angry voice, followed by an emotionless, "Tuesday, 10:08 a.m."

"That must be Allie's boss. Which means she didn't go to wor—"

Ben cut Jessie off with a wave of his hand and sat forward intently. "Here, this is the one."

It was a woman this time. Jessie's heart beat faster after the first few words. "Hi, Caboosie. Just called to tell you I won't be there for Thanksgiving, so don't hang around waiting for me. Sorry to break our date, but something came up and I have to go out of town. Oh, I left that book you wanted to borrow with Kyle at the newspaper office, since you weren't there. He's expecting you to pick it up tonight. Talk to you later.'' Click. ''Wednesday, 6:11 p.m.''

Ben turned off the machine and looked at her. ''Well?''

''That was Allie!'' Jessie said, smiling broadly. ''Thank goodness, she's all right.''

''Allie?''

''Your sister?'' Ed echoed Ben's puzzlement.

''Yes. She did something to disguise her voice, but I know it was her. That message was meant for me. 'Caboosie' is the nickname she teased me with sometimes when we were kids, when she wanted to remind me she was born first. I'm so relieved.''

Jessie noticed her companions didn't seem to share her euphoria. When neither man commented, she asked uncertainly, ''Is something wrong?''

''No, no,'' Ed hurriedly assured her. ''It's good to know that your sister's okay. We just thought we had something here that would help us with our case—a new player you might be able to help us identify. Before you told us who it was, we thought Angela—Allie, that is—might have had a coconspirator.''

''No, I'm certain it was her,'' said Jessie. ''I *am* a little confused, though, about the book she mentioned. I never asked to borrow a book from her, and it's not likely that I would. My sister's taste in reading differs from mine. She goes for that horror stuff.''

Ed leaned forward. ''That could mean something. What about this Kyle? Do you know him?''

Jessie shook her head. ''I've never met him, but if I remember right, he's a photographer who works with Allie at the paper. She's mentioned him several times. Do you think she meant for me to go and see him? That this is some kind of secret message?''

''If it is,'' Ben said, ''you've missed your rendezvous. She said he was expecting you last night.''

She looked at him in dismay. ''Oh, no. Do you think it's too late? Maybe we ought to listen to the tape again. Can we? Just Allie's part?''

Without speaking, Ben reversed the tape to the beginning of Allie's message and played it through once more.

"She *was* trying to warn me, wasn't she?" she asked after he'd stopped the machine. "I was on my way to Port Mangus by six last night. Allie must not have found out she wouldn't be home to meet me until *after* I'd left Chicago." She looked from Ben to Ed and back to Ben. "Only why on earth she thought I would listen to her phone messages is a mystery."

"Maybe the answering machine was all she had to work with," Ben answered thoughtfully. "That and her friend Kyle."

"At least I know now that nothing terrible happened to her, right? What you said before, Ben, about her knowing she was in danger and staying away must be the case."

This time Ben didn't give Jessie the reassurance she was looking for. "We'll know more after we hear what Kyle has to say. I'll phone the newspaper office to see if he's there, while you and Ed take care of the paperwork he brought along."

Ed pointed to a clipboard on the coffee table next to the tape recorder. "Just a transfer-of-property receipt," he said. "It's an acknowledgment that you received everything we brought over to you today and that nothing was missing. Do you want to take a quick look through your bags and purse before you sign it?"

Jessie followed his eyes and the lift of his chin to the wall where her suitcase, makeup tote and handbag were stacked. Grinning delightedly, she rose from the couch. "Sure, but right now the only thing I really care about is my toothbrush."

Ed rose with her and picked up the suitcase. "I'll get this one for you."

He carried it into the bedroom behind her and lifted it onto the nearest bed.

"How long have you known Ben?" she asked him casually as she unzipped the bag.

"Oh, three, four months. He's a good cop."

"Yes. He certainly got me out of a sticky situation. Do you know whether he's, uh, involved with anyone?"

Ed shrugged. "Of the female persuasion? Not that I know of. You interested?"

"Uh, no, just . . . curious."

Fleetingly that odd half smile touched his mouth, and he shook his head. "If you're a marrying woman, Jessie, you'd better look elsewhere. Ben eats and sleeps his job, and it crowds out everything else.''

"Oh, I didn't mean—''

"Hey, it's okay. Just thought I'd warn you. You see, I know his reasons for becoming a cop. There's a devil riding his back, and I doubt anything can change that.''

Jessie sensed Ed might have told her more, but good manners restrained her from asking, curious though she was. Ben had so far resisted her efforts to talk about his past. It seemed underhanded to learn about it from someone else.

After Ed left her, it took little time for her to ascertain that her belongings were intact. She took a clean outfit and underwear out of the suitcase. Carefully she arranged them over her arm so her panties and bra were covered, then picked up the cosmetics case and returned to the living room.

Ed had put on a sheepskin-lined coat and was standing close to Ben in earnest conversation when she came into the room. Abruptly they stopped talking and turned to face her. She could only hope Ed wasn't telling Ben how nosy she'd been in the bedroom.

"Everything okay?'' Ed asked.

"All here.'' She held up the articles she'd brought with her. "Don't let me interrupt. I'm just passing through on my way to get cleaned up.''

"Do you mind signing this first?'' Ed walked over and held out a clipboard and pen. "There's a patrolman waiting outside to take me back to Port Mangus, and I need to get going.''

Jessie hurriedly read the form. "My car?'' she asked when she saw the Toyota listed among her belongings.

"Out front,'' Ed said. "The keys are on the table there.''

She set the tote on the floor and scratched out her signature while he held the board for her. With a smile, she handed back his pen. "Thanks for everything,'' she said.

"No problem—glad to help,'' Ed said. "You take care of yourself now.''

"I will, thanks. You, too.''

He nodded and turned to Ben. "Guess I'll take off, then. Watch your back, partner.''

"Always." Ben slapped Ed's shoulder companionably as they shook hands, then wrapped his fingers around the door-knob and looked back at Jessie.

"Stand out of the way," he told her.

Confused, Jessie's eyes measured the six feet or so that separated them. "I'm in the way?"

"I mean, out of the way of the door. I don't want that cop out there to see you."

She frowned. "Why not? Who is he?"

"Here we go again." Ben sighed as though he were called upon to exercise great forbearance.

"What's that supposed to mean?" Jessie took immediate offense at his attitude. She *hated* it when men were condescending. She'd had two years of that from Antonio, and she wasn't going to take it from Ben.

"Look, Jessie, it doesn't matter who the guy is," he said. "Just step aside, okay? Or is that too difficult?"

"Of course not," she said with deceptive pleasantness. "No more difficult than it would be for you to explain why I should. Or if that would violate some big, important code of silence you've sworn to, just tell me it's a secret. I assure you I'll understand."

"Dammit, Jessie—"

Jessie compressed her lips and lifted her chin. Nothing now, short of an exploding grenade, could move her from this spot without an explanation. They stood locked in silent challenge.

"It's no secret."

Ed's puzzled declaration had two heads turning simultaneously in his direction. Jessie had forgotten their witness during the battle of wills; now Ed was looking from her to Ben with a mystified expression on his face. At once she saw their squabbling in a new light, and felt foolish for making an issue over such a simple matter as taking a few steps. Since Ed knew nothing of her short but volatile history with his partner, she must seem to be ridiculously uncooperative.

"Very well." She bent sideways to snatch up her tote, stalked across the room and, weighed down with her possessions, plastered her back to the wall next to the door frame where Ben was standing. From this new position she stared at her antagonist defiantly. "I trust *this* is far enough out of the way to suit you?"

Ben's face was a mask as he opened the door for Ed. Jessie didn't miss the fact that he stood well back from the opening so as not to be visible from outside.

When Ed was gone, Ben turned the dead bolt, fastened the chain and faced Jessie. Casually he leaned his shoulder against the door and regarded her with hooded eyes.

"Nobody on the Port Mangus police force but the chief has been told anything about our investigation. I'm sure the officer out there is clean and conscientious, but right now the fewer people—even cops—who know who and where we are, the better. Does that answer your question about why I asked you to get away from the door?"

"Well, why didn't you say so in the first place?"

He dragged his hand across the back of his neck inside his collar. "Damned if I know. Pure aggravation, I guess. It wasn't as though I'd asked for something that should have caused you any great moral dilemma. All I was after was to make sure nobody saw you, and you tried to make some kind of federal case out of it."

"You didn't ask—you *ordered,* as usual," Jessie reminded him.

"Okay, maybe I did. Something about you gets my back up, makes me want to score points off you."

He hadn't moved, but Jessie felt crowded, as though he had begun to invade her personal space. "Well, there's our problem. The feeling is mutual, believe me."

She pushed away from the wall. Her intention was to get around him and out of his magnetic sphere, but he caught her elbow as she came alongside. A whiff of spicy after-shave drifted past her nose.

"I guessed as much," he said. "We've been striking sparks off each other from the beginning. To be honest, I get a kick out of provoking you."

Jessie was incredulous. "You've been *trying* to make me mad?"

His fingers felt hot on her arm, and she tried to pull free. He nodded and gripped a little tighter. "Don't you know why?"

"No, I don't, but you're going to get your wish in a minute if you don't let me go."

"I can't help goading you for a reaction—*any* reaction. Only…I forgot for a minute there about Ed and what he would think if he saw the fireworks." That appealing huskiness was back in his voice, and something inside Jessie melted.

"He—he'd probably think we don't get along very well, and he'd be right."

"Uh-uh," Ben said. "Look at me, Jessie." She lifted her chin and stared into eyes burning with green fire. "He'd probably see how frustrated we both are. Isn't that what made you back down while he was here, when what you really wanted to do was push me until I grabbed you and started what we've both been dying for, ever since that kiss?"

She shook her head. "Don't talk like that."

"At least you don't deny it," Ben said more softly. "We have unfinished business between us, Jessie Webster." His hard fingers caressed the sensitive skin at the crook of her arm through the thick yarn of her sweater.

Then he dropped his hand, and his voice turned implacable. "But we can't do anything about it now. You're going back to Chicago—today."

"What?" Jessie floundered at his sudden change of mood. But when it sank in that he thought he could send her home like a naive child, her temper flared in rebellion. "Who says I'm going back?"

Ben cast his eyes upward. "See what I mean?" he remarked to an unseen audience that presumably hovered near the ceiling. He looked back at Jessie and held up his palms in a placating gesture. "Look, Jessie, it doesn't make sense for you to stick around here. For one thing, your sister has made it clear your plans for Thanksgiving are off. *She*, at least, had sense enough to get out of town. Secondly, Wisconsin is too dangerous for you right now. Whoever is after Allie may not know she has a twin sister, and I seriously doubt they'll check your ID if they nab you by mistake. On the other hand, it's not likely they'll be looking for her in Chicago, so you ought to be safe there."

"You don't know that. Anyway, even if you're right, what about Kyle? You said yourself Allie's message meant she wanted me to see him. I don't think I should leave until I do. What if Kyle plans to tell me I should do something for her, or to meet her somewhere?''

"Kyle's not at the newspaper office—nobody is. All I got is a recording when I called. It's Thanksgiving, remember?''

"Oh, that's right. Allie told me the *Sentinel* doesn't publish on Sundays or holidays.'' Jessie's disappointment stole her righteous fervor.

"That reminds me. Do you know Kyle's last name? We might be able to reach him at home.''

She shook her head. "If Allie mentioned it, I don't remember. I guess I'll have to wait and talk to him tomorrow.''

"No, Jessie, *I'll* talk to him tomorrow. I want you back in Chicago by then.''

She glared at him. "No way. It's *my* sister, *my* message, and *I'm* going to talk to him.''

"Don't be a fool. I can easily let you know what he has to say, if anything.''

"What do you mean, 'if anything'? Why else would Allie tell me to see him? And how do you know he would even talk to you?'' Realizing her temper was getting away from her again, Jessie forcibly tamped it down. "Listen, Ben, arguing about it is ludicrous. How about we compromise? If you're planning to go to the newspaper office tomorrow anyway, why don't we go together? That way I'll get to see Kyle the way Allie wanted, and since you'll be there with me, you won't have to worry about my safety.''

It was a rational solution, one that allayed Jessie's own uneasiness about plunging into unknown waters. Who knew what Kyle would tell her? She could do worse than to have a tough, experienced policeman by her side.

No matter how bullheaded he was.

Before Ben could offer the protest she saw coming, Jessie said, "Look, I've been dying for a shower for the past hour. Let me get cleaned up, and then we can hash this out all you want, okay?''

He glowered at her darkly. "All right, go ahead. But we haven't settled anything yet.''

"You think about it." She walked to the bathroom. "Just remember, you may be in charge of your investigation, but you're not in charge of *me*."

It was a parting shot to be proud of, and Jessie was still smiling over her cleverness as she smoothed her curls into waves with a brush and travel dryer twenty minutes later. She took extra care with her makeup—it was a holiday, after all—and spritzed perfume at her wrists and behind her ears before dressing.

She had selected two favorites from her suitcase, a deep turquoise silk blouse with wide shoulder pads and slimming black pleated pants. On impulse she tucked the blouse in, knowing the style would emphasize her full bosom and small waist. For some reason, Ben made her feel provocative and more alive than she'd felt in a long time.

He was on the phone again, engrossed in conversation, when Jessie came out of the bathroom. He barely glanced up as she crossed to the bedroom to put away her things. After all the fussing she'd done, anticipating his reaction, it was deflating not to rate a second look.

She double-checked her appearance in the large mirror over the bedroom dresser and sighed. She looked about as good as she was ever going to. Turquoise was one of her best colors, its richness bringing out the creaminess of her skin and the red highlights in her hair. Why hadn't Ben noticed?

It had probably been a mistake to tuck in the blouse. Her breasts didn't need enhancement. Now that she thought about it, the blouse's casually elegant lines looked dumpy with the tails inside her pants. Her buoyant, sexy mood faded fast.

Nor did it return when Ben summoned her from the bedroom after he'd hung up the phone. His eyes flicked over her once and returned to her face with no indication he'd noticed *anything* different about her.

"Well, princess," he said, "you'll be happy to know you can come along tomorrow, after all."

Already feeling defensive after her self-perusal, Jessie reacted immediately to the veiled sarcasm in his voice. "Thank you so much," she replied sweetly, "though I don't recall asking for permission. And the name is *Jessie*."

"So you've said," he acknowledged with a trace of amusement that straightened her spine. She felt as though she'd been patted on the head by an indulgent father. Nothing could have inflamed her more.

"I'll also be following you back to Chicago after we've finished with Kyle," Ben added.

"*If* I decide to go home after *I've* talked to Kyle," she returned heatedly, "I won't need an escort."

"It's no trouble," Ben said smoothly. "I just found out I have to report in to FBI headquarters tomorrow afternoon, anyway."

"Are you deaf?" Jessie exclaimed. "I said *no!*"

Ben's eyes narrowed. "Your protest is duly noted, but there's no negotiation on this. It's too dangerous for you alone."

She hated that unyielding look on his face. Jessie struggled to keep her composure. "Aren't you being a tad inconsistent, Ben? A half hour ago you were trying to push me out the door to get me out of the way. Nothing was said about the trip being dangerous *then.*"

"That was before I knew you intended to sashay up to the newspaper office tomorrow. Or didn't it cross your mind that you could pick up a tail there and never see Chicago again?"

It hadn't. Her sporadic skirmishes with Ben made her forget about the tangle of events Allie's mysterious activities had thrust upon her. She hardly welcomed the reminder now, but it did serve to bring reality crashing down.

Jessie fell silent, her teeth clenched in frustration. No matter how she looked at it, she was no longer in control of her own life.

Chapter 5

It was too much. She felt hemmed in on all sides. Suddenly the cabin, with its tightly drawn draperies and tiny rooms, seemed symbolic of her boxed-in circumstances. She had to have some air, or she would scream the walls down.

She ran to the door, only to find it solidly chained and dead-bolted. Determinedly she set to work on the locks.

"Where do you think you're going?"

"For a walk," she growled while fumbling with the chain. "And don't try to stop me." Dammit, she would have her way in *something*.

His large hand, its knuckles speckled under a masculine smattering of crisp brown hair, covered hers and gently removed it from the recalcitrant lock. With a flick of steady fingers, the chain came undone and dangled freely down the doorjamb.

"I won't stop you, I'll go with you," Ben said. "Wait here while I get your coat."

The bracing walk in the woods behind the cabin was just what Jessie needed to release her pent-up tension. She welcomed the biting cold on her cheeks and the crackle of rime-covered leaves under her boots. After ten minutes she even

topped resenting Ben's silent, watchful presence by her side.
n forty-five minutes they were back at the cabin, and Jessie's
ose, cheeks and feet were chilled almost to numbness. Not a
ingle word had passed between her and Ben the whole time
hey'd been outside.

"Feel better?" he asked when the door was closed and locked
gain.

"Yes." Jessie unzipped her parka and slipped it off her
houlders. Nothing had changed, but the invigorating exercise
nade her feel more calm and able to cope. She could get
hrough this. Soon she'd return to Chicago and be in charge of
er life again.

"Good."

She didn't notice how closely Ben was standing until he took
er jacket out of her hands and looked down at her. Her eyes
trayed to the tips of his ears, which were red from the cold, as
vere his sculpted cheekbones. He had removed his own jacket,
ut the scent of fresh air still clung to him.

Without lifting his gaze from her face, he tossed her jacket
aphazardly onto the chair. "If it's any comfort, I know how
ou feel. It never sits right when a situation is seemingly out of
our hands and you can't do anything to change it."

"It doesn't *seem* that way, it *is* that way. Anyway, how would
ou know how I feel?" she said, observing absently how at-
ractive she found his down-turned eyes.

"Things don't always go the way I want them to, either."

"You could've fooled me," she replied tartly.

A smile crinkled the corners of the eyes she'd just admired.
Their unique blend of green and yellow glimmered at her, full
f catlike mystery. Fascinated, she watched him leisurely pe-
use her face, his enigmatic gaze finally coming to rest on her
air. "It's curling again," he said irrelevantly.

Jessie's hand flew to her head. "I know, the damp air out-
ide—"

"I like it." The three words were a low, provocative rumble
n his chest. Jessie's primping fingers stopped and slowly gave
vay to Ben's larger, less deft ones as they plowed gently through
he curling strands. "It's as soft as it looks," he murmured.
'Like silk, twining around my fingers."

"Ben—"

He spread his fingers and embraced her head in his ope
palm. At the same time his other hand stole to her waist. Jes
sie waited breathlessly for him to pull her closer.

"What the hell am I going to do with you, Jess? You look s
damned adorable, with this rough-and-tumble hair and thes
elegant cheeks all rosy from being outside...." His palm sli
to her ear and he stretched his thumb to lightly graze her cheek
"And this stubborn little chin..." He cupped her jaw. "An
these lips..." Back and forth his thumb dragged across he
bottom lip. "God, these lips...tempting me...and this—" h
heated eyes drifted down "—damned beautiful body..."

His fingers tightened. Jessie closed her eyes and felt h
breath against her mouth.

"We can't finish it, not now," he whispered, "but I've g
to have one more taste."

He needed this, Ben told himself as he brushed the mois
softness of her already-parted lips with his own. Just a littl
something to hold him until he could have her completely.

She smelled fantastic, exotic—intrinsically, utterly female.

Jessie slid her hands up his chest and around his neck at h
second fleeting touch against her lips. "Hey," she protested
trying to follow his elusive mouth.

Charmed by her reaction, Ben tried a third feathery pass
This time she was clearly ready to take matters into her ow
hands, and—what the heck?—he let her have her way. Stand
ing on tiptoe, she met his lips fully, at the same time pressin
her small body into his larger, harder one.

Ben brought his arm around her waist and felt the mind
numbing crush of her breasts against his chest. The groan h
heard at the satisfying contact was his own. Hungrily his tongu
delved into the sweetness of her open mouth.

Oh, yes, baby, just like that, he told her silently when he
tongue eagerly met his, restlessly seeking. Without breaking th
kiss, he used the hand he'd burrowed into her silky hair to ti
her head to another angle. Their lips slid damply in perfe
symmetry to the new position. Ben's heart lurched when he fe
the little shudder of her body and heard the muted whimpe
that marked her pleasure.

Her ardent response fired his blood. He wanted more. Unwilling to break the union of their mouths, wordlessly but urgently he signaled his demand by rubbing and pressing his hand slowly across her back. With carnal understanding she arched into him and moved her upper body sinuously, dragging her breasts against his chest. Their firm points were like darts of fire in an undulating sea of softness. Ben's loins, already tight, surged achingly against his zipper, protesting the confinement of his clothing.

The momentary discomfort jolted him. Despite his body's charging readiness, or maybe because of it, he realized that they had better stop soon. He was in danger of forgetting all the reasons why going to bed with Jessie was a bad idea right now.

Reluctantly he eased the pressure of his arms and lifted his mouth from hers. Jessie looked at him, still a little muddled with passion, her lips softly swollen and red. Her head was thrown back in surrender, her heavy-lidded gaze lingering on his mouth. Shallow pants escaped her lips, and small but strong fingers pressed and fidgeted behind his neck, urging him back to her.

It would take a better man than Ben Sutton to resist such a lure.

"Ah, Jess," he whispered, and he bent to kiss her again. Her mouth opened to him immediately. *Just a little longer, then I'll stop,* he promised himself, sinking back into the voluptuous haze.

She felt wonderful against him. He didn't know how he'd kept from grabbing her before this, especially after she'd showered and changed clothes. Unlike that big sweater she'd worn earlier, this outfit hid nothing of the sweet, bountiful curves of her body. He hadn't been able to look at her without his palms tingling to touch her.

Her breasts had been driving him crazy. He tugged at the back of her blouse until it was pulled free and his hand found smooth, warm skin. Fingers trembling like a boy's, he dragged his palm around to her front under the blouse and cupped her lace-covered softness. Jessie leaned back slightly, lifting herself into his hand.

Ben murmured incoherent approval and fumbled without success for a front opening to her bra. Finally giving up in

frustration, he worked the strap over her shoulder instead an
reached inside the cup to scoop out the plump, womanly flesh
In spite of Jessie's ample proportions, the weighty fullness o
her breast was firm, her skin satiny. She was magnificent. Ben
fondled the luscious prize. No other woman had ever felt so
perfect.

The velvety tautness poking his palm beguiled him. With his
thumb and forefinger he plucked slowly and experimentally a
the hardened nipple. Jessie breathed a keening moan of plea
sure into his mouth, sending a renewed rush of blood into his
erect manhood. Her arms tightened around him and her tongue
became more voracious. Ben's heart nearly stopped when she
drew her leg up along the outside of his thigh.

He tensed, quelling the urge to lift her up and pump his hip
against the accessible notch she had made of her lower body
With effort he pulled his mouth from hers and withdrew his
hand from under her blouse. His arousal was excruciating
Sliding his hands down and grasping her buttocks, he held her
to him tightly and buried his face in her hair.

"What?" she asked thickly.

"Jess, honey," he murmured desperately, "please put your
leg down."

He knew the exact moment his request registered fully in her
mind. There was a brief stillness in her body, and she jerked her
leg to the floor, pushing against his shoulders with her hands.

"No, wait." He gripped her rear more firmly. "Don't move
Not yet."

She must have guessed he was still struggling for control
because mercifully she stopped trying to free herself from his
grasp. Still, her body was tense as she stood in his arms, her
cheek against his chest.

Gradually the clamoring need inside Ben began to abate. His
muscles relaxed and finally he loosened his hold. Shifting his
hands to her shoulders, he drew back and smiled ruefully.

"Damn. That nearly did me in." He lowered his head to kiss
the tip of her nose, but she turned her face so his lips landed in
the hair over her ear.

"Excuse me." She pushed him away with more force than
necessary. Then she disappeared into the bedroom and
slammed the door behind her.

Uh-oh. The lady wasn't pleased.

Ben started to go after her, but hesitated. Maybe they both ould use a little cooling off time.

Fifteen silent minutes went by. Ben's stomach growled, re-ninding him how long it had been since he'd eaten. Jessie was robably hungry, too.

He approached the bedroom door and said loudly, "It's go-ng on one o'clock, Jessie. I thought I'd call to see whether here's a pizza delivery place open around here. Any prefer-nce in toppings?"

"No anchovies."

At least she'd answered him. Ben shrugged and walked to the hone.

A half hour later he called through the door again to let Jes-ie know their meal had arrived. Then, lured by the tantalizing roma of the pizza, he dug in without manners or ceremony. He vas on his second slice when she came out.

The first thing he noticed was that she'd put the sweater back n over her blouse. The next was the determined look on her ace. Deciding it would be unwise to comment on either one, he estured with his can of cola to the flat, open box on the cof-ee table.

"Thanksgiving dinner," he said. "Large deluxe, no ancho-ies."

She gave him a tight smile as she crossed the room and sat lown. "There are a couple of things we need to talk about."

Something about her set face and firm voice told Ben he vasn't going to like what was coming.

"Eat, while it's hot," he told her before taking another bite.

She pressed her lips together. "First of all, I realize I haven't aid thank you for rescuing me last night, and I want to rectify hat. I'm ... grateful."

"All part of the job," he told her magnanimously around his nouthful of pizza.

"Yes. Well, after thinking about what happened at Allie's, believe I understand now the dangers you mentioned before. Therefore, I won't object if you feel you should accompany me ack to Chicago tomorrow."

Ben, who was in the middle of a swallow, nearly choked. "I thought we'd settled that," he said after the chewed mass was safely down his throat.

"In *your* mind, maybe—not in mine," she said pointedly. "But that's neither here nor there. The thing is, I'd like you expert opinion on something. Since I can't go back to Allie's for the night, I thought I might as well stay right here until it's tim to see Kyle tomorrow."

Ben put his pizza down and stared at her. "You're damned right you're staying here."

She nodded. "I thought as much. Should I get a room in side the motel, or try for the cabin next to this one? It doesn't appear to be occupied. Which would be safer?"

"Neither one would be safer than right here, which is where you'll be," Ben said emphatically.

Her eyes flashed. "I don't think that's a good idea."

"Oh, I get it. You're uptight about what nearly happened between us."

She arched her eyebrows haughtily. "Not at all, since it won't happen again. I just feel it would be inappropriate for me spend the night under the same roof with you."

"Inappropriate or not, it's necessary. I can't protect you you're in another building."

"I hardly think I need *protection* in the middle of the night behind locked doors!"

It was Ben's turn to raise his eyebrows. Instantly Jessie's eye lowered to her clasped hands and a soft crimson stained he cheeks. She'd caught the unintentional double entendre in he statement.

"As tempting as it is to pursue the issue of 'protection' wit you, Jessie, I'm not prepared to deal with the consequences. That wasn't quite true, unless you considered the time wasn right for Ben to get involved in an affair. Otherwise, he was we prepared, since he always kept a few foil-wrapped packages the shaving kit he carried in his car. He hadn't needed them f months, but these days a man couldn't be too careful. Uncor fortably, he recalled that he hadn't given the contents of h shaving kit a thought while he'd held Jessie in his arms.

Her blush deepened. She glanced up but didn't quite meet h eyes. "I don't want to engage in sexual innuendo with yo en. In spite of the evidence to the contrary, I'm not in the abit of behaving like that with someone I hardly know."

"Don't feel bad," Ben said. "Neither am I."

She did look at him then. "You aren't?"

Mildly indignant, he said, "No, Jessie, I don't sleep around. 'm a careful—and particular—man. Though I'll admit things ent a little further than I intended awhile ago, you can blame hat on the...unusual effect we have on each other. I won't ake that mistake again. You'll be safe tonight. I'm not going o touch you again until I'm free to finish what we started."

"What do you mean by *that?*"

Ben detected a bite in her question. "Just what I said. I'm on case. I can't be sidetracked right now, as much as I'd like to e. But later, when this is all over, there's no reason we can't xplore the chemistry between us, is there? We do live in the ame city. Oak Park isn't exactly in my backyard, but that's a ninor obstacle. I've got a feeling we're going to be great to-ether, honey."

Jessie sputtered. "Why, you arrogant, egotistical—*man!* Iow dare you make such assumptions about me!"

"What assumptions?" Ben was truly baffled by her reac-ion.

"You are the absolute limit! I've got news for you, Ben. 'elling a woman you'll come around when you've got time for er is *not* an effective prelude to seduction. If you think I'm oing to sit around waiting for you to snap your fingers when 's convenient for you, you're crazy. For one thing, how do you now I'm not already involved with someone?"

Ben's muscles tensed. "Are you?"

She wriggled uncomfortably. "Well, no, I'm not, but—"

"Good." He relaxed. The thought of Jessie with some other nan wasn't a pleasant one. "I'm not, either. So what's the roblem?"

"You're missing the point. I'm not interested in a relation-hip, particularly with a man like you."

Ben wasn't interested in a relationship beyond the most ba-ic one, either, but he didn't think telling Jessie at this juncture hat all he wanted from her was a few sizzling weeks in bed vould win him any medals.

"A man like me?" If she had a thing against cops, and a lo
of women did, there wasn't much he could do about it. He wa
what he was, and if she couldn't handle that, it was her los
Regrettably, it was his, too.

"Oh, yes, I know your type, all right," Jessie said. "I had
bellyful of your brand of machismo with my ex-husband. T
men like you, women are things to have around when you wan
a good meal or a roll in the sack. They aren't people, they're
commodity to be picked up or put down at your convenience
The rest of the time you can't be bothered, unless it's to com
plain they weren't nice enough to your boss or forgot to pick u
your suit at the cleaners or tried to have a conversation whil
you were watching television. No, thanks, I'm smarter than tha
these days. I learned from a master."

"*Now* who's making assumptions?" Ben asked softly. "
don't recall asking you to live with me, Jessie."

Her flush this time was swift and brilliant. "As if I woul
No, you simply presumed I'd be happy to fall into bed wit
you—on *your* timetable. Jerk!"

"Spare me the righteous indignation, princess. You and
both know who called a halt to things before. If I hadn't backe
off, I could've propped you against the wall and taken yo
standing up, and you would've been with me all the way. Don
try to tell me you were thinking of anybody's timetable then!

Jessie gasped and leaped to her feet. "Why, you—"

"I know, I know, I'm a jerk. But I'm a jerk with a job to d
and I'm damned well going to do it. So sit down and eat you
pizza before you burst a blood vessel. In twenty-four hour
you'll be back home in Chicago and you'll never have to see m
again. Since we're stuck with each other till then, we'll just hav
to call a truce and see if we can keep from killing each other i
the meantime."

Jessie stood looking at him, fire still flickering in her eyes. A
uncomfortable silence fell between them that he finally brok
with an impatient sigh.

"Oh, what the hell," he said. "I'm sorry for making as
sumptions, okay? *Now* will you sit down and eat?"

The thin line of Jessie's mouth softened, and she pulled he
lower lip between her teeth. Finally she took her seat in th

space Ben had left on the couch so they could both have access to the pizza.

He popped the tab on her soft drink and held it out to her. "Truce?"

She nodded, gifting him with a momentary glimpse of dark, fathomless blue before dropping her eyes to the can in his hand. Carefully avoiding his fingers, she reached out and accepted his peace offering.

"Truce," she said quietly.

Ben ate two more slices of the rapidly cooling pizza, but his mind wasn't on what he was putting into his mouth. She'd unsettled him again. This advance and retreat stuff was getting to him.

So she'd been married. That wasn't surprising; she had to be somewhere around thirty. Most people had been married at least once by that age. Ben himself was an exception at thirty-five, and even he had come close to the altar with Becky in his early twenties. Of course, he was a different man now than he'd been back then.

Uncomfortable with the direction of his thoughts, he concentrated on Jessie nibbling the crust in her hand. She must have been burned in her marriage, but good. That wasn't unusual, he knew. Few people in this day and age had the kind of enduring relationship his parents enjoyed; they were the exception, not the rule. What bothered Ben was that Jessie lumped him into the same category as her ex-husband. She had hit disturbingly close to the mark.

Ben had never thought of his infrequent liaisons with the opposite sex from the woman's point of view. He'd been more concerned with his own rules, to which he'd adhered religiously: he didn't sleep with his female co-workers, he avoided women who made excessive demands on his time, and he was careful to pick ladies who were no more interested in a permanent relationship than he was. He made sure of the latter by keeping his affairs brief.

Even so, he was a monogamous, considerate lover who believed his partner's satisfaction was as important as his own. He didn't have forever to offer a woman, but he *could* offer good sex, and for the women he'd been with, that was enough. At least, he'd never had any complaints.

He certainly didn't consider women a commodity. But he couldn't deny the time he had spent with women in the past had been at *his* convenience, not theirs. He hadn't thought of his behavior as "picking up and putting down," but now he could see the charge had some merit. For the first time he wondered whether he had ever unwittingly caused a woman pain by his actions.

Still, Ben didn't know how he could have managed things differently. A man in his line of work was a poor risk for a woman looking for commitment, and Ben was more devoted to his job than most.

Not that he hadn't ever thought of what it would be like to have a wife. He'd grown up in a solid family unit, and there had been a time when Ben believed that he, too, had a life mate out there somewhere, a woman to share his home and be his partner, living through good and bad times with him. But that expectation had died eleven years ago with Maddie.

If Ben were looking, though, Jessie wasn't a bad prospect. She was unsullied and wholesome. She could pull him into her warmth, maybe blot out for a while the slime of the underworld he prowled on the job. They'd probably fight over who was in charge ninety percent of the time, but he was starting to get the hang of bringing her around. They might even have children. Ben liked kids. And a man could grow comfortably old with someone like Jessie.

But, hell, what was he thinking? That was a pipe dream. As much as Ben might like the idea of a traditional home and family, it was no longer an option for him. His job took all his effort and concentration, and a wife deserved more than the soiled leftovers of the man he'd become. If he ever had anything with Jessie, it would have to be only a short-term, physical involvement.

Of course, there was the little matter of her cooperation, and the past few minutes didn't bode well for his success in gaining it. Ben hadn't given up, though, in spite of what he'd said earlier about never seeing her again. He'd already tasted her surrender, and he wanted the whole enchilada, at least for a while.

Now, however, wasn't the time to talk about it. Even if they came to an agreement, which wasn't likely in Jessie's current mood, they'd still have to wait until he was reassigned to his Chicago precinct.

If they did manage to get together then, Ben would have to watch himself with her. She stirred an old softness in him, made him want to hold her when she was upset, to cushion her from the harsh realities threatening her, to keep her safe. He thought he'd set aside those almost-forgotten weaknesses years ago. They dulled a man's edge, made him turn in disgust from what he'd become, made him dream of a future he no longer deserved. For her sake and his, he couldn't give in to those feelings.

Still, Jessie's poor opinion of him rankled. God knows he'd done plenty to be ashamed of. But somehow, something inside Ben wanted her to believe he was a better man than her fool of an ex-husband.

The surprisingly large newsroom of the *Sheboygan Sentinel* was sparsely populated the morning after Thanksgiving. Kyle Strickland, who came to the front and introduced himself to Jessie the minute he saw her come in, was a tall, gangly young man who hadn't quite outgrown the teenage acne phase. His long blondish hair was caught in a ponytail, and a small cross dangling from a loop in his left ear flashed in the light from his desk lamp every time he moved his head. He had the kind of looks that got better with age and maturity. Jessie thought that in ten years or so the ladies of Sheboygan would have to be on their guard against those bluer-than-blue eyes.

If he'd gotten over his crush on Allie, that is.

By the time Jessie and Ben had taken seats in front of his desk, Kyle had located and handed Jessie a sealed envelope. "I can't believe how much you look like her," he told Jessie, "even though the hair is different, and Allie is more—you know, more—" He broke off, his face turning crimson.

"I know." Jessie smiled at his infatuation. Her sister had that effect on men. "There's something about her, isn't there?"

Ben gave her a peculiar look when she said that, but her mind was on the letter in her hand. She started to open it on the spot, but he stopped her with a touch and a shake of his head. Jessie fingered the edges of the envelope restlessly, dying to know what Allie had written.

"Tell us about Allie," Ben said to Kyle.

Kyle immediately looked wary. "For one thing, she didn't tell me to expect Jessie to arrive with a man."

Jessie leaned forward confidentially. "It's all right, Kyle. You can talk freely. Ben's a friend of mine, and he wants to help my sister."

"To help her! Is she in trouble?"

"We don't think so," Ben said, "but we need to find her."

Kyle sized him up, taking his time. "You're a cop, aren't you?"

Jessie quickly glanced over at Ben, who said nothing, but simply watched Kyle impassively.

Kyle nodded knowingly but didn't press the issue. "All right, I'll tell you what I can, but I don't know where Allie is."

"Did she tell you anything about her plans?" Ben asked.

The young photographer shook his head, causing the cross to swing wildly on its hoop. "Nothing specific. Just that she was going away for a while. I tried to find out more—I knew she'd been working independently on a story in Port Mangus—but she was in too much of a hurry to answer my questions. She met me at a convenience store and asked me to come to the office and hang around until Jessie got here so I could deliver that letter. Then she made a call from the phone booth, got back in her car, and left. That's all I know."

Ben absorbed the information pensively. "This was Wednesday, right?"

"Yeah. I'd guess it was around six-thirty or so in the evening. I'd already eaten."

Jessie glanced at Ben. "The call she made must have been to her answering machine."

Ben nodded and she turned back to Kyle. "Did she seem . . . scared?"

Again Kyle shook his head, this time more thoughtfully. "No. Actually, she seemed excited, like something great was about to happen. Anyway, after she left I came here to wait like she said, but when it got to be midnight and you still hadn't shown up, I had to leave. My folks in South Bend were expecting me to spend Thanksgiving with them." He looked at Jessie apologetically.

"Oh, no, please," Jessie said. "I didn't get Allie's message until yesterday. I'm the one who's sorry you had to wait around for nothing."

"Well, at least we finally connected. Oh, there's one more thing." He turned to Ben. "There was another person in the car—a girl."

"A girl? Who?"

"I didn't recognize her, and Allie didn't introduce us. I didn't even get a good look at her, because she kind of kept her head down. She was blond, maybe in her late teens, early twenties."

"Any ideas, Jessie?"

"Not a clue," Jessie answered, more mystified than ever. Just then Kyle looked toward the back of the room in alarm. "Uh-oh," he muttered.

His warning came a split second before the deafening "*There you are!*" behind Jessie's back.

Chapter 6

Jessie jerked instinctively, and Ben leapt to his feet, his hand reaching inside his jacket. Before she even realized what had happened, he had taken a protective stance between her and the angry voice.

"Ben." She whispered tersely, rising quickly from her chair and pulling on his arm. He couldn't be thinking of drawing his gun here!

The man who had bellowed emerged from the doorway of a glassed-in office, marked Managing Editor, at the rear of the room. To Jessie's relief, Ben's hand came away empty from the hidden shoulder holster. The muscles of his arm, however, were rigid with tension, and she felt through her fingertips his readiness to spring into action.

"It's the boss," she heard Kyle say under his breath. The covert explanation was hardly necessary; Jessie had already recognized both the voice and the temper from Allie's taped phone messages. The florid-faced man's eyes were focused solely on Jessie as he strode angrily in her direction, pulling on a wrinkled topcoat.

"So you finally decided to show up for work," he said sarcastically. "Too late, as it turns out."

It was plain he had mistaken her for Allie. She spoke up seconds before he reached Kyle's desk, which was located toward the front of the newsroom. "I'm afraid you've—"

"Forget it, Webster." He kept walking, the hostility he projected seeming directed as much at the wool scarf he was stuffing inside his neckline as at Jessie. "I got too much to do to stand around listening to excuses. The accounting department already has your last check made out. You're fired."

By the time he had delivered this startling pronouncement, he had swept past Jessie. "Wait a minute," she protested to his back. "You're making a mistake."

He rounded on her suddenly and snarled. "No, Webster, *you're* the one who made the mistake. If you had time to get a new hairdo in the past three days, you had time to do your job and that means reporting the stories *I* give you, got it? My reporters don't go anywhere I don't send 'em, and they don't write anything I don't assign. I warned you. You don't play by my rules, you don't play. Take your stuff with you today when you leave. And then I don't want to see you around here again."

"But—"

"No *buts,* no *nothing!*" His stout forefinger stabbed the air in front of him. Defensively Jessie pressed closer to Ben, who put a supportive arm around her. The stubby little editor whirled around and made his way to the door. He opened it with a parting shot at Jessie over his shoulder.

"Make sure you're outta here when I get back." The windows rattled at his exit.

A silent moment greeted his absence, then the whole room seemed to sigh in relief. Uncomfortably, Jessie realized she had become the center of attention. Ben came to her rescue, turning her away from the curious eyes to face Kyle, who stood behind his desk and looked at her sympathetically.

"He gets like that," Kyle said. "Which reminds me, I have something to show you."

He led them to a corner desk in the large room. "This is— was—Allie's desk. Somebody boxed up all of her things between midnight Wednesday and this morning. It was like this when I got in today."

The desk was cleared of everything but a computer and a large cardboard box full of loose papers and miscellaneous items. There was no doubt the contents belonged to Allie, since on top of the pile was the framed twenty-fifth wedding anniversary photo of Allie and Jessie's parents. Jessie had one just like it sitting on her desk at home.

"He had her stuff packed up before he even fired her? Boy, he wasn't kidding when he said he wanted her out of here!" she exclaimed. "What did she do to make him so mad?"

"Allie and the boss were always at odds, mostly about what she considered to be fluff assignments. She kept badgering him for more meaty stories. I guess when she didn't come to work for two days, it was the last straw."

"Did he know about her story in Port Mangus?" Ben asked.

"He could have found out, I suppose. It sounded just now as though he thought she was working on something he hadn't assigned."

"Who besides you knew Allie had something going on her own?"

Kyle shrugged. "Nobody as far as I know. Allie talked to me more than anyone else in the office, and even I couldn't get anything out of her about it. She swore me to secrecy, just said she was on to something that would make her in the business. Whatever it was, it kept her busy most evenings doing research."

With an inner smile Jessie wondered what shy Kyle would think of Allie's "research" in a strip joint. He'd probably turn beet red all the way to his hair roots.

"I think you've gotten what you came for, Jess," Ben said, interrupting her thoughts. "Ready to go?"

"I guess so." Ben's tone was brisk, but warmth flooded her when he called her "Jess." She liked the intimacy implied by the shortened name.

"What about Allie's stuff? Should we take it with us?"

Guessing he probably wanted to go through her sister's papers, Jessie replied, "That's a good idea." She turned to Kyle. "I'll make sure that Allie gets it," she said, to forestall any objections.

Kyle shrugged bony shoulders. "Since everybody here thinks you're Allie, it might look a little strange if you left without it."

Ben slid the large box off the desk and into his arms with easy strength. "You've been a big help, Kyle. Just don't talk to anyone about this, or snoop around asking questions that might raise suspicions. Let everybody here take what just happened at face value. Okay?"

Kyle's brilliant blue eyes sharpened. "I'd sure like to know what's going on."

"The less you know the better, trust me," Ben said.

Kyle walked them to the parking lot, and while Ben stowed Allie's belongings in the trunk of the Trans Am, the younger man pulled out a pad and a pen and jotted something down. He tore off the paper and handed it to Jessie. "Would you let me know when you find her? Or have her call me? Considering what Ben just said, I'm more worried than ever. And now that she's not working here anymore, I, uh, wouldn't want to lose touch."

Jessie folded the paper and placed it in her purse. "Of course," she said. "Thank you for all your trouble, Kyle. I'll be sure to let Allie know what a big help you've been."

Kyle colored, and he glanced down at the ground. "I wish I could do more."

Jessie liked this young man. She hoped some sweet woman more his age would grab his attention before long; there was no way Allie might return his tender feelings. "My sister is lucky to have your friendship," she said.

She couldn't say more without embarrassing him. Anyway, Ben didn't give her a chance. He added his thanks to Jessie's, and hurried her into the car.

"The boy's in love," Ben remarked as they eased into traffic.

"It seems so, doesn't it?" Jessie's eyes fell on the letter in her hand. Quickly she strapped herself in and turned the envelope to the flap side. "Allie has collected a lot of hearts in her day."

"No more than you, surely."

She shook her head, tore open the envelope and pulled out a folded sheet of notepaper, her mind only marginally on their conversation. "We may look alike, but inside we couldn't be more different. I don't have Allie's confidence."

It took only seconds to peruse her sister's message.

Jessie—
Sorry about Thanksgiving and all this cloak-and-dagger
stuff, but it's necessary. Please do exactly what I tell you,
sis. You mustn't stay in Port Mangus tonight. You could
be in danger. Go back to Oak Park immediately, and I'll
call you at home as soon as I can. Don't worry about me.
I'm fine. I'll explain everything when I call.

Love,
A

Disappointed, Jessie sank back into the seat. Ben had maintained an obliging silence as she read, but now he glanced curiously at the paper she held.

"What does it say?"

"Nothing helpful." She read the note aloud.

"See there?" he said when she'd finished. "Didn't I tell you
she could probably take care of herself?"

"Yes, but we still don't know where she is or what she's doing. And what about that girl Kyle said was with her? There are
so many unanswered questions." Jessie sighed, refolded the
letter and put it into her purse.

"Well, my guess is we'll know soon enough what she's up
to," Ben said absently. "Damn. Would you look at all these
cars?"

Jessie glanced out the window at the streets of downtown
Sheboygan. Christmas decorations hung everywhere, reminding her that this was the first shopping day of the Christmas
season. Heavy traffic demanded all Ben's attention.

It was hard to read his mood this morning. Following yesterday's clash of wills, they had both been scrupulously polite.
When they talked at all. Jessie hadn't raised any further objections about staying in the cabin. Nor had she squabbled about
ordering in another pizza at dinnertime, or taking the bed again
instead of the couch.

She hadn't wanted to do any of those things. But she'd decided that even though physical proximity had been forced
upon them, *emotional* distance, at least, was essential after
what had nearly happened yesterday. And since arguments re-
quired a certain amount of personal involvement, they were to
be avoided at all costs, no matter how he provoked her.

By silent agreement they had put aside their differences for their visit to the *Sentinel.* Jessie remembered how he'd put his arm around her and called her "Jess" in that casually intimate way. Of course, he was just doing his job. Kyle would have been suspicious if he'd suspected they were at odds.

Firmly Jessie took herself in hand. She was right to keep her distance. When they were alone, any interaction with Ben beyond the most superficial wasn't worth the risk. She knew now how quickly and effortlessly anger could be converted into passion.

Contrarily, it bothered her that Ben hadn't shown any inclination to break through the barriers she'd erected since their argument. Certainly one part of her—the rational part—knew the pull between them was better left a question mark. But the dreamy idealist inside thrilled to the power of Ben's kisses and the touch of his hands on her body. She had never known such abandon before.

Her books were full of it, of course. She blessed every one of her heroines with a perfect partner who knew how to draw every last ounce of response from his woman and leave her blissfully sated. But that was fiction, the product of Jessie's own fairy-tale imaginings.

So she had thought. But twice now in Ben's arms she had felt herself on the precipice of a glorious realm of physical discovery that promised—or threatened—to change her forever. The frightening thing was that under the influence of Ben's compelling kisses, her instinct was to jump with heedless joy right over the edge. Yesterday, in fact, the only thing stopping her from succumbing to that urge was *his* restraint.

That was the problem. While every nerve in her body had screamed for more, Ben had pulled back. Humiliated and resentful, Jessie concluded she had been more overwhelmed than he. His greater control had given him the upper hand, something she'd vowed, after her divorce, never to grant another man.

It wasn't that Jessie was either an ardent feminist or a man hater. As miserable as it had been, her marriage hadn't put her off men altogether; she was wise enough to know that her ex-husband didn't represent his whole sex. She still planned to have a husband and children someday. Somewhere in the world the right man was waiting for her. And when fate dropped him into her lap, she would devote herself to making him happy.

But it was glaringly evident Ben wasn't the right man, any more than Antonio had been. Unwisely she'd forgotten Ed's advice. Ben's insulting insinuation that she would be willing to wait for him until he had time for her was confirmation that his partner knew him well. His job would come before any woman.

To Jessie, that attitude was worse than the way he bossed her around. She wouldn't settle again for anything less than first place in her man's life. A smart woman didn't make the same mistake twice.

Lucky for her, Ben's work right now was in Port Mangus, so after today, no further contact with him would be necessary. With a hundred and fifty-plus miles separating them, Jessie would be able to get on with her life and forget all about him. She had her work to keep her sufficiently occupied.

She had just completed her latest manuscript, *Angel's Tread*, and sent it to her agent two days ago. Ideas for her next book had been brewing for weeks while she'd finished Sydney's tale, and soon she would be embroiled in a new plot with new characters, and there wouldn't be time to think about what might have been. She was better off not knowing what she was missing.

And if her hormones regretted the loss, well, she would simply choose to ignore them.

Ben mumbled something unintelligible under his breath. Jessie noticed him glancing frequently into both the windshield and side mirrors as he drove. *Too* frequently?

"What?" she asked, alarmed. "Is someone following us?"

Ben grabbed her arm in warning. "Don't turn around. I don't know yet. Adjust your seat belt as tight as you can, just in case."

Jessie stared straight ahead and followed his instructions. He made a right turn at the next intersection, and two blocks later he turned again.

"Damn," he muttered after yet another check of the mirrors. "Let's try one more."

The bumper-to-bumper traffic caused the maneuver into the left-turn lane to take some time, but they finally made it. Ben's eyes were glued to the rearview mirror after he made the turn. Jessie sat tensely awaiting his judgment of the situation.

"Okay, we've got a tail," he said about halfway down the block.

"Oh, God," she said. "Is it the Chevy?"

"No, this one's a Mazda, I think, kind of a tan color, and it's just one man. He's hanging back one or two cars. Don't worry, though. We're lucky all the Christmas shoppers are out today. I can lose him up here at the light."

Ben stopped for the yellow signal. The car behind honked angrily, but he disregarded the other driver's annoyance. They were still in the left lane, and now Ben's Trans Am was first in line for the green light.

His eyes flitted from the pedestrians crossing in front of them, to the cars passing through the intersection, to the pickup truck waiting on their right side, to the rearview mirror, and back to begin the cycle again. When the last pedestrian had cleared the hood, he eased into the crosswalk, his hands tightening on the wheel.

"Hang on. . . ." he said softly.

Now his gaze fixed on the traffic signal. The instant the light turned green, he pressed and held the horn, floored the accelerator and entered the intersection, cutting sharply in front of the startled driver of the truck.

Jessie was stunned by the move. She squeezed her eyes shut and buried her face in her hands. Immediately her ears were filled with a cacophonous symphony of blaring horns and screeching tires. Her whole body was flung toward Ben. The twin restraints of her safety belt and harness held her in her seat, but she felt the force all the way to her bones. The acrid smell of burning rubber sifted through the mask of flesh she'd created with her fingers and bit at her nostrils.

We're going to die, she thought. Beseechingly she sent a mute prayer toward heaven.

The expected impact never came.

"It's all over, Jess. We made it," Ben said, a few seconds after the swerving motions of the car had stopped pulling at her. Only then did she uncover her face and open her eyes.

To her amazement, once again there were cars on all sides
and except for the fact they were headed in another direction
Ben's suicidal gambit might never have been executed. They'
made the illegal turn without killing anybody.

"Thank you, Lord," she whispered fervently. To Ben sh
said, "Is he still back there?"

"He's back there, all right—way back," he said with satis
faction. "By the time he gets out of that gridlock we left hir
in, he won't have the faintest idea where to find us."

Jessie drew in a huge gulp of air and exhaled slowly. "I don
think I'm cut out for this sort of thing."

Ben grinned engagingly. "You did great. Not even a squea
out of you."

"Are you kidding? My vocal cords were paralyzed in abjec
terror, just like the rest of me."

He chuckled.

"Nice driving, by the way," she told him.

"And a little luck," he said modestly.

It was a nice, congenial exchange, devoid of undercurrents
and Jessie welcomed it. She and Ben weren't playacting now
nor did she want to return to their earlier stiff politeness. The
many confrontations and the heated emotions that accompa
nied them seemed insignificant at the moment—far less im
portant than the fact that they were alive and well.

Nothing like a little mortal danger to put things in perspec
tive.

They picked up Jessie's car at the Piney Woods Motel an
drove to Chicago in caravan with only a single stop for gase
line. The trip was uneventful, but after the morning's excite
ment, Jessie was reassured each time she glanced into he
rearview mirror and found Ben's car following her trail like
faithful guard dog.

They made good time. In Oak Park, Ben pulled into he
driveway after her and she waited for him beside her car. He go
out of the Trans Am and moved toward her with a rangy, sen
sual gait. In the cold light of this winter day, the gold fleck
lightened his direct green gaze and gave him the look of
predator, not quite tame and a little dangerous. Jessie saw th

underlying hunger there, too—hunger for *her*—and a tiny thrill of excitement shot through her. He was a beautiful beast.

She smiled, wondering what he'd think if she told him her thoughts. Ben hesitated in midstep, still several feet away, his eyes on her face.

"You must be glad to be home." He returned her smile with a crooked one of his own.

Jessie decided not to correct his misinterpretation of her good mood. "Oh, I am. Can I interest you in an omelet? I'm sure I left a dozen or so eggs in the fridge."

"Sure," Ben said. "I have to call the FBI office to coordinate the meeting with my boss anyway. I'll do it from here."

He brought up her bags and riffled through the box they'd taken from Allie's office while Jessie busied herself in her small kitchenette, wishing she hadn't left things so untidy.

Except for the bathroom, there were no dividing walls in the apartment. Jessie liked it that way, even though when she was in the midst of a writing frenzy, her tendency to clutter was worse than usual and she couldn't close any doors on the accumulation. She didn't have many visitors, so usually it didn't matter. Unfortunately, she had forgotten how she had left the place when she'd invited Ben up. There had been no time for housecleaning once she'd packaged up her finished manuscript, not if she was to make it to Port Mangus before Thanksgiving.

Well, it was too late now. Jessie noticed that Ben had set aside the box and was staring at her unmade bed in the far left corner of the room.

"Excuse the mess," she told him over her shoulder as she whipped the eggs. "When I'm writing, I'm not a tidy person."

Which was a true enough statement, as far as it went. Jessie didn't add that she'd been careless about housework ever since the divorce six years ago, and it had nothing to do with her writing. While she'd been married, her ex-husband had demanded that she keep their home spotless. He would become sharply critical if so much as a throw pillow was out of place.

Antonio himself, of course, had been less than a model of neatness, habitually leaving his clothes and whatever else came to hand wherever he happened to be when he was finished with them. To top it off, he had seen no inconsistency in his exact-

ing requirements of Jessie. She was his wife, and a wife picke
up after her husband.

Now she looked at her unkempt apartment through Ben'
eyes and decided that in this aspect she might have carried he
declaration of independence from Antonio too far. Slovenli
ness was not an attractive trait.

"The phone's on the desk by the computer," she told Ben
hoping to divert him.

He made the call from her "office," but stayed in the cor
ner to idly scan the titles in her bookcase. "Did you write any
of these?"

Inwardly Jessie cringed, but she reminded herself to answe
confidently. She had nothing to be ashamed of. "The paper
backs on the third shelf from the top. I write under the pseud
onym Luciana Wells."

She turned to the stove to pour the beaten eggs into a heate
pan. The silence behind her meant Ben had probably taken a
book down and was just realizing what kind of literature she
wrote. Tensely she waited for whatever his brand of put-dow
might be.

"You wrote all these?"

"Yes," she said without turning around. "I just finishe
number eleven before going to Allie's." She cleared her throat
"That's the reason this place is such a mess. When I write I
don't clean up behind myself. Sometimes, when it's going well
I even forget to eat...." Jessie stopped, aware she was on the
verge of babbling.

"I'm impressed, Jess. How long have you been writing?"

He sounded perfectly sincere. She looked at him over her
shoulder. "All my life, actually, but I've only been published
for a little over six years."

He sauntered toward her, thumbing through a volume—oh
Lord, which one, she wondered, feeling jittery. She was too fa
away to tell. Not that it mattered. All her books were romanti
suspense, heavy on the romance. Jessie believed in giving her
mostly female fans what they wanted.

"Looking for the good parts?" she taunted, to disguise her
nervousness.

Ben looked up and raised a curious eyebrow as he closed the
distance between them. "You're an intelligent woman, I as

sume all the parts are good. I'd like to read this. Would you mind?''

Jessie returned to her eggs, feeling unaccountably defensive. He'd selected *Midnight Lies,* one of her most sensual offerings. "Of course I don't *mind.* Though I'm sure it's not your usual style of reading material.''

"I admire creative people. In my business, you don't meet too many.'' He touched her arm lightly with the book in his hand. "Hey, Jess.''

Oh, dear, there was that voice again, and calling her "Jess'' to boot. The gooseflesh rose on Jessie's arms and she had to forcibly subdue the delicious sensation that shivered through her body.

Good heavens, if the man was a late-night radio announcer, he could make a fortune! He'd have all the women in Chicago panting in their beds as they listened. He'd be so popular, they'd probably syndicate him, and after that, Masters and Johnson would report a sharp rise in feminine erotic dreams and fantasies across the country, all centered around Ben Sutton's husky, evocative voice.

Jessie stirred the eggs briskly, then, realizing she was turning an omelet into scrambled eggs, slammed the spoon down on the stove and spun on her heel to face him. Wishing she didn't have to look up so far to meet his eyes, she said, "Go ahead and read it. I warn you, though, it's women's fiction. You may not like it.''

Ben searched her face. "Why do I feel like I'm taking the hits for some other guy?''

The fire drained out of Jessie as she realized he was right. "Okay, guilty. My ex-husband thought my stories too earthy and trivial—too *female*—for a lawyer's wife. He was embarrassed to have anyone know about them, so I was forbidden to talk about my writing to any of his friends or colleagues. I suppose I'm a little touchy on the subject.''

"Just a little.''

The look on Ben's face was so pained Jessie laughed sheepishly. He smiled back, their eyes caught, and smiles wavered as the air between them began to throb.

"Jess . . .'' Ben murmured.

Whatever he planned to say was lost forever when the phone rang. Jessie reluctantly excused herself and walked to the desk.

"Hello?"

"Jessie. Thank God. Where have you been?"

Her sister's anxious voice cut through the fog in Jessie's brain. "Allie?" Her two hands gripped the receiver, and she glanced back at Ben joyously. "Ben, it's Allie."

Then she noticed the smoke behind him. "Oh, no! The eggs!"

Ben turned around at her dismayed outburst and reacted instantly, grabbing the smoking skillet by its insulated handle and placing it on a nearby cutting board.

"Who's with you, Jessie? What's happening? Are you all right? Jessie!"

"It's okay now," she said into the receiver as Ben flung open a window to let the gathering smoke escape. "Just a little cooking mishap. Ben's taking care of it."

Ben said something to her over his shoulder as she spoke. Unable to make out the words above her own voice, she tucked the receiver under her chin and asked, "What?"

As he repeated whatever he had said, Allie, sounding frantic, shouted, "Ben? Who's Ben? Jessie, who's with you?"

"Take it easy, Al. I'm all right," Jessie soothed. "Hold on a sec, will you?" She put her hand over the mouthpiece. "Sorry, Ben, I couldn't hear you."

Ben stopped waving the smoke toward the window long enough to tell her again, "I said, wait a minute before you talk to her about the investigation. Make sure it's off-the-record first."

"You're joking, right?" she scoffed. "She's my *sister.*"

"No joke, Jess," he said. "Allie's a reporter, remember, and I don't want her interfering with this case any more than she already has."

"She won't, once I tell her what's going on."

Even across the room Jessie could detect the set of Ben's jaw at her protest.

"Off-the-record, Jessie, or you can give me that phone right now, and *I'll* talk to her."

She clenched her teeth. He did it to her every time. Just when she was beginning to think he wasn't half-bad, he started bossing her around again.

"You can dump those eggs in the wastebasket under the sink, and run some water in the pan. That should get rid of the smoke faster," she said frostily. Then she deliberately turned her back on him.

"Okay, Allie, everything's under control now. Ben says he knows you from that club where you were working as a waitress. Did you know he's a policeman? Why didn't you tell me what you were doing? I mean, a *strip joint,* for Pete's sake!"

There was a telling silence from Allie's end of the line, then, "Are you talking about Ben, the bouncer? He's a cop? Are you sure, Jessie?"

"I'm sure." Jessie heard rasping noises behind her and turned to watched him scrape the burnt eggs into the covered container she kept under the sink for garbage. "He's been working undercover, just like you. And, Allie, don't get mad, but he says the only way I can talk to you about what's been happening is if you agree it's off-the-record."

"What? Who does he think he is?"

"He's a cop doing his job, I guess." She was surprised to hear herself defending him. "I think he just means to protect his investigation until he and the FBI have all the evidence they need. They know you're a reporter."

"Just my luck. What's been going on there, anyway?"

"Off-the-record?"

"Yes, off-the-record!" Allie shot back. "Jeez Louise!"

Jessie grinned at the childish interjection, relieved that her sister had capitulated so easily. "So much has happened, I hardly know where to start. I guess you already know somebody was after you in Port Mangus?"

"No! That is, I knew there was a chance, but—"

"Well, anyway, listen to this. They thought I was you, Allie, and Ben had to come and save me. Where did you go?"

"Oh, Jessie! You didn't listen to the messages on my answering machine, did you? And that means Kyle didn't give you my note."

"Not until today, but it wasn't his fault. He's been worried about you, Allie. Where are you, anyway?"

"Uh-uh, sis, you first. I've been trying to call you for *two days*. I was scared to death something terrible had happened."

"It might have, if Ben hadn't come to my rescue." Jessie settled into a chair beside the phone. Starting with her arrival in Port Mangus, she hit the high spots of her two days of adventure, omitting the more personal aspects of her story.

While she talked, the smoke cleared. Ben closed the window and joined her in the living area, where he neatly stacked the scattered newspapers on the sofa and set them aside so he had a place to sit.

"So the chauvinistic pea-brain fired me," Allie said after Jessie had related the events in the newsroom. "I figured as much."

"Ask her if she had anything in her desk about the story at Club Duan," Ben said. "I didn't find anything in the box."

Jessie was still put out with him, but she refrained from sticking out her tongue at his edict. "Ben wants to know if you kept notes in your desk about the club."

"Absolutely not," Allie said. "I kept my notes in the trunk of my car, and I didn't tell anything to a soul. This is *my* story."

Jessie relayed Allie's negative response with a shake of her head at Ben. "But you don't have a job anymore," she said into the phone.

"Then I'll free-lance it." Jessie recognized that stubborn determination in her sister's voice.

"Every paper in the Midwest will be after me when I write this thing up. It's big, Jessie, bigger than I dreamed when I first got wind of it. I've got something that'll knock the police *and* the FBI on their collective fannies. I found a journal in Mai Duan's safe."

"A journal? What were you doing in her safe?" Jessie shrugged at Ben, who had sat up straight when he heard her words.

"Well, to make a long story short," Allie answered, "I sneaked into her office to look around while she was busy elsewhere. To my surprise, one of the strippers, a girl named Christie Carter, had gotten there before me and was robbing the safe. She told me later she was the one who had arranged for Mai to be called out of her office in the middle of counting the night's receipts. She was stealing money for a plane ticket to

Kansas, where her parents live. Jessie, Christie's only seventeen, can you believe it? She was *stripping,* for God's sake, to keep her sleazy boyfriend in dope.''

"Seventeen! Didn't anyone check her ID?'' Jessie noticed Ben signaling her, but she was too interested in what her twin was saying to interrupt the flow of the story.

"She has a very convincing set of ID that says she's twenty-two,'' Allie said. ''Anyway, the two of us struck a deal. I agreed not to give her away if she'd put the money back. Then I persuaded her to tell me her story while I drove her home to Kansas.''

"That's where you are, in Kansas?'' Jessie frowned at Ben and nodded impatiently to let him know she was well aware he wanted a report and she'd get around to it in a minute.

"Yes, at Christie's parents. The poor kid has had a rough time of it, and I'm acting as sort of a buffer right now. But there's more, Jessie. While I was in Mai's office, well, since the safe was already open, I couldn't resist checking a few papers. I came across a journal written mostly in Vietnamese, except for some lists of names and numbers. And you won't believe the names I saw, including my slimy boss's—ex-boss, that is. Mai must have been keeping records for some kind of exposé, or something.''

"Wow! You *stole* it?'' Jessie could see that Ben was on tenterhooks to know what Allie was saying. ''Hold on a minute, Allie. I need to tell Ben about this.''

"No! You might not be able to trust him.''

Jessie considered the scowling man sitting on her couch. ''I trust him, Allie. He saved my life, remember?''

Over her sister's protests, Jessie concisely related the gist of what Allie had told her. Ben's face grew more and more grim as she spoke. He shook his head when she'd finished.

"Good Lord. Tell her to go to the nearest FBI office or the local police and turn that journal over to them *right now.*''

Dutifully she repeated his directive.

"Does he think I'm stupid?'' Allie exclaimed. ''If I do that, my inside access to the biggest story of my life is history. Tell him no way, Jessie. I'm going to deliver that baby to the authorities in Chicago myself—*after* they give me some guarantees. I've got a bargaining chip, and I'm going to use it to get an exclusive.''

"Are you sure that's wise, Allie?" Jessie asked worriedly.

"What did she say?" Ben wanted to know.

"She says she's going to bring the journal back herself."

"Give me that." He got up and grabbed the receiver out of Jessie's hand. "Allie, this is Ben. Allie? Allie?" With a muttered expletive, he handed the phone back to Jessie. "She hung up. Did she say where she is, at least?"

Jessie recradled the handset. "In Kansas."

"I know, but *where* in Kansas?"

She thought back, then shook her head. "Sorry, I don't know."

"Great," Ben said. "Kansas. That really narrows it down."

He walked to a nearby window and stared out, hands in his back pockets in a masculine, unconsciously sensual pose. Six years of celibacy was finally getting to her, Jessie thought. Did thirty-one-year-old women have middle-age crises? There had to be *some* explanation for why she was drawn to a man so manifestly wrong for her.

"What now?" she asked in an attempt to distract herself.

He combed his fingers through his thick hair. "How about I help you fix us something to eat while we go over everything Allie told you again? Before I report in downtown, I need to know all of it." He glanced at his watch. "My boss on this case has meetings this afternoon and we still have a couple of hours till he's in his office. Okay?"

Without waiting for Jessie's answer, he headed for the refrigerator. In spite of his typical presumption that she would fall in with his plans, she followed him into her little kitchenette without rancor. He'd taken her acquiescence for granted, to be sure, but at least he'd asked this time.

As she brushed by the counter, Jessie's eyes snagged on the forgotten copy of *Midnight Lies*. A secret smile warmed her insides. Unlike Antonio, Ben seemed to approve of her writing career. Maybe there was hope for him yet.

Chapter 7

Chief Agent Cal Leutzinger placed the notes he'd taken during Ben's report on the corner of his desk and sat back in his chair.

Ben thought the stereotyped image most people had of government agents sat on Cal's shoulders with particular ease. He was an unpretentious-looking man. But his wire-rimmed glasses hid a sharp intellect, as well as a wealth of hard experience gained over years in fieldwork for the bureau.

He had a legendary reputation in the Chicago office as a relentless agent with no patience for ineptitude, and was regarded with judicious respect by his co-workers. Since there was inherently an adversarial relationship between feds and local cops, even when they were cooperating on a case, Ben couldn't say he liked the man. Still, he'd sensed from the start of the Club Duan investigation that Leutzinger took his work seriously. Ben could relate to that.

For the past hour and a half, the agent had put him through a grueling debriefing on the case and now regarded him with serious eyes. "I got a call from Ed Brock this afternoon, right after yours, Sutton. Somebody broke into that duplex where you've been staying in Port Mangus."

Ben quickly adapted to the switch in topic. "A burglary?"

"That's what it looked like at first. A neighbor noticed a broken window open on your side of the place, got suspicious and called the police. When the cops saw you weren't there, your landlord was notified. He let them in to investigate."

"And?"

"Nothing was taken that they could tell, at least none of the things that burglars are usually interested in. Whoever broke in was looking for something else. Every room had been ransacked."

Ben ignored the curl of distaste in his stomach. The few possessions he'd kept in the furnished duplex were not valuable, but being a cop didn't preclude him from a sense of violation at strangers pawing through his belongings. "Any clues as to who did it?"

Leutzinger shook his head. "According to the police chief, the Port Mangus boys investigated, and nobody saw anything. A light-colored car a few neighbors noticed parked on the street a couple of doors down from the duplex might be involved, but that's not much to go on."

Ben's instincts perked. "Was the car a Mazda?"

"I thought of that, too, when you told me about the tail you picked up in Sheboygan. Could be. But since nothing was taken, I doubt they'll pursue it any further, even if we tell them about the Mazda. It's a long shot that would require a lot of man-hours to check out. Not worth it for a simple break-in with no property loss."

This didn't feel right, Ben thought. "If whoever broke in wasn't your average small-time junkie after a quick buck for his next fix, what was he looking for? It's not likely he was there by mistake or coincidence."

"Could the Duan woman be behind it, just checking you out?"

"Uh-uh. Too late in the game. I've been working for her for more than two months."

"But what about the journal that reporter says she has?"

Ben nodded. The agent's train of thought matched his own. "If that's what they were looking for, it could mean Mai's found out somehow I'm a cop."

"Maybe. Or she might have just been looking for a connection between you and that reporter. Could be she thinks you're a reporter, too. Or that there would be something at your place that would lead her to the Webster woman."

Ben just looked at him. His intuition told him differently.

"Or else," Leutzinger continued bleakly, "we're totally off base and Mai had nothing to do with the break-in at all. Maybe it *was* a burglary, and the thieves were scared off by something before they had a chance to take anything. Coincidences *do* happen." He sighed. "What a mess. So far in this case we haven't got a single thing we can use in court. Instead we've got a hotshot reporter who's managed to run off right under our noses with a potentially important piece of evidence we didn't even know existed. She's somewhere in the state of Kansas with some girl whose name may or may not be Carter, and we don't have even the name of a city to help run her down. Not that that would necessarily help, because said reporter is showing distinct signs of noncooperation."

He took off his glasses and rubbed his eyes before settling the wire rims back into place. "For all I know, I could wake up tomorrow and find our case spread all over the front page of every newspaper in the country. Now, to top it off, there's a good chance the cover of my primary operator has been compromised. This investigation is going to hell in a hand basket, Sutton."

Ben wasn't happy about how things were going, either, and he felt more than a little responsible. He should have seen through Allie Webster's machinations. And if, as he suspected, his cover had been blown, that left the questions how and by whom? Had he been careless without realizing it?

"I'm going to pull you off the case," Leutzinger said. "You can report back to your old precinct on Monday."

Ben blinked. He hadn't expected this. "Why?"

"The only reason we called you in was for the undercover piece, and my gut tells me you've been made. Even if you haven't, your chances of getting Mai to trust you after somebody stole her journal are almost nil. She's going to be suspicious of everybody for a long time. So I can't use you there anymore, and there's no other reason to keep you—none that I can justify to your commander, anyway. I have to let you go."

Ben tightened his jaw. In eleven years working undercover, this was the first time he'd been pulled in the middle of an investigation. He didn't like it.

"You know," Leutzinger went on thoughtfully, "maybe the situation isn't as black as it looks. We can start checking out this editor in Sheboygan, for one thing. Besides him, this journal, if we can get our hands on it, raises possibilities for establishing Duan's link to organized crime. I'll have a Vietnamese translator standing by. The thing is, it might not be good evidence, given the way the Webster woman got it. I'll have to check with the prosecutor on the legalities. They've assigned us a new one, by the way. Ted Simmons is still in a coma, and it's doubtful now that he's going to make it."

"I heard." The news about the assistant U.S. attorney's automobile accident Thanksgiving morning had been part of Ed's update at the cabin.

"In fact—" Leutzinger reached for his telephone and punched in some numbers "—the U.S. Attorney's Office was supposed to send the new guy over today to get filled in on Simmons's caseload. Maybe he's still around. Sandy," he said into the phone, "has Rory Douglas checked out of the building yet...? No, I'll wait."

Rory Douglas, Ben thought. A familiar name from his teenage years. Could the new attorney be his old rival? *Who cares? You're off the case,* he reminded himself.

There was just one last thing to take care of before he got back to Jessie. She'd waited for almost two hours, and was probably wondering what had happened to him.

Leutzinger didn't miss the surreptitious peek Ben gave his watch. "I'll let you go in a minute. I just need to get—" He broke off, his attention diverted to the phone again. "He is? Find him for me, will you? I want to see him."

He replaced the receiver and asked Ben, "How can I get in touch with the other Webster woman—the twin? You said she lives in Oak Park?"

"Yeah," Ben said. "I'm glad you mentioned her, as a matter of fact. I didn't want to leave her alone, so I brought her with me today. She needs protection till this is over. If her sister hadn't taken that journal, she'd probably be safe at her place, but it won't take long for the wrong people to put the pieces together. If they haven't already. Jessie's in as much danger as her sister, since the two of them look so much alike."

Leutzinger frowned. "I see what you mean, but I haven't got a man to spare. And until I show my superiors some concrete evidence that we're dealing with organized crime here, my budget won't stretch to the expense of a safe house. I suppose we could send her out of town to stay with relatives or something, though I'd rather have her available to help us deal with her sister if necessary."

"She wouldn't go, anyway," Ben replied. "I tried to talk her into visiting her mother in Florida, but she refused. She thinks Allie might need her." Actually, he hadn't pressed Jessie too hard over the whole thing, because he'd figured Leutzinger would assume responsibility for her protection. Besides, if they were dealing with the mob as they suspected, there were no guarantees she'd be any safer in Florida.

"Come to think of it, I do have an extra man." Leutzinger looked at Ben reflectively. "I haven't called your captain yet to tell him I've released you. How about it? Are you up for a baby-sitting job?"

"Me?"

"I realize it's probably been a long time since you were asked to pull guard duty, but it would just be till her sister turns over the journal."

Ben decided in less than a minute.

He found Jessie where he'd left her, in a glassed-in waiting room near the reception desk. She was writing furiously in a small notebook propped on the purse in her lap. Since she seemed unaware of him standing outside the strip of windows looking at her, he paused a moment to appreciate the chic uptown look she'd adopted for her visit to the bureau. Her outfit, a slim navy skirt and short plaid jacket, was businesslike, but Ben suspected he'd find her sexy in anything she wore.

Jessie looked up and smiled when he entered the room.

"Hi. Sorry I took so long," he said.

"It's okay. I've been busy. Sandy at the desk got a nice young man to show me around, and I was just writing down my observations and taking notes for future research." When he looked at her blankly, she said, "You know, for a book. I've been thinking of an FBI agent as a heroine. I haven't done that before. I like the idea so much, I may table the next book I had planned to write and do this one right away.''

Enthusiasm glowed at him out of her dark eyes. Ben came close to kissing her right there in the open waiting room. Since they'd shaken that tail today, Jessie's prickly defensiveness had disappeared, and he was finding it harder than ever to resist her. In one way or another she challenged all the rules he'd fashioned for himself.

Realizing he was standing there just looking at her, he cleared his throat. "Leutzinger wants to talk to you."

Jessie closed the notebook and got to her feet. "What does he want with me?"

"Got me. I'm just a messenger."

He reached out to smooth an errant auburn curl over her ear. The gesture was a poor substitute for what he really wanted to do.

Jessie stared at him, her eyes soft, turbulent and bottomless. Then, with a faint blush on her cheeks, she smoothed her skirt and checked to see that the visitor identification tag she'd been given by security was still clipped to her lapel. She smiled up at him. "I'm ready."

Me, too, baby, he thought.

He was careful not to touch her as they walked through the hallways. Even in those heels she was a little thing. A surge of protectiveness swelled in his breast. Suddenly he was fiercely glad he'd been handed the job of taking care of her. By God, he'd fight the devil himself to keep her safe. She deserved to write about her female FBI agent with nothing more to worry about than where to put the next comma.

But how was he supposed to keep fighting himself? No way in hell could he be with Jessie twenty-four hours a day and stay away from her; besides, the effort of resisting her was taking a toll on his focus and objectivity. Maybe if he took her to bed, he'd stop wondering what it would be like with her, and he could concentrate on his job again. Fate had intervened and made him her bodyguard, so why not make the most of it?

Jessie used their trek through a series of corridors to marshal her equilibrium. Ben had only touched her hair, a simple nonsexual gesture. Yet, coupled with the unmistakable message in his gaze, its impact was as erotic as if he had reached under her skirt. Something had changed. Somehow she had the feeling that, on a basic man-to-woman level, he'd claimed her.

Before she had a chance to decide exactly what that meant, Ben guided her into a small, shabby office. Two men rose simultaneously at her entrance.

"Jessie, this is Cal Leutzinger," Ben said, indicating the man behind the desk.

"Miss Webster." Leutzinger held out his hand and Jessie shook it.

"And this is Rory Douglas." Ben touched her waist and turned her to the carefully groomed man nearest her. Douglas smiled broadly, eyeing Jessie with masculine approval.

He was almost as tall as Ben, she noted. His dark hair was sedately graying at the temples and showed early signs of receding in points from his forehead.

"Rory just told me that you two are old friends," Leutzinger said to Ben as Jessie placed her palm against the one Douglas offered her.

Douglas's hand was large but almost womanly soft to the touch. He pressed her fingers a little too warmly and held on longer than necessary. A feeling of mild revulsion snaked down Jessie's spine.

"We went to high school together," Ben said, "but since then our paths haven't crossed much. Rory."

The handshake that followed was brief. Douglas said congenially, "It *has* been a long time, hasn't it?"

"Cal tells me you've been assigned to take over Simmons's cases," Ben said.

"Yeah, the poor bastard. I hear he's in a coma. Still, the wheels of justice must grind on. I don't mind telling you I'm glad to finally have the chance to prove myself in the U.S. Attorney's Office. Up till now they've given me penny-ante stuff to work with."

"You always were ambitious, Rory. I guess one man's misfortune is just another man's opportunity."

Douglas raised neatly trimmed eyebrows. "In this case, yes, though of course I regret that Mr. Simmons fell asleep at the wheel of his automobile and crashed into a tree."

"I'm sure you do," Ben replied.

"Well." Douglas rubbed his hands together. "It's getting late and I need to get going. I'll get back to you, Cal, after I've researched the issue we discussed. In the meantime, I'd appreciate it if you'd keep me informed about any new developments in the case."

"Of course," said Leutzinger. "Thanks for stopping by."

"No trouble. Good to see you again, Ben. Miss Webster, it's been a real pleasure. Perhaps we'll meet again."

Not if I can help it, Jessie thought as she smiled her goodbye. She'd take Ben's arrogance over oily charm any day.

"It sounds as though there's some history between you two," Leutzinger said when Douglas was gone.

Ben waved his hand dismissively. "Just kid stuff. You wanted to talk to Jessie?"

Leutzinger reclaimed his seat and made himself comfortable. "Yes, I do. Sit down, both of you. Your twin sister is causing us a few problems, Miss Webster."

"Yes, I know." Jessie sat down, hoping she didn't sound as intimidated as she felt under Leutzinger's penetrating gaze.

"Ben has told me about this journal she claims to have. I understand she has shown some reluctance to give it to the police."

Jessie looked at Ben accusingly before answering. "That's not exactly correct," she told Leutzinger. "What Allie said was she wants to deliver it to you *in person.* She fully intends you to have it."

"Did your sister tell you anything she'd read in the journal?"

This was ground Jessie had already covered with Ben, but she patiently repeated the information Allie had given her on the phone. When she'd finished, Leutzinger leaned forward and rested his folded hands on the desk.

"I don't want to alarm you, Miss Webster, but evidence like this in your sister's possession could place her in danger. It's vital that she turn it over to the authorities as soon as possible."

"I agree."

"We may need your help with that."

"My help? I don't understand."

"Right now you're the only link we have to that journal or to your sister," Leutzinger said. "If she calls you again, I'd like you to find out exactly where she is. Try to persuade her to drop the journal at the nearest police station. Tell her she can call me from there and I'll arrange for her safe return home. Then, even if she refuses, I want you to call me immediately. Will you do that?"

Uncomfortably aware that the full weight of the United States government rested behind his request, Jessie asked, "What will you do if she refuses?"

"Do you think she might?"

"It's possible. Allie is a good citizen, Agent Leutzinger, but she's also a reporter who's just lost her job. Remember, Ben already suggested that she give the journal to the authorities in Kansas. Her answer was she didn't want to chance being cut out of the story. She wants you to guarantee her an exclusive."

"Or what?"

"I beg your pardon?"

"Or what, Miss Webster? If your sister doesn't get what she wants, do you think she'll be foolish enough to hang on to that journal and risk charges of withholding evidence and obstruction of justice? I *will* bring charges, make no mistake."

"Now, wait a minute, Cal—" Ben said.

"My sister is not a criminal, Agent Leutzinger." Jessie was angry.

"I'm glad to hear that, Miss Webster. A good citizen cooperates with law enforcement officials out of a sense of duty. She doesn't cut deals like an informer on the streets."

Jessie gathered her dignity around her and stood up. Infuriated by the unexpected threat to her sister, she was hardly aware that Ben rose beside her.

"I see your point," she said in a stilted voice. "I'll do what I can if Allie calls, but I can't promise anything."

"Your effort will be greatly appreciated," Leutzinger said amiably. "Ben knows how to reach me."

"All right. If there's nothing else, then—"

"One more thing, Miss Webster. Ben believes your resemblance to your twin places you at risk from certain unknown and undesirable sources. I'm inclined to agree. Until we learn otherwise, I've assigned him to stay with you for your protection."

"Stay with me!" Jessie looked up and Ben's eyes burned into hers. "But—"

"It's only precautionary," Leutzinger said. "He'll watch out for you until we know there's no further threat."

Jessie tore her gaze from Ben's, engulfed once again, as she'd been at the cabin, by the overwhelming feeling that she was a powerless pawn in a game where someone else was moving the pieces.

"Very well. Goodbye, Agent Leutzinger." She struggled to keep her voice even. Then she turned sharply and left the office, not caring whether Ben accompanied her or not. The ring of Leutzinger's phone followed her out the door.

She had reached the end of the long hallway and realized that she didn't know the way out, when she heard Ben call, "Hold up a minute, Jess."

Impatiently she waited, barely able to control the roiling emotions that demanded release, while Ben stood at the open door of the office she'd just vacated, talking in muted tones to Leutzinger. He seemed in no hurry to leave.

She was contemplating whether to brave the maze of corridors on her own or to simply give in to her frustration and kick the wall beside her when Ben called to her again.

"Jessie, do you have call forwarding on your phone?"

"No," she called back. "Why?"

She flinched when she heard her amplified voice. There were closed doors all up and down the hallway. How many people had heard her shouting down these dignified corridors like a rowdy child?

Ben turned his head and spoke again to Leutzinger. *Hurry up!* she urged him mentally. *I want to get out of here!* Finally he joined her, his face grim.

"What's the matter?" she asked.

Grabbing her by the elbow, he muttered, "Later." He practically dragged her down the right-hand corridor, his stride long and purposeful. By the time they reached the reception area, Jessie was winded from trying to keep up. Sandy, the friendly gray-haired receptionist, had apparently left for the day, and a security guard sat in her place behind the desk.

"Slow down a little, will you?" she gasped. "I may be anxious to leave, but I'm not dressed for a marathon."

"Sorry." Ben unclipped the identification tag on his jacket collar. "You should have said something sooner."

"I'm saying it now. I hate all this. I feel like slugging somebody."

Ben grinned and flicked the tip of her nose with his finger. "Hold your fire, Jess. Give the man your pass and sign your name."

"Orders, orders, orders," Jessie mumbled, pleased and a little flustered by his affectionate gesture. She did as he said, then faced him, placing her fists on her hips in not-quite-feigned pique. "When am I going to get some say again in running my own life?"

"Come on, princess. Let's blow this low-class joint." Ben circled the back of her neck with his big hand, pulling her to his side, and hooked his arm casually across her shoulders as they walked to his car. This time she kept pace with him easily.

Jessie felt giddy as a schoolgirl with Ben's arm around her in public. And confused. Where was the man who issued orders like a field marshal and delighted in goading her to madness? Had he stopped fighting the attraction between them? If he had, she was going to have a hard time resisting. This gentle possessiveness was far too tempting.

Still, she made no effort to step away from his loose hold. She was even sorry when they reached the car and he withdrew his arm to open the door.

Jessie's bemusement fled soon after Ben pulled into traffic and turned onto a southbound expressway. She looked at him quizzically. "I assume you know this isn't the way back to Oak Park."

Ben kept his eyes on the road. "I'm not taking you home, Jess."

"Why not?"

"Leutzinger got a call from Ed in Port Mangus as we were leaving his office. Some employees at Club Duan reported Mai missing this morning. Nobody's seen or heard from her since Wednesday night, when Ed tapped into that call about Allie."

His answer puzzled Jessie. "So? Maybe she spent Thanksgiving with her family and is late getting back. What does that have to do with me?"

"No, she's Vietnamese, remember? She doesn't have family here in the States. She had arranged to eat Thanksgiving dinner at a cafeteria with some of her girls but didn't show up, nor at the restaurant yesterday or this morning for work."

Suddenly Jessie thought of the journal her sister had taken from Mai's office and quailed. "What do you think it means? That she went after Allie?"

Ben took his hand off the wheel and wrapped it around hers, giving her fingers a reassuring squeeze. "No, honey, the police there suspect foul play. Both Mai's office and her apartment upstairs were trashed when they went in to investigate. Plus wherever she is, she didn't take her car. It was sitting outside where she always parked it." Ben's hold on Jessie's hand tightened. "They also found Allie's name written on a notepad in her office, Jess. There's no question now that she knows exactly who your sister is."

Jessie's heart lurched.

"Other people—dangerous people—probably know now too," Ben went on, "and Allie's trail is going to lead right to you. That's why I'm not taking you back to Oak Park. We're going to my house instead. Leutzinger is sending someone over to your place to fix the phone so all your calls are forwarded to my number. That way, if Allie phones again, you won't miss her."

Jessie absorbed this new information in numbed silence. Her head was reeling.

"Hey," Ben said after several minutes had passed. He wiggled her hand. "You still with me?"

She sighed tiredly. "This doesn't seem real, Ben. Things like this don't happen to ordinary people like me."

"If only that were true. Nobody is immune from the thieves and pushers and murderers in the world. Sooner or later everybody is touched in one way or another by their dirt."

"That sounds so cynical." In spite of her circumstances, Jessie didn't want to believe he was right.

"Hell, Jessie—I *am* cynical. Most cops are. The real world is not a pretty place."

He took his hand away, and Jessie regretted the loss. She wondered what memories he'd buried to give him such a bleak outlook on life. So far he'd told her very little about himself.

Uncomfortably she was reminded of Antonio, who, even after two years of marriage, had remained a distant stranger. Not once had he shared anything of emotional significance with her. She'd been an adjunct to her ex-husband's life, not a real part of it.

To be fair, she hadn't known Ben very long, so maybe she hadn't given him enough of a chance to open up to her. Or was she just making excuses for him, the way she had for Antonio for so long?

In spite of the brevity of their acquaintance, she cared for Ben far more than was good for her. How on earth would she protect herself against him now that they'd be together in the same house for heaven only knows how long? Especially if he kept acting as though they were a couple. It was hard enough guarding her emotions when they were at odds.

Jessie was beginning to feel doomed to repeat her mistakes. Maybe it was already too late to save herself.

Perhaps she'd been too pleased with herself for gaining her independence after her divorce. Maybe somebody up there was showing her she'd been fooling herself to think she commanded her own destiny. There was certainly no way out of her current predicament.

"Am I going to be like a prisoner now?" she asked abruptly. "If I can't go home, how am I going to work? What about clothes and things? This is the second time you've whisked me away with only the shirt on my back."

In contrast to his brooding silence a minute ago, a grin tugged at Ben's lips. "You're not going to start arguing with me again, are you?"

"That depends," she warned. "I'm used to doing as I please. As I told you before, having my every movement dictated reminds me of a very unpleasant period in my life. Don't be surprised if I get a little testy."

He laughed outright at that. "No, I won't be surprised."

Chapter 8

A half hour later Jessie got her first glimpse of Ben's home and realized her image of him would have to be adjusted.

"*This* is where you live?"

"This is it."

"It looks like a farmhouse."

Ben threw her an amused look. "It *is* a farmhouse. Though the farm around it has long since been cut into little pieces for all the other homes in the neighborhood."

Jessie had to look through the rear window to see the homes to which he alluded. His property was set back from the others by a long driveway and nearly hidden by a copse of winter naked trees. She could see that this residential area on the southern outskirts of the city was an old one, less urban than rural in character. With the exception of Ben's, though, all the houses were crowded together on city-sized lots.

Ben's yard was huge by contrast, dotted with large trees that had long ago spread their roots and established their ownership of the rich Illinois soil beneath their branches. The house itself, wearing dignified white siding and black trim, exuded the stately permanence of an old society matron, comfortably out of fashion with the times.

The sole discordant note—and the only outward evidence that a security-conscious cop might live here—was the high, forbidding chain link fence enclosing the property.

Ben stopped the car outside the gate to retrieve a complicated-looking control mechanism from the glove compartment.

"What's that?" Jessie asked.

"A remote for my alarm system." He pressed a succession of buttons on the device and a red light in the top corner flashed. Then he punched in another code, the light blinked again, and the wide gate separated in the middle. With smooth efficiency, the two parts of the barrier slid on runners into retaining pockets.

"Pretty slick," Jessie commented as Ben drove through. She turned in her seat to watch the gate close behind them. "Is this a high-crime area?"

"It used to be. But we started a community program several years back involving both residents and the police department. The number of personal and property crimes has dropped off a good bit since then."

"Oh, like Neighborhood Watch. We have that where I live, too."

Ben nodded. "Something like that. Neighborhood Watch is good as far as it goes, but our program expands on it. We have more interaction between cops and civilians. The police here have bases throughout the community, two men to a substation, instead of everybody at a central location. One guy mans the substation with a phone and a car, while the other patrols the neighborhood on foot or on a bicycle."

"Like the old beat cop?"

"Right. Plus there are regular meetings where the police give tips on home security and personal safety. There's also a free exchange of information about crime in the area. I thought if cops got to spend more time around the good, honest folks they're protecting, and if the residents got to know the decent men and women who joined the police force because they wanted to help people, it would be a natural thing for everybody to join forces against the *real* bad guys. And it worked."

Ben pulled around to the back of the house and parked in the carport.

"The program was your idea, then?" Jessie asked.

He looked at her. "Did I say that?"

"You said *you* thought it would work that way, as though you came up with the plan."

"You don't miss much, do you? Wait there, I'll get you door."

Jessie recognized a diversion when it smacked her in the face but Ben left the car before she could call him on it. Perhaps he was being modest. She was afraid, though, that his refusal to talk about even so impersonal a matter as a crime prevention program he'd conceived was his way of keeping barriers in place.

Preoccupied with his evasion, Jessie followed him to the house and watched him unlock the back door. He pushed it open and stood back to let her precede him. She walked through but turned around just inside the door, thinking she might as well find out right now whether he would shut her out as Antonio had.

"So was it your idea? The cop on the beat, I mean."

He stopped short and looked down at her with a frown of mild exasperation. "As a matter of fact, it was. The program was set up here in this neighborhood as a pilot for the whole city. Look, Jessie, I'll tell you about it later if you're really interested, but right now let's get inside. It's cold out here."

He nudged her out of the way. With a hand at her back, he hustled her through the spacious country kitchen before she could note anything other than the cheerfully checkered tile floor and a backyard view through the breakfast nook windows. In the living room, he stepped away, leaving her to look around while he slipped out of his jacket and removed the holster strapped to his shoulder.

"What a gorgeous room!" she exclaimed.

"Thanks," he said nonchalantly, though she sensed he was pleased. "The furniture is kind of hodgepodge, but since I live alone, I don't have to suit anyone but myself."

"You mean *you* decorated this? Ben, it's wonderful." Jessie was amazed but sincere in her praise. The high-ceilinged room was open and airy, the traditional furnishings chosen for expansive comfort and utility. Nothing jarred the senses or called attention to itself. Even the decidedly modern, freestanding fireplace occupying the corner looked homey.

"I'll take care of this and be right back. Look around, if you want." Still holding the leather-encased gun, Ben disappeared down a hallway, and Jessie had a chance to leisurely study her surroundings.

She liked the color scheme, a mix of blues and muted reds against light walls and a gleaming parquet floor. Ben had achieved an atmosphere both pleasing to the eye and restful to the spirit. Two picture windows flanked what must at one time have been an exterior door, but which now opened onto a glassed-in sun porch. Through plain, translucent curtains, she caught a glimpse of dark branches beyond the porch's wall of windows. She would have wandered out to investigate if Ben had not returned to the living room just then.

"Was this your parents' home?" she asked.

"No, I bought it several years ago as a fixer-upper. So far I've only renovated the downstairs. I don't feel rushed to do the second floor since there's a bedroom down here."

Jessie absorbed that surprising information. Ben, a handyman? "Darn. I had almost managed to visualize you as a rosy-cheeked little boy climbing all those trees out in the yard. Now I have to rearrange my thinking again."

His mouth tilted. "Well, I was a little boy, once upon a time, but otherwise you're way off base. There weren't any trees where I grew up, or even a yard, for that matter. My father and mother were missionaries with an inner-city ministry. We lived over a Salvation Army-type mission in a pretty rough section of Chicago."

Dumbfounded, Jessie exclaimed, "Are you serious?"

"What's the matter? You can't picture me as a preacher's kid?"

She was trying, but it was hard. "What was it like?"

Ben plucked his jacket from the back of the couch and walked to a narrow louvered closet by the front door Jessie had noticed earlier. "I can't complain. I had it pretty good compared to the other kids in my neighborhood."

"I mean being a preacher's kid. Was that difficult?"

He shrugged as he hung up his jacket. "I suppose it set me apart. When your parents are ministers, you don't have much in common with the homeboys. I learned early on to make it on my own. I didn't mind that so much as I did sharing my mom and dad with every drunk and junkie on the street.''

He crossed the room to the thermostat and made a quick adjustment. The furnace clicked on.

"So you were alone even then," Jessie said quietly.

Ben's eyes warmed as he looked at her. "What's going on inside that beautiful head of yours, Jess? Have I touched a chord of sympathy inside your soft heart? Are you thinking I had an unhappy childhood?"

"Well, it couldn't have been easy, with no friends and having to compete for your parents' attention."

"It's tempting to let you think so, just to find out what form your sympathy would take."

Somehow he had shifted closer, and Jessie looked up and saw the devilish glint in his eyes. She stepped back and made a face at him. "You've been putting me on, haven't you?"

He broke into a teeth-flashing grin. "Not really, but I couldn't resist teasing you. You looked so earnestly concerned."

As far as Jessie could tell, he hadn't moved as he spoke, but somehow he'd managed once again to invade her personal space. She resisted the urge to take another step back. "So what was it *really* like?"

He tapped her nose. "Don't tell anybody, but I was a normal, selfish kid who didn't realize how special my parents were or how lucky I was."

"Were they there for you when you needed them?"

He lifted a careless shoulder. "Not always. But they did the best they could. Truthfully, I couldn't appreciate their work until I was old enough to understand. My folks gave people hope, as well as food and clothes and a place to sleep for the night. There were plenty of victims around who needed them more than I did."

"Baloney." Jessie was indignant. "You were just a child. Children need to know they're the most important thing in the world to their parents. Somebody should have set them straight on that point."

Ben smiled crookedly. "C'mere."

He reached for her, and after a brief hesitation, Jessie let him draw her close. *This isn't smart,* she told herself. But she didn't resist when he gently pressed her head to his chest. Instead she rested her hands on his biceps, closed her eyes and savored the strength and the hardness of him as she imagined the lonely little boy he'd once been.

"You're determined to champion my cause, aren't you?" he said against her hair. "I like it—even if you're just doing it for the sake of argument."

"I'm not."

She jerked back in protest and the top of her head connected solidly with Ben's chin. Yellow spots pirouetted in front of her eyes as his arms fell away.

"Ow! Dammit, woman!" Gingerly he kneaded the underside of his jaw with the heel of one hand.

Still reeling, Jessie rubbed her own sore spot. "Sorry," she muttered.

"Me, too," Ben said with comic remorse. "So much for taking advantage of your gentle sensibilities."

"Is that what you were doing?"

"If I was, you launched a pretty good defense. My aching chin tells me you're not in the mood."

"I didn't do it on purpose," Jessie protested.

Ben studied her for a charged moment and asked evenly, "Does that mean you *are* in the mood?"

She bristled at the soft, vaguely threatening question, torn between relief and regret that the poignant moment was over. "Don't be ridiculous. I was just . . . you were just—"

Unsure herself about what would have happened if she hadn't been so clumsy, Jessie floundered for an explanation.

"Never mind," Ben said, coming to her rescue. "I'm hungry, aren't you? It's been a long time since lunch."

Jessie accepted the new subject gratefully. "Are you cooking?"

"Sorry, all I have to offer is your choice of TV dinners. Sometimes I think I single-handedly keep the frozen food folks in business."

"I've eaten my share, too," she said lightly. "Cooking for one isn't very rewarding, is it? Very well, show me to your freezer."

He turned and headed for the kitchen. Jessie followed, her mind going back to the way he'd told her about his childhood. She couldn't suppress a thrill of pleasure at the memory. Whatever his motivation for telling her, she'd bet there weren't too many people who knew how he had grown up. He'd given her an important piece of himself without hedging or putting up roadblocks. Having lived for two years with an uncommunicative man, Jessie treasured that relative openness.

Inside the kitchen doorway, Ben flipped on a light, reminding her that darkness fell quickly during midwestern winters. Until the artificial brightness chased away the gray shadows in the room, she'd hardly noticed the gathering dusk outside the windows.

The phone rang as Ben reached to open a door on his side-by-side refrigerator-freezer, and Jessie's thoughts flew immediately to her twin.

"I'll get that," Ben said. "You go ahead and pick out what you want to eat from the freezer."

"Do you think Agent Leutzinger had time to get my calls forwarded to your number?"

"It's possible. I'll let you know if it's Allie."

He left her alone, and seconds later the glow of a lamp from the other room lit the doorway. Jessie heard his low voice murmur a greeting. She waited a moment for his summons. When it didn't come, she relaxed and glanced around the kitchen. Like the living room, the kitchen was unpretentious and homey, but its overall atmosphere was more cheerful than serene. Simple blue-and-white gingham curtains graced the windows, complementing eggshell walls, the checkerboard floor, and a multitude of wooden cabinets and almond-toned appliances. Ben's "fix-up" had apparently been extensive.

Jessie walked to the refrigerator, opened the freezer section and smiled. He hadn't been kidding about eating frozen meals. The freezer was crammed with several brands and varieties of breakfasts, sandwiches and dinner entrées. Ben had a fondness for beef, she decided.

She scanned each of the shelves and spotted a lone turkey dinner at the bottom of the lowest shelf.

"Aha!" she said under her breath. With some awkwardness she stooped to extricate her dinner choice from the pile of boxes, her leg muscles reminding her of the high heels she wore. She berated herself for the preening foolishness that had motivated her to dress up for the trip to the FBI office. If she'd been less occupied with her own vanity—or, more to the point, with impressing Ben—she might be comfortable now in jeans and sneakers.

She hoped there would be a way to pick up some things from her apartment tomorrow. Even if she was here for only a short time, she didn't want to spend it in a suit and heels. The way her life had been going lately, she ought to start carrying a fully stocked duffel bag wherever she went.

On that thought, she freed the turkey with two hands and somehow managed not to break a fingernail in the process.

"Finally," she muttered.

Clutching her dinner triumphantly in one hand, she straightened and arched her back to get the kinks out before closing the freezer door. When she turned around, there was Ben.

Embarrassed that she'd just given him a fine view of the backs of her knees, not to mention her too-rounded fanny, Jessie cast about in her mind for something to break the silence. "Who was on the phone?"

"A neighbor kid, Stevie, who lives in the house we passed just before turning into my driveway. He saw us come in earlier and wanted to know if I'd play catch with him tomorrow."

Ben's gold-green eyes gleamed dangerously. Jessie fiddled with the buttons on her stylish but suddenly warm jacket. "Won't it be too cold?"

"Not for Stevie. But I had to tell him no. I'm working, remember?"

"Oh, right." She'd do well to remember that, she cautioned herself. She wouldn't be here if Ben hadn't been assigned to take care of her. "I hope he wasn't disappointed."

"There's plenty of time for me to practice with him before the summer Little League season. He wants to be a pitcher, and I told him I'd help him. His dad died a few years ago."

"That's nice of you."

"Not really. It gives me an excuse to play ball, and Stevie's a fun little kid."

"Still. Some men wouldn't even consider it. Not every man likes children. My ex-husband didn't."

Ben folded his arms and leaned back against the counter, his eyes following the fluttering movement of her fingers on her buttons. "Did the two of you disagree about having kids?"

Glad to have even Antonio as a topic of conversation, Jessie nodded. "That was one of the many reasons I left him. Although it's not his fault entirely. I was young and starry-eyed and never told him what I expected before we got married."

"How old were you?"

"A very young twenty-three. I hadn't ever lived away from home—Allie and I had commuted to the University of Chicago—and I was married shortly after I graduated. I'd never been on my own, never had any hard knocks. I guess I thought marriage would just be a continuation of my uncomplicated life, only better. Pretty dumb, huh?"

"But hardly unusual."

Jessie tipped her head in acknowledgment. "I suppose not. I had in mind a big happy family with lots of babies. I thought most Latin males loved children, but somehow that trait bypassed Antonio's genes."

"How did you meet him?"

"He was a Bolivian exchange student at the university. He charmed me into marrying him, became a U.S. citizen, and never went back home. I was just part of his great plan. You can't know how stupid I felt when I realized how I'd been used."

Ben was watching her intently as she spoke, and abruptly Jessie was reminded of her ex-husband's rapt attentions while he'd courted her. The uncomfortable thought struck her that she had taken Antonio at face value and never questioned the motivation behind his attention. Did Ben have another agenda besides protecting her? Would she find, when this was over, that she'd been used again? *It's not the same thing,* she assured herself, brushing the fleeting suspicion aside.

"When did you figure out he had taken advantage of you?" Ben asked.

Jessie hardly noticed that she had begun to work her top jacket button in and out of its buttonhole. "It didn't take long, once we were married. He was possessive of me from the start.

I thought he didn't want children because he didn't want to share me. I tried to accept it, telling myself I should be flattered that he loved me so much." She shook her head. "But Antonio loved only Antonio. Ultimately I realized any slave would have suited him, as long as she was American, female, and willing to jump as often and as high as he dictated. I'm afraid that toward the end, I wasn't very good at that. But by then, he'd already picked out my replacement."

Suddenly Jessie felt ill at ease. "Listen to me, would you? I hadn't intended to tell you all *that.*"

Ben's smile was almost tender. "You're not boring me."

"Maybe not, but Allie's the only one I've ever confided in about my divorce. Even my mother doesn't know the whole story."

"You don't have to tell me if you don't want to."

Jessie shrugged. "There's not much more—you might as well hear the rest. Antonio had an affair with a meek little secretary in his office. A better woman than I, he was quick to tell me, one who knew a wife's duty, something I had forgotten. They're still married, as far as I know, so maybe she's made of stronger stuff than I am."

"Or weaker."

"I don't think so. I heard they had a baby a couple of years ago. Apparently she was able to influence him, something I could never manage."

"Or maybe she was just more devious."

Jessie brightened. "You mean she might have tricked him into fatherhood?"

She spared Antonio's current wife a moment of empathetic congratulations, then grew thoughtful. "You know what? I just realized I don't feel angry or humiliated about any of it anymore. I think I'm finally over the whole thing. After six years, it's about time, don't you think?"

"Antonio's a scumbag," he muttered, pushing himself away from the counter and approaching her. "You're well rid of him."

"I couldn't...agree more," Jessie said, her voice faltering when, instead of stopping, he entered her personal space and took the frozen dinner from her hand. Tossing it behind him onto a countertop, he backed her against the refrigerator.

"What . . . What are you doing, Ben?"

"I don't want to talk about your ex anymore, Jess," he growled. He propped his forearms against the enameled door, blocking her in. "And if you don't stop fooling around with that button . . ."

His eyes fell to her busy fingers. Instantly Jessie stilled them and caught her breath as she looked into Ben's hungry gaze.

"It's too late, honey. I'm already imagining what I'd see if you opened up that jacket . . . for me."

"I'm . . . not going to do that," she whispered. Her respiration quickened. With each indrawn breath, her wool-covered breasts brushed against his encroaching body. They swelled and grew heavy inside her bra, the nipples tightening.

"Aren't you?" Warm air from his mouth caressed her lips. Jessie felt her body grow liquid from his nearness.

"Ben . . . I thought we decided not to . . ."

"We were stupid." His voice was raw with tightly leashed passion. "I can't be with you without wanting you. I'm going crazy with it. Tell me you feel the same."

Jessie swallowed and recalled his kisses, the feel of his hands, the spiraling pleasure he'd ignited in her body that had yet to be fulfilled. Oh, yes, she wanted him.

"Tell me," he said again.

This strong, hard man knew his power over her; she wouldn't resist were he to take what he wanted.

But he didn't take. Instinctively she knew she could say no, and he'd honor her refusal. It was that which tipped her over the edge and fully seduced her.

Surrender was all the sweeter for being freely given. Jessie slipped her hand up his chest and cradled his stubborn jaw in her hand. "I do want you, Ben."

Masculine lips captured hers on the whisper of his name. Unconsciously mewing deep in her throat, she opened her mouth in invitation. Without hesitation his tongue swept inside, scouring the moist cavern with sweet ravishment.

The whole of Jessie's being was centered on the greedy joining of their mouths and the heated yearning in secret places inside her newly awakened body. The past two days of fighting her desire had kept the lusty coals smoldering, and in seconds she was once again on fire for him.

Ben pinned her against the refrigerator, practically lifting her out of her shoes as he imprinted his hard planes against the yielding curves of her body. Jessie strained against his arousal, frustrated by the thick clothing that prevented a more satisfying meeting of flesh to flesh.

He wrenched his mouth from hers to rasp, "Not here," then swooped her into his arms and out of the kitchen. She buried her face in his neck. She nuzzled his throat, seeking out his warm skin with her lips and tongue as he carried her. Excited by his moan of pleasure, she kissed and nibbled and licked at the sensitive nerve endings between his shoulder and ear until, with desperate, coaxing movements of his cheek against her hair, he nudged her head back and found her mouth again.

Jessie wasn't aware they'd reached his bedroom until her feet touched the floor. Unsteadily Ben stepped back, clicked on the bedside lamp and started to unbutton his shirt.

"Take off your clothes," he said, a rough edge to his voice. "Hurry."

His rush to get undressed testified to the urgency driving him. Jessie recognized it, shared it, and understood that there would be no visual savoring of the baring of their bodies, no inclination toward gentle exploration. She didn't want it, either. Need propelled her shaking hands to the buttons of her jacket.

Ben had less to take off and had stripped completely by the time Jessie managed to remove only her outer clothing. Her eyes swept down his well-honed frame and settled on his powerfully engorged erection as she stepped out of her skirt. With a thrill of anticipation she celebrated his size and strength.

Soon, soon, her heart sang dizzily.

"Protection," he muttered between gritted teeth. "I'll be right back. Hurry."

Jessie didn't know whether he'd meant the last command for her or for himself, but she tackled her lacy camisole and bra with renewed, if inept, energy. She was fumbling with her panty hose when he returned with the square packet. He ripped the foil open with his teeth and prepared himself in the seconds it took her to rake the hosiery clumsily off her feet.

Ben didn't wait for her to remove the bikini panties that remained. In one fluid motion he grasped her under the arms, lifted her crosswise onto the nearby bed and slid the panties down her legs and off. Then he joined her on the bed. Spreading her thighs wide with his knees, he reached down to test her readiness. Jessie cried out when he explored her swollen petals and found the slippery evidence of her desire.

"Jessie," he breathed.

"Please," she begged, close to delirium from the probing of his fingers. She tried to help as he positioned himself between her legs, and he laughed shakily when her hands only got in the way.

"Here, let me," he said unsteadily.

Then he was there, blunt and hard, squeezing his way into her, stretching her until he was buried to the hilt inside her feminine sheath. Her legs bent and wrapped themselves around his buttocks, settling him deeper.

"Jess," he growled, eyes tightly closed in agonized pleasure. "Nothing has ever felt this good before."

She scarcely heard him. *At last,* she was thinking ecstatically. It was more—*he* was more—than she'd ever known, ever dreamed possible.

Then, unbelievably, as he held himself rigidly in control inside her, Jessie felt the gathering tightness that signaled the initial shudders of her release. Thrilled, amazed, unable to stop the compelling rush to completion, she ground her hips against him and reached to embrace it, crying out as the undulating waves rolled over her.

"Don't move yet, baby," Ben moaned. "Oh, Jess."

Then he was moving, too, fast and deep, thrusting his hips into the cradle of her thighs until in a final lunge, he found his own prolonged fulfillment. He met it with a strangled groan of satisfaction and collapsed on top of her.

Jessie caught him in her arms and lay under his damp heaviness, happy and replete, listening to the thunder of his heart.

Chapter 9

Way to go, Flash, Ben complimented himself derisively when he could think straight again. *You really know how to show a lady a good time.*

He'd been a mindless pig, and that was putting it mildly. In his headlong race to get inside her, he'd skipped all the parts that made sex good for a woman. Hell, he'd been so carried away, he'd barely remembered to protect her. And once he'd gotten in—the thought was uncomfortable enough to make him wince—it had been all over in an embarrassingly short period of time.

Even so, it had been heaven while it lasted. Ben's modest sampling of women in the world hadn't prepared him for what he'd felt with Jessie. He'd always enjoyed sex, but never before had a woman's body received him so sweetly; never had an orgasm rocked him so intensely. Never had he lost control.

This frantic taking was not his usual style at all. As one woman in his past had told him, he had what that old song called "a slow hand." He liked to draw out the preliminaries, to savor the gradual climb to climax. His partners had seemed to appreciate it.

But he'd taken Jessie like an animal.

Carefully he eased up and off the quiescent woman under him, his sticky skin peeling reluctantly away from her naked body. Jessie opened her eyes and shivered when the cool air hit her. She was flushed and damp and incredibly beautiful lying there in lavish nudity, wet little tendrils of hair clinging to her cheeks and temples.

"Whew!" She smiled. "We didn't waste any time, did we?"

Ben felt heat climb his neck to spread in his face. "Yeah, well—"

"Ooh, I feel...." She stretched sumptuously, her raised arms lifting her lush breasts into perfectly rounded mounds on her chest. "Energized! Like I could—build a house, or something."

Ben's eyes flew to her face. "You do?"

"Damn that Antonio, anyway," she said cheerfully. "I guess we showed him!"

"We did?" Ben heard his puzzled question and grimaced. He was starting to sound like a fool without an original thought in his head.

"We did." Jessie put her hand behind his neck and pulled him down for a soft kiss. "You're quite a man, Ben Sutton."

Ben almost said, "I am?" but caught himself in time. Her hand drifted down to dally in his chest hair. Little tracks of heat trailed behind her fingers.

"You aren't disappointed, then?"

Feathery lashes lifted and blue eyes, dark and glowing with mischief, pulled him into their mystery. "Fishing for compliments?"

Compliments?

Her lips curved into a sultry smile. "Well, much as I hate to feed your ego, I have to oblige. How could I be disappointed? I didn't know making love could be so...so...."

"Quick?"

She laughed seductively deep in her throat. "Uh-uh," she corrected with a shake of her short curls. "More like... explosive. I'll tell you a secret." Her voice softened and she blushed becomingly. "That was the first time I ever...you know. Thank you."

Her ingenuous disclosure caused Ben's chest to expand, and he felt a queer tightening in the region of his heart. He should say something, but there were no words for the relief, tenderness, pride and other more indefinable emotions pulling at him. Taking refuge in action, he stole a brief kiss and drew back with a smile that felt lopsided. "I'm glad you were satisfied, honey, but that was only the appetizer."

"Oh?" Jessie looked at him from under half-closed eyelids and a naughty smile curved her lips. "Then I can't wait for the banquet."

Her playful challenge arrowed straight to his manhood. Ben leaned over and caught her mouth once more. Deliberately he limited his tongue to a single, teasing dip inside, then forced himself to back away.

"You'll have to give me a minute. Don't move so much as a centimeter from this spot until I get back."

She grinned saucily. Ben jumped from the bed and hurried into the bathroom. Quickly he took care of necessities and fumbled for another foil packet from the box he hadn't bothered to put away earlier. Then he paused. A vision of Jessie as he'd left her, stretched out on his bed clothed only in her skin, filled his brain. He grabbed the whole box and rushed back to the bedroom.

There he found her under the covers, the sheet tucked up to her chin.

"You moved!" he complained.

She smiled at him, but the devilish glimmer was nowhere in evidence. Instead she looked unsure. "I got a little chilly."

Ben walked to the bed and put the box of condoms on the nightstand. "Having second thoughts?"

"I don't think so," she said cautiously. "I'm a little nervous, though."

"How come?" He lifted the covers and slipped in beside her. To his relief, she didn't resist when he drew her into his arms.

"It's just that I've never been very good at this. What happened before was really a fluke. It might not happen again."

He chuckled and gave her a squeeze, causing her breasts to move up delectably against his upper arm and chest muscles.

"No, I'm serious," she said. "I'm just loaded with inhibitions, and I never know what to do...."

Ben understood. Someone—he was pretty sure he knew who—had done a number on her confidence. Too bad she'd had time to remember it. Her ex-husband had a lot to answer for.

"Tell you what," he said, nuzzling into the curls at her temple. "Just make believe we're on an expedition, sort of like Lewis and Clark mapping out the Northwest Territory."

She gurgled. "What?"

"You know, explorers. We'll pretend there's all this unknown terrain in front of us, and all we have to do is find our way through it."

"What a concept for foreplay. Did you get it out of a manual?"

"Nope. Just thought of it. What do you say? You'll like it, I promise."

She pretended to think. "Lewis and Clark. Are we looking for anything in particular?"

"Well, the end point of the journey, the...climax, so to speak, is the Pacific Ocean. But our real objective is to chart the wonders we find along the way. We can't hurry past a majestic mountain or an enchanting little valley without giving it our full attention." Ben's hands were busy as he lectured.

Jessie tilted her head back and warm blue eyes sparkled into his. "Mountains and valleys, huh?"

"Right. Plains are nice, too, of course. Not really flat like a lot of people think. They're actually full of interesting swells and ridges and hollows."

"Hmm. I see what you mean. I believe I may have discovered a swelling ridge already."

"See what a natural you are?" Ben inhaled sharply. "Uh, Jess, we'd better leave that for now and come back to it later." He moved her hand to his chest and she giggled adorably. "In fact," he said with a kiss to the tip of her nose, "why don't you just lie back and let me lead this expedition for a while?"

"Okay."

Jessie rolled onto her back, her uncertainty gone. Anticipation brightened her eyes.

He threw back the covers. "Turn over, sweetheart."

Like a curious bird, she cocked her head. Then, with an implicit trust that caused the same squeezing sensation in his heart he'd felt before, she smiled at him and turned onto her stomach.

By heaven, Ben vowed, he'd make this the most memorable night of her life. She was a desirable, passionate woman and he would prove it to her. He surveyed the beautiful offering displayed before him and bent to his pleasurable task.

Her responses were hesitant at first, the clutch of a pillow, the catch of a breath, a muffled cry. But he was patient. He traced the curves of her feminine form, outlining it with his hands from the indentations under her arms to her slender ankles. He ran his fingers over the smooth line of her calf and thigh. He kissed the tender hollows behind her knees and the twin dimples at the base of her spine. He rubbed his cheeks savoringly across the voluptuous swells of her buttocks.

With each caress, every kiss, he praised her beauty, her satiny skin, her softness.

Her first moan came when he nibbled his way up her backbone. She moaned louder and managed to prop herself on her arms when he found the juncture of her neck and shoulder with his tongue and teeth. He tormented that sweet spot until she threw her head back and began planting clumsy, desperate kisses in his hair, on his ear, and anywhere else her lips would reach, punctuating each with a breathless cry. Sensing her need, Ben dragged his mouth to hers and gave her his tongue, at the same time slipping a hand under her arm to cradle her warm, heavy breast in his palm. She covered his hand with hers and pressed. She was awkward, unskilled. Wonderful.

"Jess," he whispered. "Do you know how it feels to have you want me this way?"

"Please, please," she whimpered. "Let me turn over."

Ben raised his upper body and she flipped neatly to her back, reaching immediately to wind her arms around his neck and pull him down for a soul-deep kiss. She groaned, she panted, she writhed under him until he was close to losing his head. He wanted nothing more than to nestle between her legs and let his straining, eager hardness find its snug haven.

Somehow he mustered the strength to break the kiss. "Wait, honey."

He levered his body to the side of the bed and made himself ready for her. Jessie watched, her slender rib cage lifting her opulent breasts with each unsteady breath she took. His pulse quickened. The feast he'd been waiting for was just ahead.

Ignoring the throbbing in his groin, he winked at her. "Now this side."

He'd saved the best for last. He pleasured her breasts in every way he knew, wallowing in their glory. They were sensitive to his thumbs, palms and trailing fingertips. He buried his nose in their fragrant cleft and Jessie delighted him by pushing them in from the sides to trap his face in a prison of softness. And when he put his mouth to the pale, delicate nipples, she nearly went crazy.

She made him greedy. He tongued his way down her rib cage and stomach, kneeling between her legs. He paused to linger at her navel and had just dropped a first soft kiss on the puff of hair guarding her womanly secrets when he noticed her sudden stillness.

"Jess? Does this bother you?"

"I . . . don't know."

"Should I stop?"

"Yes. I don't know. Maybe."

Ben grinned when he saw her eyes were tightly closed. "Can we just try it? I want all of you."

She lifted her lashes. "Really?"

"Really. If you don't like it, I'll stop. Just tell me."

"O-okay, then."

Her attack of nerves was short-lived. He separated the feminine folds with his fingers and placed his tongue on her sensitive flesh. She gasped. Ben's own arousal grew as her enjoyment rose by degrees from sighs to cries. In minutes her hips were arching to meet him, and he felt the singular tightening under his mouth, foreshadowing her release. Excitement gripped him as he applied himself more diligently to her pleasure. She gave a lusty shout and the contractions began.

Ben was ready. He was on her and in her before it was over. He held himself high and unmoving within her heat, close to dying with the pleasure of feeling the fluttering aftershocks of her climax around him.

When at last she was still, he rested on his elbows and kissed her tenderly. "You're beautiful."

"You don't have to say that." She was flushed and breathless.

"It's true."

Just then his strict control slipped. Without warning, he jerked inside her.

"Oh!" Jessie's eyes widened.

Ben smiled. "Hello. Think you can handle some more?"

She squeezed him with her inner muscles and he closed his eyes. "Oh, baby, that feels good."

He withdrew slightly and she squeezed him again, holding tight this time while he pushed his way back.

Ben groaned. "Jess, honey, I wanted this to last."

She looked pleased with herself. "Should I stop?"

"Hell, no. I'll try to bear up."

To his delight, Jessie caught fire again and made the ascent with him. It didn't last as long as he wanted, but by the time he reached the top, Ben didn't care.

"So what do you think of exploring?" he asked her when they lay recuperating in each other's arms.

"Don't bother me—I'm lying on the beach," she said dreamily. "And the ocean is beautiful today."

"What time is it?"

"Dunno. Nine or ten maybe. Past supper time. Are you hungry?"

"Not hungry enough to get out of bed."

"Good. Me, either."

"I wonder what Allie's doing."

"I'd just as soon forget about your sister right now."

"Oh, no! I did forget—for hours. Ben, my twin sister is in terrible trouble, and I've scarcely given her a thought."

"And it hasn't made her situation any better or worse. Relax, Jess. There's nothing you can do for her until she calls. I, on the other hand, could use a little body heat, and would greatly appreciate it if you'd lie back down."

"I suppose you're right."

"That's better. Damn right I'm right."

"Ben? Were you dating Allie?"

"Uh-uh."

"You kissed her, though."

"Her car broke down one night and I gave her a ride home from work. *She* kissed *me*. Once."

"Do you think she's . . . interested in you?"

"Nope. It wouldn't do her any good if she was."

"Why not?"

"What kind of question is that? I think I've made my choice between the Webster twins pretty clear."

"Still . . . most men like Allie better, even though we look alike. Even Antonio said he married the wrong twin. At least when we were in the bedroom."

"Your ex-husband is a selfish, stupid son of a bitch. And anybody who picked Allie over you obviously hadn't conducted a kiss comparison."

"Ha! As far as I know, *you're* the only one who managed that."

"I'm a very enterprising kind of guy."

"Yes, you are. You're also a very . . . good . . . kisser."

"You . . . inspire me . . . ."

"I'm embarrassed."

"Why?"

"I've never been so . . . unrestrained."

"Yeah, you're pretty loud."

"You needn't sound so smug."

"Why not? I deserve some of the credit for all that panting and groaning."

"When I think back, I can hardly believe that was me."

"It was you, all right. The woman who said she was inhibited."

"I'm serious now, Ben. Did I make you feel—awkward? Did I make a fool of myself?"

"Honey, you turned me on like I've never been turned on in my life. I love it that I can make you forget yourself like that. You're wonderful."

"You almost make me believe it. I think you're wonderful, too. You have a beautiful body."

"You have a thing for freckles?"

"For yours, I do. I wondered when I first saw you if you had them all over."

"Now you know. I would've been happy to bare my chest sooner, if you'd asked."

"No doubt. You're disgracefully immodest. It's a very nice chest, though. All these muscles, and just enough manly hair to run my fingers through."

"I'm glad you like it. I'm rather fond of yours, myself."

"I noticed. You pay it an inordinate amount of attention."

"It's worthy of a double portion of consideration. Ouch! Easy on my manly chest hair!"

"That was a very bad joke."

"Be honest. You love my attention."

"To my shame, I do. Tonight's the first time in my life since puberty that I've been pleased with the way I'm built."

"I don't believe it."

"No, it's true. I don't remember a single male in high school who ever looked me in the face. Allie didn't mind—she always liked our figure. But it made me self-conscious. Do you know what we were called? The Hooter Twins. Don't you dare laugh."

"I apologize on behalf of all horny teenage boys everywhere."

"You're forgiven. Tell me about your neighborhood program."

"Back to that again, are we? What do you want to know?"

"What do people think of it? Have you gotten the credit for a brilliant idea?"

"I'm not looking for credit. I'd just like to see it put into effect throughout the city. I think it would make a big difference, not only in improved relations between the police department and the public, but also in the crime rate, like it has here."

"If that's true, why don't they do it? Don't they know how well it works?"

"The city council has the statistics, but there's a money problem. Once the program's in place, it doesn't cost any more to run than what we have now, but there's extra expense in setting it up that has to come out of the city budget. We're talking a major revamping, and money is tight. Besides that, not everyone agrees the program would work in the inner city like it does out here in the suburbs. The police commissioner is all for it, but there's enough opposition in the ranks to keep the issue from even being brought to a vote of the council."

"How do you feel about that?"

"Damned frustrated, if you want to know the truth. Somebody's got to do something, and soon, or the gangs and criminals are going to take over our cities altogether. A whole generation of kids could be lost. It's pretty clear the cops can't do it alone.''

"You feel strongly about this, don't you?"

"For good reason. Can we change the subject, Jess? Or better yet, stop talking period. . . ."

"Ben?"

"Hmm?"

"Are you sleeping?"

"Uh-uh."

"What's it like being undercover?"

"Not nearly as nice as being under the covers with you."

"Be serious. I want to know. Is it terribly dangerous?"

"Sometimes. If you're careless. You learn pretty quick not to be."

"Are you one of those men who gets off on danger and close calls?"

"No way. I'm a peace-lovin' man."

"You have to be a good actor, don't you?"

"Get the stars out of those pretty eyes, Jess. Undercover work isn't a movie. There's nothing glamorous about it."

"Come on, tell me. What's it like?"

"I'll tell you this once, Jess, and then I don't want to talk about it anymore. It's lousy, if you want to know the truth. Being undercover is living a lie every day of your life. It's hobnobbing with the lowest kind of scum and pretending you like it because you're just like them. You meet people—good people—while you're on a job, and you have to ignore them or ridicule them or even hurt them to keep them and anybody else watching from finding out who you are. You get to see the scorn in their eyes, or worse, fear. It's living with the knowledge that things could go bad at any minute and you've got to be ready. Sometimes it's almost forgetting who you are, you play your part so well. Sometimes you feel like you're a criminal yourself."

"Why do you do it, if you feel that way about it?"

"Because it's usually the only way to get the top dogs in an organization so you can shut it down. For that you need evidence. An undercover cop can get it. Jess?"

"What?"

"I'd rather not talk about this now."

"Oh. Well, then, can I ask you about something else? You're one of the most interesting people I've ever met."

"Interesting, huh? Considering what we've been doing for the past several hours, I'm not sure how to take that."

"It's a compliment, of course. I appreciate *all* your many facets. Were you ever married?"

"Uh-uh. I came close once, though, when I was younger."

"Who was she?"

"A girl I met in college. Her name was Becky."

"What happened?"

"A lot of things. But mostly it was that Becky didn't want to be the wife of a policeman. It's just as well she broke the engagement. Cops don't make good husbands."

"Did you love her?"

"Not enough to give up my plans to be a cop."

"Ed told me you're very dedicated. He said you have a devil on your back."

"I'm not too pleased he was discussing me with you, but that's a fair description, I suppose."

"Don't blame Ed. I asked about you. Have you wanted to be a policeman since you were a little boy?"

"No."

"Why, then? Or am I being too nosy?"

"Now, why would you think that?"

"You're being sarcastic. Sorry. I didn't think you minded my curiosity."

"Careful. Here, I've got it."

"Whad are you dooink, Bed? Leggo of by dose."

"I'm just trying to help. It was starting to slip out of joint."

"Very funny. Okay, I won't ask any more questions."

"That'll be the day."

"You know, Antonio never wanted to tell me anything."

"Can we keep your ex-husband out of this bed, Jess?"

"Oops. Sorry."

"I'm a cop because of my sister."

"Your sister? Didn't you tell me you were an only child?"

"I am now. She's dead."

"Oh, Ben, I really am sorry. No wonder you wouldn't answer me. You don't have to say any more."

"It's all right. It's been eleven years."

"Was she younger or older than you?"

"Younger. Her name was Maddie."

"I like that."

"She had freckles, like me, but her hair was copper-colored. In the sunlight, it shone like a new penny."

"You loved her."

"Yeah. I didn't realize how much till she was gone. She thought her big brother set the world and all the planets in motion. And I let her down when she needed me most."

"What happened?"

"She was killed—beaten and stabbed by a boy she thought was her friend—when she was fifteen."

"Ben, how awful!"

"The kid was high on cocaine. He hung himself when it was over."

"It must have been terrible for you and your parents."

"It was hard. Dad and Mom got through it on their faith, but I didn't have any faith left to draw on. Maddie was gone, she'd suffered, and I couldn't turn to God for comfort when he'd allowed it to happen in the first place. I blamed him for not keeping her safe. And I blamed myself, too."

"Why?"

"I was away at college, and Maddie had called me that week wanting me to come home for the weekend. It was the second time she'd asked. But I told her no, even though I hadn't seen her or my parents for a couple of months. I was too busy with classes and polishing up my master's thesis and helping Becky plan our wedding. Maybe in a few weeks, I told her. In three days she was dead."

"Ben, that wasn't your fault."

"It was. If I'd come home, she'd have been with me at my parents' place instead of with that crazy junkie. She was always so glad to see me, she hardly let me out of her sight when I was there."

"Would you have gone home that weekend if you had known what was going to happen?"

"Hell, yes. I would've left right after Maddie's call if I'd known."

"Of course you would. But you didn't know, and neither did she. Maybe I'm wrong, but it seems to me you had good reasons for not going home—finishing your education, planning your future with your fiancée. That's important stuff."

"Not more important than my sister's life."

"No, but . . . things happen, Ben. People live their lives the best they know how, and sometimes, like Maddie, they're in the wrong place at the wrong time through no fault of their own. You can't change that. I think you must have been a wonderful brother for her to have loved you like she did. Remember that, and let the other go."

"I can't let it go. You don't know how it was. You're right about one thing—I couldn't change what happened. That enraged me. I wanted revenge, something, anything to get rid of the pent-up feelings inside. The boy who killed her was already dead, so that avenue was closed. But I found a way to make it up to Maddie by going after the people who sold the drugs to that kid."

"You became a policeman."

"Not then. The police had closed the case as a drug-related murder-suicide, and as far as they were concerned, that was that. But I wasn't satisfied. I wanted to know where the boy had gotten the drugs. So I did a little snooping around on my own, got a few leads, and took matters into my own hands. I never did go back to finish my master's. Instead I enrolled in the private high school Maddie's killer had attended. It was my first undercover job."

"Enrolled? As a student?"

"Uh-huh."

"That's incredible! How old were you?"

"Twenty-four. But I was pretty fresh-faced back then, and with a wild haircut and all these freckles, I passed for a kid who was big for his age. After four months I had enough information so the police would listen to me. Then I had their help, and in another four months we broke a big ring of dealers who sold mainly to kids. We were lucky enough to get a substantial cache of drugs and drug money at the same time. I'll never forget the day the arrests were made. That night I slept the whole night through for the first time since Maddie died. Doing what I'd done helped. It was for Maddie. *Then* I became a cop—for her."

"What happened to Becky?"

"Her plans for her life didn't include being a cop's wife, so she called it quits. It's kind of ironic, now that I think about it."

"What?"

"I told Maddie I couldn't come home because of school and Becky. After all the dust settled, I never got my master's degree and never got married. Crazy how things work out sometimes. Hey, what's this? You're not going to cry, are you?"

"I'm trying my darnedest not to. Come here, you."

"Mmm. You do feel nice all squashed up against me. Don't cry for me, Jess. Just think, if things had been different, tonight would never have happened. We probably wouldn't have even met. On second thought, maybe I'll cry with you."

"You devil. Stop trampling on my tender feelings. I'm trying to comfort you."

"Hmm. Maybe you're right. Wouldn't want to shoot myself in the foot here. Go on with what you were doing. I'm starting to feel better already."

Carefully Jessie reached over Ben's sprawled, slumbering body to turn off the lamp. He mumbled unintelligibly as her breasts brushed his chest. She felt his big hand sweep up her side to gently squeeze her before he settled back into sleep.

Poor baby, she thought as she pulled up the covers and snuggled down next to him. He was exhausted, and no wonder. She'd lost count of the times they'd made love.

Jessie was tired, too, her body pleasantly aching from the night's workout. She still couldn't believe the responses Ben had pulled from her or her own greedy demands—demands he'd met and fulfilled without exception. He'd awakened her sleeping sexuality and turned her into a woman she didn't recognize. In the process he'd given her something she hadn't even known she was missing—her womanhood. She was exhilarated with the prize.

Infinitely more precious, though, were the quiet moments of discovery when the two of them had lain entwined in lovers' intimacy, touching the nakedness of their souls along with that of their bodies. In one night she'd learned more about Ben than she had about Antonio in years. To Jessie, that simple act of sharing their most private selves was far more significant than their physical joining, spectacular as that had been. In fact, for her it was what had made the sex so wonderful. She'd never felt so close to another human being, not even Allie.

Now it was hard to believe she'd fought the attraction between them. The only explanation was that the lingering scars of her marriage had blinded her to everything but her inability to control the fast-moving events that had brought Ben into her life. He was there, a handy outlet for her frustration, and she'd stupidly blamed him for all of it. It just showed that in some ways, she was still letting Antonio call the shots.

But her eyes were wide open now. The night had proved that Ben was nothing like her ex-husband.

Well, he *was* a little bossy, but only at those times when he was trying to do his job and keep her safe. How could she condemn him for that? He had told her how important his work was to him, and she understood, probably more than he thought she did. He was fighting demons of guilt and obligation over something that hadn't been his fault at all.

His tough-cop persona hid a warm, caring man who felt things deeply. Up till now he'd fought his battles alone, but no longer, Jessie vowed. Maybe he didn't realize it yet, but he needed her, he needed her love. Just as he had freed her from the constricting bonds left over from her past, she would help him to break loose from his self-imposed penance over Maddie. He'd been living under that cloud for too long.

She loved him; they were meant to be together. Jessie knew it in every fiber of her being.

Chapter 10

Ben's eyes shot open when the phone rang. Jessie stirred in his arms and murmured drowsily. Reluctantly he disentangled himself from her sweet warmth and whispered, "Go back to sleep, Jess. I'll get it."

He slipped out of bed and turned off the ringer on the bedside phone. Naked, he padded to the telephone in the living room, catching it in the middle of a ring.

"Hello?"

There was a brief hesitation on the other end, and a female voice said, "Who is this?"

"Allie?" At once Ben's hazy mind cleared. "This is Ben. Where are you calling from?"

"Never mind where *I* am—where's my sister? Why are you answering her phone?"

"We had her calls forwarded to my number. She's staying with me." Ben's brain identified the background noise coming through the earpiece as highway traffic. "Where are you?"

"Why is she staying with you? Oh, never mind. Let me talk to her."

"She's still in bed."

Another telling silence. "You're *sleeping* with her?"

Avoiding a direct answer, Ben snapped, "I'm doing precious little sleeping these days. Thanks to you, your sister needs bodyguard, and I've been elected for the job. Now the sooner you turn that journal over to the authorities, the sooner life can get back to normal for all of us."

"That's what I'm trying to do. Look, Ben, I'm on the road back to Chicago, and somebody is waiting to use this phone, so I don't have a lot of time to talk. Jessie says you're a cop, and you sure as hell sound like one all of a sudden, so I want to make a deal. An exclusive for the journal. Can you do that?"

"No, I can't. I'm not authorized to make any deals. The best thing for you to do is find the nearest police station and—"

"No, dammit! I'll hand it over to whoever *can* promise me his story and nobody else. So you might as well tell me who that is."

"What happened to the breezy, free-wheeling Angela we all now and love?" Ben asked sarcastically.

"Give me a name, Ben."

"An FBI agent named Cal Leutzinger," he said. "But I wouldn't count on a deal if I were you."

"Just have him ready to see me. I'll take care of the rest."

"Don't be dumb, Allie. You can't come into town on your own. It's not safe."

"Let me worry about that. I have a plan. Jeez, I'd better hurry—it's cold, and this woman out here is getting impatient. Tell that FBI guy to meet me at two o'clock today, okay? Oh, and thanks for taking care of Jessie. I didn't mean for her to get involved."

"Wait a minute—"

"Gotta go now. Bye."

"Wait! Allie—" But Allie had already hung up. He wondered how long it would take her to figure out she hadn't designated a meeting place. "Damn."

Ben put the receiver into its cradle, thought a second and picked it back up to press in Leutzinger's home phone number.

Five minutes later he hung up the phone, damning Allie Webster, Cal Leutzinger and life in general. He hadn't anticipated this turn of events.

He didn't notice Jessie standing just inside the hallway until she spoke.

"Good morning."

He turned, his irritation forgotten. Wearing a shy smile and the shirt he had tossed aside last night in his haste, Jessie looked rumpled and very, very sexy.

For a moment the adoring look in her eyes gave him pause, but he pushed aside the unsettling feeling and went to her. She came into his arms willingly, turning up her mouth for a soft fleeting kiss.

"Good morning." He kept his face close and nuzzled his nose against hers. "You taste like mint."

"I borrowed your toothbrush."

"And my shirt, too, I see." She had left the three top buttons undone, providing him with a tempting view. Ben leaned away and ogled it blatantly.

"I hope you don't mind."

They kissed again, long and deep. Soon Jessie's arms were clasped around Ben's neck and his hands were moving under the too-big shirt. The feel of her soft skin sent a vibration of possessiveness shuddering through him, unexplainable but urgent. He hoisted her up by her bottom and pulled his lips away only long enough to gasp, "Put your legs around me." Compliantly she enclosed his waist in a sweet girdle of smooth feminine muscle. He carried her back to the bedroom and tumbled her onto the mussed bedding.

As he reached for protection he studied her, wondering about the need she effortlessly drew from him. Even after last night he wanted her.

It was just the sex, he told himself. It wouldn't do to get carried away with dreams and emotions he had no business entertaining. He'd better watch it, or before he knew it, he'd be in too deep to get out comfortably. But it felt too good to stop now.

Jessie reached for him. Ben came down on top of her, his niggling concerns forgotten as he lay claim yet again to the secrets of her body.

Later he rolled to his back, pulling Jessie with him. Wearily he arranged her pliant body along his side and declared with a sigh, "I am a satisfied man."

Jessie flopped a limp hand onto his chest and stroked his damp skin and hair lethargically. "Does that mean we're not going to do it anymore?"

Ben, whose eyes were closed, heard the sated note in her droll wisecrack and chuckled. "You'll be the death of me, woman."

"You're safe for a while," she murmured, and yawned. "I think I'll sleep the day away."

"No, you can't." Ben's feeling of well-being fled. "Don't go to sleep, Jess. We've got company coming."

"We do? Who?"

"Cal Leutzinger. I forgot to tell you—Allie called earlier, while you were still asleep."

Jessie raised her head. "Why didn't you wake me? I wanted to talk to her."

"You probably should have. *I* sure didn't get anywhere with her."

"What did she say?"

"Not enough." Ben related abbreviated versions of Allie's call and his subsequent conversation with Leutzinger. "When he calls back to set a meeting place, he wants to be here so he can talk to her himself."

Jessie listened thoughtfully. "How dangerous do you think it is for Allie to come to Chicago by herself?"

"I don't know, Jess. Leutzinger did say if anyone is trying to find that journal, they're probably watching for her in Port Mangus and Sheboygan rather than Chicago."

"Why does he think that?"

"Because there's been an APB out on Allie's car in three states since yesterday. No one has reported spotting her. Plus she was smart enough to make a withdrawal of several hundred dollars from her account on Wednesday and hasn't used any credit cards in the meantime. Which shows she's doing *some* thinking."

Jessie's brows knit together in a frown. "When did they find out all that stuff?"

"They've been working on it since yesterday afternoon. What it means is, if the FBI hasn't been able to trace her movements, it's not likely anyone else has, either. From what you've told me, you're her only obvious connection in Chicago. So if the worst case happens and the wrong people know you're sisters, Allie knows you're here with me. There's no reason for her to go to your apartment. My guess is she'll be okay. Hopefully when she calls again, you'll be able to talk her into turning the journal and herself in.''·

"'Turn herself in'? You make her sound like someone who's committed a crime. Agent Leutzinger hinted at the same thing yesterday. You're both wrong about her."

"Easy, Jess. You know what I meant. Allie hasn't exactly been cooperative with us, but I believe she does intend to turn over the journal. And so far she hasn't broken any laws. At least none that she'll be charged with."

"What does *that* mean?"

"Well, she stole that journal. But without Mai Duan to press charges against her, she won't be arrested. And Mai's missing, remember? Even if she shows up again, I doubt she'll want to call police attention to a piece of evidence that would almost certainly incriminate her."

Jessie fell silent. Having given her that bit of oversimplified hedging to chew on, Ben stretched out his arm and patted her bare bottom.

"Try not to think about it, honey. We have other things to worry about right now, like getting up and dressed before Leutzinger gets here. I don't know about you, but I could use a shower. How about it? I wash your back, you wash mine?" He waggled his eyebrows.

Jessie's stomach chose that moment to growl expansively.

He grinned down at her. "On second thought, breakfast first."

Together they raided Ben's bounteous freezer. At his request, Jessie ate her microwave pancakes dressed only in his shirt. He'd found her a pair of heavy wool socks to keep her legs and feet warm, a consideration that charmed her.

They spoke little during the meal. Obviously tired from their night of passion, Ben was indifferently groomed in an old gray sweatshirt and yesterday's jeans. He hadn't shaved, and his hair was rumpled from a haphazard finger-combing. But the slumberous cast of his tilted eyes put Jessie in mind of hot need and sweet release. Just looking at him was enough to keep her warm.

"You're very quiet," she observed when they'd finished eating. "Is it something I said?"

He pushed his chair back and started gathering their dishes. "Not you—Leutzinger. Having him come over here makes me edgy."

"You surprise me. I didn't think you were the type to be intimidated by your boss. Here, let me help with that." Jessie got up from the table and joined him at the kitchen sink.

"I'm not intimidated. I just don't like it. You want to rinse and stack these in the dishwasher?"

"Sure." She nudged him out of the way.

Ben took on the remaining chores, wordlessly putting away the syrup and wiping down the table and countertops. As he worked, his tension seemed to increase until it emanated from his body like shimmering waves of heat from sunbaked asphalt.

Bemused by his brooding silence, Jessie finished her job quickly and reached to dry her hands. Without warning, Ben came up behind her, his lean, hard body crowding her stomach against the edge of the counter. She felt him, solid and male, all up and down her backside as he folded the cloth he'd been using and hung it with exaggerated care beside the towel.

He must have shaken off his dark mood, Jessie thought. She wriggled her rear end against his fly and grinned, leaning back to look at him.

His mouth came down hard on hers, pushing her head into his shoulder. She felt his palms on her bare thighs, sliding up under her shirt and nestling like spoons beneath her breasts. His tongue tasted of syrup and greedy pleasure.

"Sweet, sweet Jess," he whispered into her ear. "You know what I wish?"

"What?"

"I wish Leutzinger and your sister and everybody else in the whole damn world would just go away and leave us alone."

"What a lovely thought." Jessie turned in his arms and searched his face. She didn't fully understand the message she read there, but suddenly the words that had been hovering in her heart since the early morning rose and pushed against her tongue.

"I love you, Ben."

His eyes flickered the second before he averted them. "You don't love me, Jess," he said gently.

A fist squeezed Jessie's heart. "I don't?"

He shook his head. "You're confusing love with lust. Sex is a powerful thing, and I'm the first man to really satisfy you in bed, so..."

"You needn't talk to me like I'm still in kindergarten, Ben." Jessie stepped out of his arms. "And I don't need you to tell me what I feel. I'm a grown woman."

A stupid grown woman who doesn't know when to keep her mouth shut, she clarified silently.

"Believe me, I *know* you are. And I'm not the kind of man you...you deserve...." His raking fingers messed up his hair even more, and he shook his head soberly. "Don't fall in love with me, Jessie. There's no future in it. Just enjoy what we've got."

Jessie's confidence slipped in the face of his absolute statement. His bluntness hurt. No future? Was she wrong to love him? Had he lived without love so long, he had none to give back? Maybe she was a fool to think hers could erase his darkness and make him happy.

But she rallied when she remembered her early morning vow. She couldn't give up on him so soon. One thing she'd learned from her marriage was to fight for what she wanted. Ben cared for her, she knew he did. She couldn't have been mistaken in what she'd felt from him last night. No, *he* was the one who didn't know the difference between love and lust.

Jessie shored up her determination. "Maybe you're right," she told him lightly. "Now how about that shower? I'll give you first dibs."

Ben looked doubtful, as though unsure he had gotten his point across, but then he shrugged. Apparently he'd decided to leave well enough alone. "You're not joining me?"

"Uh-uh. Time's awasting, and I'd probably be tempted to jump your bones again."

"I might be tempted to let you."

His eyes took on a familiar gleam that Jessie was relieved to see. She hadn't scared him off.

She summoned a laugh and shooed him out of the kitchen.

*   *   *

Two cars buzzed in at Ben's gate at about ten. Leutzinger drove the first, and the second, to Ben's annoyance, held Rory Douglas.

Ben held the agent back at the door, letting Douglas enter the house ahead of them. "What's *he* doing here?"

Leutzinger looked at him quizzically. "When I called to tell him what was going on, he asked to come along. As prosecutor, he has a vested interest in this case, so I didn't see any reason to say no. Was I wrong?"

It would suit Ben just fine to never see the man again, but he shook his head. "Nah. It doesn't matter."

They entered the house just in time to see Douglas's eyes light up when he spotted Jessie, who was looking gorgeous in the suit she'd worn yesterday. Ben quickly moved in to stand beside her. He endured the handshake Douglas forced on her, even though he felt like lopping off the man's arm at the elbow. Jessie didn't dawdle over the greeting; she turned at once to extend the same courtesy to Leutzinger.

With the amenities over, an awkward silence fell. Jessie looked at Ben, eyebrows raised. She indicated the topcoats both men wore against the near-freezing temperature outside. "These gentlemen would probably like to take off their coats."

Ben lifted his shoulders in an I-could-care-less shrug. He'd be damned if he'd play the role of fawning host to a couple of intruders. He pointed. "There's the closet, gentlemen."

Jessie cast a puzzled glance at him when Leutzinger and Douglas turned their backs. Ben pretended to ignore her by sauntering over to a window and staring out.

"Nice place," Leutzinger said after hanging up his coat. "Has the woman called yet?"

"Not since this morning."

Ben's succinct retort did not invite further comment; thankfully, none was offered.

He felt jumpy inside, uneasy. This feeling that something was unraveling had started when he realized he couldn't dissuade Leutzinger from coming over today. It had increased every time he thought about that uncomfortable scene in the kitchen with Jessie earlier. And now that his boss had showed up with Rory Douglas in tow, it was worse than ever.

The two men inside these walls felt like a violation. For the first time since Ben had bought this place for a sanctuary, the separate parts of his segmented existence were coming together, overlapping.

He'd never been one to frequent the hangouts where cops gathered to let off steam over a few beers, nor did he accept invitations to the homes of fellow officers. That kind of socializing was fine for others, even necessary, but Ben had never felt that he truly belonged to the unique brotherhood of his profession.

He'd found his own way of dealing with the pressures of the job—here, under the roof of this old farmhouse. Except for the plumbing and electrical work, every bit of renovation was the product of his own planning and the labor of his own hands, plotted and executed exactly, down to the shade of varnish on the baseboards. It was straightforward, rewarding work over which he exerted absolute control.

Ben took a great deal of satisfaction from the results.

The house was a haven he had so far kept segregated from his life as an undercover cop. Here he could almost forget who he was in that other, dirtier world where lies prevailed and anything could happen.

Leutzinger and Douglas didn't belong in his peaceful refuge.

"Wouldn't it be more comfortable if we all sat down?" The strained suggestion came from Jessie. Apparently they'd all been waiting for an engraved invitation to use his sofa and chairs.

"By all means," Ben said grudgingly. "Have a seat."

Some of his annoyance faded when he saw Jessie's pink cheeks. She was embarrassed over his less-than-welcoming attitude. Something inside him gave a little.

"There's a fresh pot of coffee in the kitchen," he said. "Since we don't know how long we have to wait until Allie calls, I'll get everybody their first cup. After that, you're on your own. Give me a hand, Jess?"

When they were alone in the kitchen, she folded her arms and studied him. "If you're bucking for host of the year, I think you need a little polishing up."

"Hey, I didn't invite them. I'd just as soon they didn't get too comfortable."

"I don't think you have to worry about that. They probably feel about as welcome as the swine flu."

"Good. Then they'll leave as soon as possible." Ben poured coffee into the mugs he'd lined up on the counter.

"Come on, Ben. The time is going to creep by for all of us if you don't show some common courtesy."

"Why should I? This is my home. I come here to get away from reminders of my work, not to have them knocking on my front door."

Jessie compressed her lips. "Is it those two in particular, or does that apply to all your guests—including me? *I'm* connected to the case you're working on."

Ben's hand slipped and a tiny puddle of coffee splashed onto the counter. She had him there. He'd broken his own rules by suggesting to Leutzinger that he guard Jessie in his well-fortified home. This was the one place where he tried to forget he was a cop, and Jessie's presence brought countless reminders. Why hadn't she spoiled the peace he found here, as Leutzinger and Douglas had?

It must be the sex, of course, he assured himself for the second time that day. Which was one more reason to wish the two men in the living room to perdition.

"Well?" Jessie demanded impatiently. "Do you resent my being here?"

She looked cute when she was mad at him, but Ben knew better than to tell her that. He placed a steaming mug into each of her hands and picked up the other two.

"No," he said, dropping a quick kiss on her mouth, "I don't." He turned and strode into the living room, leaving a befuddled-looking Jessie to follow.

"Rory here tells me the two of you played football together in high school, Ben." Leutzinger accepted the mug Ben handed him.

Ben glanced at Rory. "Yeah, we did."

"That's right," his old rival said heartily. "Old Ben here was our star quarterback, weren't you, Ben? They called him 'Struttin' Sutton.'"

Ben shrugged and took a sip of his coffee.

"Come on, don't be modest." Douglas smiled at him and said to Leutzinger, "The teachers and coaches all loved this guy. They used to hold him up to the rest of us as a model of what we all should be."

"That's a slight exaggeration," Ben said warily.

"Not too many of us were cut out to be men of the cloth, though, not like Ben," Rory went on doggedly. "Did you know that Ben had studied to be a minister, Miss Webster?"

Jessie said faintly, "No, I didn't, but I don't think—"

"What happened, Ben? You could have knocked me over with a feather when a buddy told me at our ten-year reunion that you'd become a cop. Everybody in the old gym was hoping you'd show up that night, so we could get the scoop on what changed your mind."

Ben masked his irritation behind a tight smile. Douglas's eyes were fairly glowing with unholy speculation. Evidently he was nursing old grudges and still retained his bullying tendencies from the old days. Well, Ben thought, this time he had underestimated his opponent. Ben Sutton had stopped turning the other cheek a long time ago.

"It's a dull story," he said. "Yours is far more interesting, Rory. Why don't we talk about the old neighborhood? The stories we could tell, right? I'm sure Cal and Jessie would be fascinated."

Douglas opened his mouth, then closed it. Ben mentally chalked up the point. Just as he suspected, Rory was touchy about his humble beginnings.

Ben let the silence go on for an uncomfortably long time before he said, "No? Oh, well, come to think of it, high school nostalgia is pretty boring stuff to outsiders. Sorry, Jessie . . . Cal."

Rory looked furious, but Leutzinger only shrugged.

Jessie caught Ben's eye and he winked at her. She winked back, surprising a grin out of him.

Ben suddenly felt expansive toward his guests, even Rory. "Anyone for more coffee?"

Sometime later, Jessie wandered to a window to gaze out at the November morning. The sky was overcast, and she could almost see the frost in the stiff wind that bent the bare branches of the trees in Ben's yard.

"Bored?" Ben asked softly. She turned around and found him standing close.

"I'm not into golf," she whispered back, glancing over her shoulder at the match Douglas and Leutzinger were watching on TV. Neither man seemed aware of the conversation going on behind them.

"What's between you and Rory Douglas, anyway?" she asked.

"A lot of bad memories I'd just as soon not talk about," Ben said. He, like Jessie, kept his voice low.

"I knew there was something I didn't like about the man. What did he do to you?" She was firmly on Ben's side, whatever had happened.

"Nothing, really, at least nothing specific. You know kids. We were friends once, but then he turned against me. He grabbed every chance he could to make me look stupid or uncomfortable in front of other people."

Jessie remembered Douglas's type from her own school years. "He was probably jealous of you and tried to put you down to make himself look better. When he didn't succeed, he disliked you all the more."

Ben smiled and brushed her cheek with his knuckle. "You could be right. I was an overachiever in those days and usually got what I went after. More times than not I was in competition with Rory."

"Is it true you wanted to be a minister?"

The smile disappeared, and Jessie saw the shadow in his eyes just before he turned away to look out the window. The light from outside turned the coffee-colored locks at his forehead to shining strands of silver. "That was a long time ago," he said quietly. "I realized when Maddie died it was a bad career choi—"

The telephone rang, and their eyes locked. Jessie said, "Allie."

Ben hurried to answer. The caller was indeed her twin, Jessie gathered. Ben wasted no time in introducing Leutzinger and passing the phone over to him.

Allie apparently had her speech prepared, because after identifying himself, the agent stood listening for what seemed to Jessie a long time. Finally he glanced at Rory Douglas and said, "I have the prosecutor for this case right here. I'll have to okay it with him first. Where do you want us to meet you?"

Allie's answer did not please him. He lowered the phone and covered the mouthpiece with his palm. "She won't give us a location until we agree to her terms," he told Douglas grimly. "And that's not all. She says she's got enough dirt for a hell of a story whether we play her way or not."

"Meaning?" Douglas asked.

"Meaning we give her what she wants, or she writes the story *before* she hands over the evidence."

"And there goes our case," Ben said.

"Your case? What about Allie's safety?" Jessie's voice was strident. "Don't any of you care that somebody may be out there looking for her and that journal?"

"Of course we care," Leutzinger told her patiently. "But your sister is being extremely bullheaded, Miss Webster. We've offered her protection, and she's refused by choice, strictly out of her own interests. Now she's jeopardizing an investigation that could put away some major crime figures. It takes time to build sufficient evidence to convict in these cases, time that your sister is threatening to take away from us."

"She's giving us a good case for obstruction of justice," Douglas added.

Jessie began to see the magnitude of the trouble Allie was in. "Let me talk to her." She took the phone. "Allie?"

"Jessie? Jeez, I was beginning to think Leutzinger had fallen asleep over there. He's not tracing this call, is he?"

"No, of course not. Listen to me, Allie. You've got to forget about this story and cooperate with the FBI. They told me you're breaking the law. Please, tell them where you are so they can come and get you. There are people who would kill you to get that journal. I want you to be safe!"

There was a long silence. "Don't worry, sis, I'm safe. I'm wearing a disguise so good even you wouldn't recognize me," Allie finally said in an sardonic voice. "But I don't get it. These guys make deals with criminals all the time—why not with me?"

"*Forget* about the deal! Your life is in danger!"

"Settle down, Jessie. I'm okay, really. Listen, do you think these guys are really serious about charging me with something?"

Jessie looked at the three men watching her. "I don't know. I think so."

"Then you tell Leutzinger I've just upped the ante. The journal *plus* freedom from prosecution for my exclusive. Damn, this is no good over the phone. What does this guy look like?"

"Who, Leutzinger?"

"Oh, never mind what he looks like. Tell him to wear a flower in his lapel and stand by the elephants in the museum at two o'clock sharp. I'll find him. Bye, Jessie. Don't worry about me."

Jessie took the phone from her ear. "She hung up."

"Dammit!" That was Leutzinger.

"Did she give you a meeting place?" Douglas asked.

"Yes, but there's more." Jessie related Allie's demands.

The men looked at one another.

"She has us over a barrel," Douglas said.

Leutzinger snapped, "So she thinks. I'm still concerned about the integrity of our investigation. This woman is hungry to make a name for herself. I don't think we can trust her to hold the story until we're ready for it to break."

"We can if we keep her in protective custody," Ben said.

"Wouldn't she have to agree to that?" Allie asked.

"Good point," said Douglas. "She doesn't seem to be overly concerned about her safety, and there's not much chance she'll voluntarily turn herself over just so we can keep an eye on her. You'll have to arrest her."

"But what about the deal?" Jessie was alarmed by the turn of the conversation.

Leutzinger said, "We haven't *made* a deal yet. Where does your sister want us to meet her?"

She thought fast. "You'll have to get a flower for your lapel so she'll know who you are."

"A flower!" Leutzinger rolled his eyes. "Okay, where will she be?"

Jessie crossed her fingers behind her back. "By the elephants," she said, quavering inside, "at Brookfield Zoo."

Chapter 11

Heart pounding, Jessie struggled to keep her deception from showing on her face. She'd never been a good liar, and now she avoided looking Ben in the eye. Of the three men, he was the one most likely to see through her subterfuge.

Though she wasn't sure where to go from here, she had to try to keep Allie from walking into what amounted to a trap. For once her twin needed her help, and Jessie couldn't let her down.

Ben, apparently remembering his duties as host at last, went to the closet and handed the other men their topcoats. Leutzinger checked his watch, grumbling that Allie hadn't given him much time to set things up, a meeting outdoors in November was damned idiotic, and where in the hell was he going to find a flower?

Jessie had a bad moment when she realized Rory Douglas was watching her during Leutzinger's complaining, but she looked at him with an innocent smile. He returned a bland one of his own and prepared to leave without comment.

If she wasn't challenged, she'd be fine, she told herself. She just had to hang on.

In the general flurry of activity, she noticed Ben slipping into his leather jacket. "Are you going, too?" she asked hopefully.

That would certainly simplify her task. She knew it wasn't enough just to send Leutzinger and Douglas on a wild-goose— make that *elephant*—chase. Somehow she had to get to Allie with a warning.

"Nope." Ben yanked his jacket zipper all the way to the collar. "My job is to look after *you*. I'm just walking Cal and Rory to their cars."

So she would have to deal with him, after all, she thought with an inner sigh. Well, she didn't have time to talk him into helping her, if that was even possible. She'd have to work around him.

He pressed a large squarish button next to the doorjamb.

"What's that?"

"It opens the front gate. You stay put. I'll be right back."

Jessie waited until he'd followed the other men out, then eyed the button he'd just pushed. She hadn't given the gate a thought until now. What else was there lurking in her path that she hadn't considered? For an instant her determination wavered.

But she shook off her apprehension, deciding that finding out how the gate opened from the inside was a good omen. That was one obstacle she didn't have to face. Anything else, she would confront as it came.

Knowing there was no time to waste, she hurried to the phone to call a cab. Momentarily stymied when the dispatcher asked for an address, she spied a news journal on the table next to Ben's recliner. A subscription magazine with an address label. She read the address into the phone and hung up, relieved. That took care of transportation.

Now all she had to do was figure out a way to keep her bodyguard occupied while she sneaked away.

She was in the kitchen heating a couple of cans of thick, beefy soup when Ben spoke from the kitchen doorway. "What're you up to in here?"

Jessie glanced over her shoulder, her insides churning. She hated what she was doing, necessary though it was. "Fixing lunch. This whole thing with Allie has made me headachy, and I thought food might help. Is it okay that I snooped and found this soup in the pantry?"

Ben came up beside her and took the wooden spoon out of her hand. "Do you need some aspirin?"

"Oh, no, I'm sure I'll be all right once I've eaten."

"Let me do this. You sit down by the table and rest."

He sounded so solicitous, Jessie felt doubly guilty as she let him gently push her away from the stove. Then she remembered what he and his cohorts had planned for Allie. She took a seat at the table, her resolve hardening.

"You were gone a long time," she said. "What did you have to talk about out there that you couldn't say in front of me?"

"We weren't hiding anything from you," Ben said. "I was just saving time by walking Cal out. He only has a little over an hour to coordinate the rendezvous and I wanted to see what he had planned." He filled two bowls from the steaming pan, grabbed a couple of spoons out of a drawer, and brought soup and utensils to the table in one trip.

Jessie picked up her spoon. "What *does* he have planned?"

Ben stirred the brothy mixture in his bowl. "It's a pretty standard operation. Nothing more than a couple of extra men to ensure Allie's safety."

Jessie snorted. "Oh, sure, her safety is a big problem. Right after getting her handcuffed."

"Hopefully, she'll go along with them and it won't come to that."

Jessie's head snapped up. "You mean, they would actually put handcuffs on her? In public?"

"There's a lot at stake here, Jess. Surely you understand that protecting Allie from public embarrassment doesn't rank very high in importance right now. Leutzinger will have to do whatever is necessary to get that journal and keep our investigation quiet. Anyway, it's not likely there will be many witnesses at the zoo in this weather."

Upset at his callous disregard of Allie's sensibilities, Jessie stood up, ready to tell him just what he could do with his investigation. Barely in time she remembered her plan and swallowed her angry words. It was more crucial than ever that her ruse be successful. "Oh!" she cried, lifting a hand to her eyes as though she were in pain.

In an instant Ben was beside her, one arm around her waist while his other hand gently brushed the hair away from her face. "What's the matter, honey? Are you dizzy?"

"No," she said weakly, watching him through slitted eyes for a sign of suspicion. "It's this darned headache. Maybe I'd better lie down for a while."

He made no move to let her go. "Let me get you those aspirin."

"No, please—I'll be fine. I have something in my purse in the bedroom."

"You sure?"

"Really, it's only a headache. All this tension and everything…I'm sure I'll be fine once I lie down. You go ahead and eat."

Reluctantly he gave in and let her move away. "Leave the bedroom door open and call if you need anything."

"I will," she said.

She had done it! And now it was all Jessie could do not to run from the kitchen, away from the kind sympathy in Ben's eyes.

Once in the living room and out of his sight, however, she hurried to the porch door to press the gate button. The mechanism engaged with a muted click under her unsteady fingers. Jessie looked over her shoulder to the kitchen, relieved to see or hear no sign of Ben.

Having opened the gate, she spared a long second wishing she dared to walk out the front door, but rejected that idea as too risky. Ben might hear or walk in from the kitchen unexpectedly. Instead she tiptoed down the hallway to the bedroom. There, contrary to her promise to Ben moments ago, she not only closed the door, but also turned the lock in the doorknob. It was a flimsy barrier at best, and Jessie didn't deceive herself that it would stop him if he should come looking for her. However, it could provide her a few more precious minutes to meet her cab. After that, she would be home free.

Once again she stopped and listened, her ear pressed to the door. Nothing. So far, so good.

Jessie dashed first to the dresser to snatch up her purse— she'd need cab money—then to her next hurdle, the window. Uncounted seconds were frittered away while she fumbled to lift the sash. Finally she realized it was locked. In a burst of frustration, she flipped the latch.

And froze.

A high, penetrating tone, unbroken and persistent, reached her ears from another part of the house. Oh, no, she'd activated an alarm!

Panic gripped her, and Jessie was never able to recall afterward any details of how she'd climbed out the window and made her way to the end of the driveway. Only the bitter cold and her mental chant of *hurry, hurry, hurry* made lasting impressions. Her cab pulled up only seconds after she reached the street.

"The Field Museum!" she said to the driver as she got into the back seat.

She heard a shrill, attention-grabbing whistle just before she slammed the door closed.

"Who's that?" The driver looked up the driveway to the house. Jessie saw Ben running toward them like a sprinter in a race.

"Never mind! Just go!" she cried, sitting forward on the seat in a futile effort to get the cab moving.

"We better wait," the cabbie said. "Maybe you forgot something."

"What?" Jessie looked at the back of his bald head incredulously. She couldn't have been unlucky enough to draw the only considerate cab driver in the universe.

"See? He's yellin' something."

Jessie wanted to reach over the seat and tear the man's ears off. "I didn't forget anything! Go! Go, dammit!"

But it was too late. Ben opened the door and leaned in with fire in his eyes. "Where the hell do you think you're going?"

"None of your business!" she snapped.

"It sure as hell *is* my business! Get out of this cab!"

"Hey, is this guy givin' you trouble?" The Good Samaritan in the front seat finally realized he might have miscalculated. Jessie shot him a dirty look.

"There's something I have to do," she told Ben frigidly. She had no alternatives left, not if she was going to meet Allie in time. "Either get in or get out. This cab—" she paused significantly and met the cabbie's eyes with a venomous glare ''—will be moving in ten seconds.''

Ben swore and climbed in.

''You sure he's okay?'' the driver asked her warily.

Jessie rolled her eyes. This guy was the limit. ''Just go.''

Ben shivered, and Jessie noticed for the first time that he was in shirtsleeves. She hadn't stopped for her coat, either, but at least her suit jacket was wool. Even so, the icy air outside had cut through her clothing as she'd run to the taxi. Ben must have nearly frozen.

''How's your headache?'' he asked her snidely as they pulled away from the curb.

Guilt stabbed her, but Jessie turned her head away and took refuge in silence. For all she knew, Ben could still stop the cab and get word to Leutzinger that Allie was nowhere near the zoo. She couldn't take that chance.

''Where in the hell are we going, anyway?'' was Ben's next question. When she didn't answer, he thunked the back of the driver's seat. ''Hey, cabbie, where are we going?''

''Don't tell him,'' Jessie ordered.

The driver looked into his mirror at Ben and shrugged. ''You heard the lady.''

''Listen, fella, I'm a cop,'' Ben told him threateningly, ''so it's in your best interest to tell me where we're headed.''

''Yeah? Show me your badge,'' the driver challenged.

''I don't have it—I'm working undercover. Tell him, Jessie.''

She raised get-serious eyebrows and looked away obstinately. Ben swore again and slumped back into his seat. Jessie felt his eyes boring into her.

''This is pretty damned stupid, you know,'' he said tightly. ''I'd like to know what the hell is going on. Why did you sneak out?''

She kept her face turned to the window and refused to speak.

''C'mon, Jess, where are we going? I don't even have my weapon with me. How am I supposed to protect you? Does this have something to do with Allie?''

Stubbornly she maintained her silence, though her conviction that she was doing the right thing wobbled. Until now, she'd pushed the possible danger in her actions out of her mind.

"Tell me, dammit! What did the two of you cook up on the phone?" Ben caught the involuntary stiffening of her body. "That's it, isn't it? You weren't straight about what Allie said to you. She's not at the zoo, is she? Jess, I'm not the enemy, dammit. Talk to me. Where is she?"

Jessie's eyes filled with tears. She detested this whole business and was probably going about it all wrong. Still, she couldn't throw Allie to the wolves. "I can't tell you."

"Oh, this is great, just great," Ben snarled.

She wheeled on him. "They were going to *arrest* her. I have to warn her, don't you understand, Ben? She'll change her mind about things if I can just talk to her face-to-face. She's...she's my sister!"

The adrenaline that had propelled Jessie for the past half hour was depleted, and her tears overflowed.

"Aw, hell," Ben muttered. He held out his arms to her and she flung herself against his chest, sobbing.

With the onset of Jessie's tears, the urge to wring her damnably elegant neck evaporated. Ben wrapped her in his arms and let her weep, his emotions in as much a turmoil as hers seemed to be. He should be angry—he *was* angry—but in spite of her trickery, he was unable to quell the impulse to comfort her.

He laid his cheek in her hair and rubbed his jaw against it as he stroked her back, shushing her quietly. She tied him in knots. She'd duped him—hard-nosed, I'm-no-fool Sutton—and here he was, soothing her tears. Worse, he even felt a touch of admiration for her audacity. She'd outwitted two seasoned law enforcement officers and a U.S. attorney, after all.

By a stroke of luck she hadn't known about the warning signal his alarm system gave off when door and window locks were released from the inside. When Ben had heard that, he'd thought she was only opening the window to get some air to help her headache. He'd hurried to the bedroom to close it again, since he'd fully engaged the system right after Leutzinger and Douglas had left and in ninety seconds both the alarm outside and one at the security monitoring headquarters a few miles away would sound, bringing the police. He'd found the bedroom door locked, and Jessie hadn't answered his calls.

Suspicious at last, Ben had kicked in the door, taking in the damning scene at a glance. The window was open, all right, but Jessie was gone.

At least he'd caught on in time, even though he hadn't had the foresight to grab a weapon before running after her. By then it had been too late to do any more than take care of the alarm without losing her.

But it could have been worse. She could have been out here on her own. At that disturbing thought, Ben's arms tightened around her.

"Here, buddy, give 'er these."

Ben took the small box of tissues the driver handed over the seat. "Thanks."

Jessie's sobs had quieted to ragged sighs and sniffs against his shirt. He pulled a couple of tissues out of the box and pressed them to her damp cheek.

"Want to blow your nose, princess?"

"Uh-uh," she said in a small, rueful voice, nestling in closer. "I think I'll just stay here until your shirt dries."

Ben chuckled and peeled her away from his chest. "Come on, time to mop up."

She allowed him to dry her flushed cheeks, sitting as still as a child having her face washed. Her eyes were wet and luminous, her lips adorably pouty from her bout of weeping.

"Blow," he told her when he was finished, placing the tissues in her hand. She sat back obediently and blew her nose.

"Better?"

Jessie nodded. "I'm sorry. I don't know why I broke down like that."

"*I* do. It was a guilt attack and you deserve it," he said gruffly.

A chagrined smile fluttered on her lips.

"So are you ready to tell me the truth now? Where's Allie?"

Her eyes locked with his uncertainly. Ben wondered how in hell he'd been taken in before, when her emotions were displayed on her face like headlines. He'd been unwary as a rookie, thinking with his gonads, not his brain. He wouldn't make that mistake again.

"If I tell you—" Jessie started.

"Here you are, folks." The cabbie pulled to a stop by a curb.

Ben recognized the enormous building at once. Every child who'd ever gone to school in Chicago had toured the fascinating Field Museum of Natural History, probably several times, and Ben was no exception. The wonders inside, from dinosaur bones to Egyptian mummies, were enough to keep even unruly boys wide-eyed and awestruck for hours.

"She's here?" He turned to Jessie.

But she had already opened the door. "I'm sorry," she whispered, and exited the cab.

Ben lost precious time scooting across the seat. "Wait a minute. Jessie, get back here! You can't—dammit!"

She was one-third of the way up the massive bank of tiered steps, and moving fast.

"Looks like she stuck you with the tab," the driver smirked.

Ben gritted his teeth as he realized his gun was not the only thing he'd left behind. His wallet—and his money—were sitting uselessly on his dresser at home. He scrambled out of the cab on Jessie's side, keeping his eyes on her as she climbed the steps. "Wait for us. We'll need a ride back."

"Wha—? Hey, wait a minute, dammit!" the cabbie sputtered, then called threateningly after Ben, "The meter's runnin'."

Ben watched the plaid top of Jessie's suit being swallowed up by the entrance doors. A heartfelt curse exploded from his lips. He took the steps three at a time, aware that the woman he was supposed to be protecting could disappear in seconds into the huge labyrinth of corridors inside. He'd already known she was going to meet Allie; why hadn't he pressed her harder about their meeting place? If someone had followed Allie, hoping to get that damned journal...

Fear for Jessie and fury that he'd let this happen drove Ben to the top of the steps and through the ornate portals of the museum into the vast lobby. He stopped just inside, the reverberating echoes of uncounted voices bouncing off the high ceiling and walls and assaulting his ears with remembrance. In his boyhood he had delighted in shouting "hey!" into the yawning, seemingly limitless space above him in this massive room, to hear his own voice come back to him louder and somehow larger than his original utterance. But his only interest now was to locate Jessie.

The lobby was undulating with patrons of all ages and nationalities this Thanksgiving weekend, making Ben's task all the more difficult. His eyes swept wide over the marked hallways leading to exhibits in the museum's bowels, trying to catch a glimpse of his prey before she eluded him completely. Methodically he scanned the crowd—left, right, then back again. Desperation rose in his chest with each unsuccessful pass of his eyes.

Suddenly his brain registered a flash of plaid and he swung his gaze in a return arc to the center lobby. There was Jessie, dwarfed under the display of battling woolly mammoths, or "hairy elephants," as he'd called them when he was a boy. Oh, yeah—elephants. Ben shook his head and started toward Jessie.

He had just noticed the unkempt gray-haired woman dressed in shabby clothing standing next to her, when two things happened at once. Jessie glanced over at him with a start of recognition, and a small, exuberant boy of four or five ran into his path and tripped, his momentum catapulting his small body forward over Ben's leg. Ben heard the dull crack as the boy's head struck the stone floor, and a woman shrieked, "Joey!"

The next few minutes were pandemonium. The hollow acoustics of the enormous room amplified little Joey's cries, and the frantic mother rushed over, wild-eyed with fright. Ben started to pick the child up, but the mother attacked him with her purse. "Why don't you watch where you're going? Leave him alone!"

Ben raised his arms to protect himself, moving as quickly as he could out of the line of fire. As soon as he was outside the woman's reach, she gathered Joey in her arms, bombarding him with worried questions about where it hurt and maternal reassurances that he'd be all right, mommy was here now. All the while she shot dirty looks at Ben. When they were joined by an anxious museum official, Ben's involvement was forgotten, and he looked over to where he'd last seen Jessie.

She was gone.

So was the old lady to whom she'd been so earnestly talking. Sudden realization struck him as he replayed his brief glimpse of the two women in the moments before Joey had collided with his leg. His mind ticked off what he'd seen. A frumpish old woman's face, garishly pale with makeup against the dark plastic frames of her glasses. A too-long coat hanging shapelessly on a stout body, hiding definitive lines of bone and muscle. Hands clasping Jessie's, telling of more than casual acquaintance.

Allie.

If there had been a wall handy to put his fist through, Ben would probably have broken his fingers in that moment. Instead his knuckles pummeled the more forgiving flesh of his own palm.

What now? None of his options held much hope of finding either Jessie or her sister. If he'd had his badge, he might have ordered the museum sealed off until Leutzinger could come with some men to search the place. Without it, he had about as much chance of convincing whoever ran this place that he was a cop as he had that cab driver. Anyway, both women could easily have slipped out unnoticed in all the confusion of the past few minutes.

Ben left the crowd around the boy and dashed outside. His gaze skimmed the steps, the wide stretch of pavement in front of the museum, and up and down the street as far as he could see. Nothing.

Damn! Not only had he lost Allie and the journal, he'd let Jessie, their only link to the woman with the evidence, slip away as well. There was going to be hell to pay when he reported in. Ben walked back into the museum, thinking of Leutzinger and his men waiting pointlessly in the biting cold at Brookfield Zoo.

Jessie almost crashed into him inside the door. She pulled up short, looking relieved to see him. "I—I thought you were going to leave without me," she said.

Ben grabbed her shoulders, unsure whether to hug or shake her. "Where did Allie go?"

Alarm colored her eyes. "You recognized her?"

"I'm not stupid, Jess," he said harshly. "Is she still in here?"

"I d-don't know."

"The hell you don't!" Ben rasped. He was dangerously close to shaking her teeth loose. "Stop shielding her, dammit! This is a *criminal investigation,* for God's sake, not a game of one-upmanship. Every minute that Allie is on the loose with that journal is one minute more that the wrong people have to find her and take it away.''

"She didn't have it," Jessie said miserably.

"What?"

"The journal. She didn't even bring it."

"She didn't—hell, why not? I thought the whole idea behind this rendezvous was to turn over the journal."

"So did I."

"Yeah, right."

"I did!" she insisted. "In fact, I was trying to get Allie to give *me* the book to take to Agent Leutzinger, along with her promise not to write her story prematurely." She sighed. "But it was all for nothing. She couldn't do what I asked even if she wanted to, she said, because she didn't bring the journal along. She wanted to make sure first that Leutzinger was willing to work with her on the story. She intended to take him to where she's hidden it after they'd talked things over face-to-face."

"Where is that?"

Jessie shook her head. "She wouldn't tell me."

Ben tipped her chin up with his forefinger and searched her eyes. They were troubled, but clear and direct. She was telling the truth.

"Where is she now, Jess? No, look at me." He nudged her chin higher when her lashes fell. "Time's running out now, for all of us, especially Allie. Where did she go? Or is she still here, waiting for us to leave?"

"She left the museum during all the commotion. And before you ask, I don't know where she went. There wasn't time to find out where she's staying, not once we'd seen you. Allie was anxious to get away before you could arrest her."

"You told her."

"Yes, I did!" Jessie said. "She deserved to know what would happen if she kept trying to cut a deal." Wilting a little then, she added, "Not that it did any good. My sister has more courage than sense sometimes."

Privately Ben thought stupidity, not courage, drove Allie Webster, but he kept his opinion to himself. Allie could be headed anywhere in the city by now, and thanks to Jessie's misplaced loyalty, she would be wary of the law. They might as well be back to square one.

"Well, what's done is done. Come on, let's find a phone. I've got to break the news to Leutzinger that you've been jerking him around."

Jessie's cheeks pinkened guiltily, but she followed him to a bank of pay phones nearby.

Ben talked to the duty agent at FBI headquarters and was assured that word of what had just happened would be immediately relayed to Leutzinger out in the field. That done, he took Jessie's elbow and escorted her out of the museum.

"We'll have to go over everything Allie said to you when we get home, probably several times," he told her as they descended the wide concrete stairs. He kept her close, his practiced eyes thoroughly checking the surrounding area but seeing nothing out of the ordinary. "She may have said something that will help us to find her."

"All right." Jessie sounded subdued.

Their cab still waited at the curb, and as they got in, the driver grumbled, "Took you long enough. I was beginning to think you were going to stiff me."

"I told you I'm a cop," Ben said. "I'm sworn to uphold the law, not break it. Take us back home."

He settled back as the cabbie pulled into traffic, thankful for the blessed heat that flowed through the taxi's interior. He was cold as a corpse.

Jessie sat quietly in the seat beside him, hands fidgeting with her purse. Finally she spoke up. "I shouldn't have interfered."

"You got that right," Ben grunted.

"I thought I was doing the best thing for Allie."

"Yeah, well, you weren't."

She looked at him defiantly. "I won't grovel."

"Who asked you to?"

"A simple apology is all you'll get."

Ben waited.

"I'm sorry." She sounded more obstinate than remorseful.

"Apology accepted. Now let's forget it."

She glanced over at him, wariness in her eyes. "That's it? Just like that?"

"What do you want, a brass band?"

She shook her head. "I'm just—surprised. After what I did and the way it turned out, I expected...well, some kind of retribution—the silent treatment, at the very least."

"You know, Jess," Ben said with deceptive evenness, "I'm getting damned tired of being thrown into the same basket of rotten apples as your ex-husband."

She looked startled for a moment, then said meekly, "You're right. I shouldn't do that."

"I make it a practice to forget the last hand dealt to me and play the one I've got. One thing, though..."

She looked up at him with questioning eyes.

"If you ever try to run off by yourself again, I'll handcuff you to the bed for a month."

She risked a teasing smile. "As threats go, I've heard worse."

Ben wasn't playing. "Promise me."

The smile disappeared and Jessie drew an X on her breast with a forefinger. "Cross my heart."

"Come over here." He lifted his arm to make a place for her. Amenably she scooted across the seat to his side and adjusted her curves to the planes of his torso before settling with a sigh against him, her palm resting over his heart.

Ben's hand fell naturally to her hip and pulled her closer. Thank God, she was safe.

She'd made a mess of things.

The whole situation reminded Jessie of her childhood, when she'd stood on the sidelines while her wonderful, foolhardy twin courted disaster in order to prove some point. She felt just as ineffectual today as she had then. She never had been able to turn Allie off course once her mind was made up. Why hadn't she remembered that?

After today's fiasco, Jessie decided she'd better forgo adventurous living and stick to writing about it. Easier on the pocketbook, for one thing, she thought with a flash of humor as she shelled out close to seventy-five dollars for cab fare.

The fact was, if she'd kept her nose out of the whole business, her sister would now be in Leutzinger's custody, which Jessie concluded was no more than Allie deserved. Maybe being arrested would finally open her eyes to what was at stake.

Ben's gate had stood open the whole time they were gone, and after dismissing their cab, he made her huddle in the cold outside the unlocked front door while he made sure there was no one inside the house. Which was no more than *she* deserved after the trouble she'd caused.

At least Ben wasn't holding her temporary insanity against her. That was pretty remarkable, all things considered.

"Come on in, Jess. Everything's okay."

"That's a relief." She hurried into the warmth of the house. "I'd never forgive myself if someone had come in and damaged or stolen something."

"I wasn't as concerned about ordinary vandals or thieves as much as I was about whoever wants the journal," he told her. Jessie followed him into the kitchen, where the remains of their aborted lunch had congealed on the table. Ben gathered up the bowls and carried them to the sink.

"But... why would anybody think it was here?"

"Oh, yeah, I didn't tell you." He scraped and rinsed while relating what he'd learned at the FBI office about the break-in at his Port Mangus duplex. "Given all that," he concluded, "we have to assume the bad guys have figured out I'm a cop. Or at least that I have an interest in Mai's journal."

"Which means you're in as much danger as Allie. And I made you follow me around the city without any protection at all."

Jessie launched herself at Ben and wound her arms tightly around his middle, her cheek pressed against his solid back. She was horrified that her afternoon's folly might have ended in tragedy for him.

"I couldn't stand it if anything happened to you," she told him fiercely.

In spite of her clinging embrace, he managed to turn around and face her. "Hey, nothing happened," he said. "And it won't. I've been taking care of myself for a long time. Anyway, as it turns out, something good came out of your escapade. Nobody came in here while we were gone. You know what that means, Jess?"

"That nobody's after us?" Jessie asked hopefully.

"I wouldn't go that far yet, but at least we can be pretty sure they don't know where you are. Bringing you here was the right thing to do." He lifted her chin and his down-turned eyes crinkled into a smile. "Not to mention extremely enjoyable."

He brushed his thumb across her bottom lip and hooked it in the corner, nudging her lips and teeth apart as his mouth descended. His tongue stroked and coaxed, languidly seducing. Jessie was ready to let the erotic kiss take them where it would, but Ben restrained his hunger and set her away before their passion could mount.

"Don't tempt me. We still have to go over what Allie told you today." He took her hand, led her into the living room and sat her down on the sofa.

Jessie repeated everything she remembered at least three times—some parts even more, due to Ben's prompting—without coming up with anything that might help locate Allie or the journal. Afterward Ben called Leutzinger to brief him on the afternoon's events.

"Was he terribly angry?" Jessie asked when he'd hung up.

"Just hope you don't see him for a while," he said. "Come on, I want to show you something."

He took her down the hall to a room, opposite his bedroom, that had been closed up until now. It was a study of sorts, a utilitarian room with a plain but sturdy desk, a wall of half-empty bookshelves, and a long table upon which was spread a computer with several components unfamiliar to her. The single window was unadorned except for tightly closed miniblinds. Though everything was neatly arranged and orderly, decoration in here was nonexistent, if one excluded the thick carpet carried through from the adjacent hallway. Jessie guessed that Ben didn't spend much time in here.

He walked to the computer and beckoned her over. "This is the heart of my security system."

Jessie recognized grist for her always-hungry writer's mill in the elaborate setup. "How does it work?"

"Very effectively, as you found out today," he replied with a quirk of his lips. "This computer is linked to sensors both outside and inside the house. When the system is fully activated, no one can so much as step foot into the yard or move around in the house without an alarm going off. There are several different levels of security, each requiring its own numbered code."

She was impressed and a little sheepish. "I didn't stand a chance of sneaking away today, did I?"

"Remember that. But that's not why I brought you in here. This machine came with a few pieces of software, including a word processor. You're welcome to use it while you're here, if you'd like to work on your writing."

"Why, Ben, thank you," Jessie said, touched by his thoughtfulness. "But won't that interfere with the alarm system?"

"No. If an alarm goes off, though, *your* work will be interrupted, and the system will take over the machine."

Ben showed her how to access the word processing program and the little he knew about its operation. While Jessie was learning the commands, he left to answer the phone in the living room. She'd been alone for quite a while before he returned.

"Jess."

She turned in the swivel chair at the peculiar tone in his voice. A sudden chill riveted her in place. "What's happened? Is it Allie?"

Ben nodded. "Don't panic—she's all right."

"Tell me."

"After she left the museum, she went back to the motel where she's staying and was assaulted as she was going into her room."

"Oh, no." Shocked into motion, Jessie jumped out of her chair. "Where is she? I have to go to her."

He grabbed her before she could race out the door. "Settle down, honey. I called Leutzinger and he's going to send somebody to pick her up and bring her over here. I'm supposed to keep her out of trouble until he gets back from questioning the assailant at the city jail."

"They got the guy who did it?"

"Uh-huh. Your sister must be a hell of a fighter. She knocked him out, tied him up and presented him to the police on a silver platter. I can't wait to hear the whole story." His eyes sparkled with amusement.

Jessie shook her head wonderingly. "That's Allie for you."

"You okay now? Want a drink to settle your nerves?"

"No, I'm all right. Who was it? Did Allie know him?"

His eyes went abruptly cold. "Allie didn't, but we do. It was Rory Douglas."

Chapter 12

Less than an hour later, Allie, still in disguise, burst into Ben's living room. Jessie grabbed her and hugged her like a mother reclaiming a kidnapped child. Allie clung a little desperately herself before she eased away.

"I'm okay, sis." She slipped her shoulder bag to the floor at their feet and took off her coat.

"Did he hurt you?" Jessie's anxious eyes inspected her for injuries.

A bark of male laughter split the air and a familiar voice said, "You should see the other guy."

Jessie turned toward the voice just in time to see Ed Brock's somber mouth remarkably curved in an all-out, teeth-exposing grin as he set Allie's suitcase next to the couch.

"Hello, Ed."

"Jessie." Ed nodded to her, his face settling back into its normal sagging lines.

"He speaks," Allie said derisively. "You know this cretin, Jessie?"

"Allie!" Jessie chided.

"Never mind, Jessie," Ed said mildly. "Your sister's just irritated because I wouldn't answer any of her fifty million questions on the way over here."

Ben, who had been observing the reunion from the doorway, closed the door and walked over to join the party. "What're you doing in Chicago, Ed? I didn't expect *you* to be playing delivery boy."

"Delivery boy just about sums it up," Ed said. "I brought some evidence down to headquarters earlier, and Leutzinger tagged me to pick up Ms. Webster as I was checking it in."

"What evidence?" The sharp question came from Allie.

Ed's eyes twinkled in his hound-doggy face. "Is there someplace private we can talk, Ben? I'm under orders not to give any information to the press."

Allie's breath hissed through her teeth with exasperation.

Ben touched Jessie's arm. "Why don't you show Allie where the bedroom is, Jess?" His voice deepened when he addressed her, containing a gentle note far different from the one he'd used with Ed. "She'd probably like to change out of that getup she's wearing."

Jessie's cheeks warmed and she avoided looking directly at Allie. "All right. Will you get the other suitcase, Allie?" She stooped to pick up the shoulder bag and waited until her twin collected the bag Ed had brought in.

"By the way," Ben said to Allie, "all the alarms are set, so don't try to run."

"Don't worry," Allie said determinedly. "I'm not going anywhere until I see Leutzinger." She turned to Jessie. "Let's go...*Jess.*"

All the way down the hall, Jessie felt sisterly eyes boring holes into her back.

Inside the bedroom, she turned around to see the door Allie had tried to close bounce back open.

"What happened here?"

Jessie looked at the splintered door frame with dismay. "Oh, no! Ben must have broken it when he chased after me today. I should never have locked it before I climbed out the window. It's not too bad, is it?"

She set the shoulder bag on the bed and came over for a closer examination. Allie blocked her path.

"Forget the door. What's going on between you and the bouncer?" It was her you-have-some-explaining-to-do-Jessie-Webster voice.

"He's not a bouncer, he's a policeman," Jessie said. "Anyway, I refuse to talk to you while you're wearing that disguise. How can you expect me to bare my soul when I can't tell you from a bag lady in the street?"

"Oh." Allie glanced down at her still-padded body in its tawdry dress. "Well, okay, but don't think you're weaseling out of anything."

She strode determinedly to the bed and hoisted her suitcase up. It landed on the covers with a thump.

Suddenly reminded of where she and Ben had spent a large portion of the past twenty-four hours, Jessie gave the bed a quick once-over to reassure herself that she had restored it to pristine condition earlier.

"So," Allie said casually. "Ben told me on the phone he's your bodyguard. Just what does that entail?"

"Protection," Jessie replied, but her cheeks flamed.

"You *are* sleeping with him. I knew it!" Allie held up an arresting palm before Jessie could answer. "No, don't say a word. Give me a minute in the bathroom, and then I want to hear everything from the beginning."

Quickly she opened the suitcase, pulled out a fresh set of clothes, then lifted her hands to the gray hair on her head. "Push that chair in front of the door, will you?" She removed the wig and tossed it negligently to the bed before affixing Jessie with a narrow-eyed glare. "And don't you dare leave this room."

She grabbed her clothes and shoulder bag and disappeared into the bathroom. A minute later, Jessie heard the shower running.

"You're gonna have your hands full with that one," Ed told Ben after the women were gone.

"Who, Allie? I'm not keeping her," Ben said. "She's just here until Leutzinger gets done at the jail, at least I hope so. Want a beer?"

"No, I'm not off duty yet. Gotta go to the jail myself to check out this Rory Douglas. Leutzinger wants to know if I ever saw him during our surveillance of the club. He thinks the guy might be tied in either with this end of Mai's operation or in Wisconsin."

"I agree. Douglas must be dirty, or he wouldn't have gone after Allie. But I already told Leutzinger I don't remember ever seeing him in Port Mangus, so unless you know him, I doubt you'll recognize him, either. Why didn't you get a look at him when you picked up Allie at the motel where he attacked her?"

"They'd already hauled him off when I got there." Ed unbuttoned his jacket. "I got an earful about his bloody nose and the lump on his head from the cop who was taking Allie's statement, though. Hard to believe, a little thing like that doing so much damage. Anyway, they're going to put Douglas in a lineup for me, and after I'm through at the jail, I'm bringing Leutzinger back here. That should be my last 'delivery' of the day."

Ben saw the humor in Ed's eyes. He'd learned over the past months that, contrary to appearances, Ed had a fully functioning, albeit droll, wit. They'd spent long hours of surveillance together before deciding Ben's best cover for the Duan investigation, and now knew each other pretty well.

Ben had worked with feds before, and Ed was the first one he'd met who didn't have that I'm-in-charge-here attitude. He'd immediately accepted Ben as an equal and given him credit for knowing his job. There had been no jockeying for power in their partnership.

In many ways Ed reminded him of his father, if Ben discounted the cynicism characteristic of a man who had seen too much of the seedy side of life. Maybe that was why, for the first time since becoming a cop, Ben had let down his barriers in a professional association and opened himself up to friendship. Ed knew things about him he'd never shared with another fellow officer. Just like he knew personal things about Ed.

"How about coffee, then? It'll only take a minute to fix a pot."

"Sure, sounds good," Ed said, trailing behind into the kitchen. "This place is real nice, buddy. Big, though. Kinda wasted on a confirmed bachelor, isn't it?"

"I just use the downstairs," Ben said. He thought about the second-story bedrooms he'd ignored in his renovations. No doubt they'd held generations of children before he'd bought the house, but he'd closed off the whole floor. A man alone needed only one bedroom. "Tell me what's happening in Port Mangus. Any word on Mai?"

"Not yet. We hit pay dirt of another sort, though, on a shakedown of the marina this morning."

Ben looked up from scooping freshly ground beans into the coffeemaker. "Who did you get?"

"Not *who*. Sad to say there was no welcoming committee to greet us. It was locked up tight, even the bait shop. Mai's disappearance must have spooked everybody into steering clear of the place. Ask me *what* we got, though, and the answer's a little better."

Ben's mouth quirked. "A whole lot better, I'd say, from that look in your eye. *What*, then?"

"A real bonanza. You shoulda been there, Ben. There was this tunnel leading from one of the stalls in the men's john to a building that looked like a storage shed behind the marina proper. False door, no windows. Inside was an office with an empty desk and filing cabinets, and a teller's cage, like a bank, also empty. At first it looked like the place had been cleaned out, but then a youngster with the Port Mangus P.D. found a hole in the floor under the files, just chock-full of goodies. Greenbacks and white powder—lots of both."

Ben leaned against the counter while the coffee machine gurgled beside him. "Well, well."

Ed allowed his lips to curve slightly. "I don't need to tell you, we started moving furniture like crazy after that. There were two more holes, the biggest one under the counter in the teller's cage, where we figure they dealt to individual customers. Under there we found smaller packets of pot, coke, heroin, pills, even some designer stuff. Plus all the paraphernalia for your preferred mode of ingesting the stuff—a regular junkie's pharmacy."

"How much did you take?"

"Eighty-one thousand and change in cash. Probably ten times that in drugs, maybe more."

Ben whistled through his teeth. "Nice going."

"It would have been nicer if we'd gotten some live bodies to go with it," Ed said somewhat disgustedly. "As it stands, we haven't arrested so much as a gofer, let alone anybody close to the top of the operation. We'd have had a lot more leverage to put these guys away if we'd found somebody on the premises. We really needed more time on this one."

After a brief silence he shook his head. "You know, I looked at all that dirty money stacked up today and it made me sick. It's not right that guys like you and me work damned hard—even risk our lives—for a pittance, while crooks like Mai Duan and her cronies are stacking it up by the wheelbarrow dealing dope and sex."

Ben understood the older man's frustration. "But you did shut down their operation. You cost them a healthy amount of cash and dope in the process, too. Count this one a win."

"Yeah. And how long will it take 'em to bounce back with a new setup somewhere else?"

Ben had no answer for that.

"Oh, well," Ed said. "I gotta admit, it *felt* like a win for a while. It's just too bad you were taken off the case right before things got interesting. Even though we didn't get to arrest anybody, I would've hated missing out on finding that stash this morning."

Ben thought about what he had been doing early that morning and wasn't sorry at all. "There are still some loose ends that might lead to convictions, remember. Mai, for one."

The older man snorted. "If you ask me, that's not a *loose* end, it's a *dead* end. My guess is she ticked off somebody in the organization and is floating facedown in the lake right now."

"Maybe," Ben acknowledged, "but there's still her journal. I'm thinking maybe that's what Rory Douglas was after when he attacked Allie. Since he's the new prosecutor on Mai's case, the plot thickens. This thing isn't over yet."

Ed's eyes brightened inquisitively. "Yeah, fill me in on that. Leutzinger only had time to give me the bare bones."

"I don't know much more than that myself. We should probably wait to see what Leutzinger can get out of Allie Webster when he gets here." As Ben spoke, the coffeemaker expelled a prolonged, sputtering hiss. He pushed himself away from the counter. "Coffee's done. Black as sin, right?"

"And hot as hell," finished Ed, quoting his often-repeated preference. "Couldn't take it any other way."

* * *

Jessie decided to ignore Allie's order to stay in the bedroom, reasoning that a seventeen-minute advantage in age did not give her twin dictatorial rights over her. Ordinarily she wouldn't have minded Allie's curiosity, but somehow she didn't feel inclined to reduce what she'd shared with Ben to the frivolous topic of girlish confidences.

She didn't leave the room immediately, however. With a silent apology to Allie, she rifled through the clothes in her sister's suitcase and changed into a pair of jeans and a forest green sweatshirt she found there. The jeans fit more snugly than those she usually wore; the sweatshirt, bedecked with black *faux* gems set in a starburst around the neckline, wasn't one she would have chosen for herself. Still, the outfit was far more comfortable than her suit and she was grateful for it.

She looked over several pairs of plastic-wrapped shoes and boots in the suitcase and selected a pair of tennis shoes. The shower shut off as she was slipping them onto her feet. Quickly she grabbed her suit and panty hose off the bed and hung them on a single hanger in the closet.

"Jessie, do you know where Ben keeps the towels? . . . Jessie?"

The bathroom door opened and Allie's head popped out just as Jessie was making her exit. "Where are you going? Darn it, Jessie, you get back in here!"

Jessie laughed and waved cheerfully before pulling the broken door as near to closed as it would go. Allie yelled her name once more in frustration, but Jessie continued down the hall. She didn't feel a bit guilty about thwarting her sister's intended third degree. Allie, after all, had a lot to answer for herself.

Jessie found Ben and Ed talking quietly at the kitchen table. "Ugh! Coffee, again?" She grimaced. "I was hoping for some food."

Ed stood with a chuckle and put on the jacket he'd slung over the back of his chair. "Thanks for reminding me it's supper time. I should just have time to stop for a hamburger on my way over to the jail."

"There's a fast-food place on the access road on your way out," Ben said.

Jessie's mouth watered at the thought. "That sounds wonderful. I could go for a juicy cheeseburger myself."

Ben shook his head. "Sorry, Jess. I can't leave you and Allie alone, and it's not safe for either of you to go out. We'll have to make do with frozen dinners."

"Well, now, I don't guess it would hurt anything if I picked up some burgers and fries for all of you before I take off," Ed said. "Another half hour one way or the other won't matter too much, since I'm probably going to have to wait around until Leutzinger finishes interrogating the suspect, anyway."

"In that case," Ben said, rising from his chair, "I'll let you take the spare remote to the security system so you won't have to get out of your car to buzz in when you get back. Come on, I'll get it and show you how it works."

The deed was accomplished swiftly, and Ed left through the back door with a promise to be back before they knew it. In his hand he carried a remote like the one Jessie had seen in Ben's car.

After the door closed behind him, Jessie told Ben, "You're a fraud, you know."

"Say what?"

"That was a thoughtful gesture, giving Ed the remote, just to keep him from getting a little chilled."

"Is that right." Ben moved closer.

"Mmm-hmm. You're not so tough, after al-"

Her last word was cut off as Ben reached out and pulled her middle flat against his. "You're dynamite in these jeans, princess." His strong, splayed fingers rhythmically squeezed her denim-clad seat. "What were you saying?"

For the life of her, Jessie couldn't remember. The excitement only Ben could generate blossomed where their bodies touched. She batted her eyelashes.

"Why, Officer Sutton, what fast moves you have."

"Don't flirt with me, woman, or I may show you just how fast I really am." A wicked light glinted in Ben's eyes. "Ever do it on the kitchen table?"

Jessie whispered back naughtily, "Not with my sister in residence." She hooked her hands behind his elbows and used the leverage to undulate her pelvis provocatively. Ben grunted his pleasure, his lashes dropped, and she felt his manhood grow firm.

Suddenly his eyes opened wide, as though he'd just heard what she'd said. He looked dumbfounded. "You've done it on a *table?*"

Jessie laughed up at him. "Of course not. You're talking to the winner of the Miss Sexually Inhibited award for years running. You'll have to show me how it's done."

"Miss Sexually Inhibited, is it?" said a wry feminine voice from Jessie's right. "Don't look now, sis, but I think you're going to lose the title this year."

Two pairs of eyes swung to the doorway. The vision standing there was pure Allie, from the long, sensuously tossed hair brushing her face and neck to the tips of her neat ballet slippers. In between were skintight leggings and a hip-hugging, wide-necked sweater falling carelessly off one creamy shoulder.

Ben swore. Jessie pushed out of his hold and put a respectable distance between them, still feeling the imprint of his fingers on her backside as though they'd been cast in plaster.

"Sorry," Allie said, grinning mischievously. "I thought I'd better remind you two that you have company. Where's my deaf and dumb chauffeur, by the way?"

Embarrassed and more than a little irritated that her sister had overheard the lovers' teasing between her and Ben, Jessie would have answered sharply. Ben, however, beat her to it.

"His name is *Ed,* and he kindly offered to take time out of his busy schedule to go out and get your dinner. So I'd watch the insults, if I were you."

"Oh, good—food." Allie airily disregarded his annoyed tone. "I hope he gets back soon. I'm starved. Do you have cable, Ben? It's been days since I've seen a newscast." Without waiting for an answer, she turned and walked away, her voice drifting back into the kitchen. "Never mind, I'll figure it out."

Ben and Jessie shared a rueful smile.

"She really is a nice person," Jessie said, apologizing.

"She could be Mother Teresa, and I'd still wish her to Hades right now."

"Mother Teresa she's not," Jessie stated, so emphatically they both chuckled. Ben caught her in an impulsive hug and placed a brief, sweet kiss on her smiling lips.

"Even so, I guess we'd better be good," he said. "Shall we watch the news until Ed gets back?"

"We might as well." Jessie floated into the living room, not caring whether Allie saw the stars in her eyes.

Ed returned shortly after that with cheeseburgers, French fries and colas for three, staying only long enough to place the aromatic bags on the table and hand the security remote back to Ben. Ben refused it, suggesting he hold on to it until he came back with Leutzinger later, so Ed slipped it into his pocket and left.

During dinner Ben made a futile stab at getting information out of Allie. Stubbornly, whenever he brought up her activities in Port Mangus over the past several weeks, she rebuffed his questions with her own queries about the FBI investigation. Ben, of course, was equally unwilling to answer.

Jessie decided to stay out of it. She loved her twin and she loved Ben. After the travesty at the museum, she wasn't about to take sides again.

In spite of her earlier claim of pending starvation, Allie pushed away from the table after eating less than half her food. "I'd like to lie down for a while, maybe take a nap, if it's all right. I haven't been getting much sleep lately."

"Go ahead," Ben told her.

"If you have a spare blanket, I'll use the bed and just lie on top of the bedspread."

"There's a blanket on the overhead shelf in the closet."

"Oh, I'd rather not rummage through your things. Would you get it for me, please?"

Allie's sweet politeness caused Jessie's antennae to quiver. Her twin was up to something.

Ben put down the last bite of his sandwich and rose from the table. As they left the kitchen together, Jessie heard him warn Allie again that the alarm was set, so she'd better not try sneaking out the window. Her sister laughed, but they were too far down the hall for Jessie to make out what she said after.

For a moment the legacy of self-doubt left by Antonio gripped her, but she dismissed it immediately. In spite of that kiss Ben had told her about, she had sensed absolutely no sparks between her sister and her lover; besides, she knew Allie would never deliberately hurt her.

When Ben returned to the kitchen, he looked preoccupied.

"What?" she asked.

He sat down and shoved the remaining bite of his cheeseburger into his mouth. She waited while he chewed and swallowed. "Your sister is very protective of you, isn't she? Aren't you going to eat the rest of that?"

"Here." She pushed the uneaten portions of her sandwich and fries across the table. "What did Allie say to you?"

He dumped her leftovers onto his paper plate and resumed eating as he talked. "Basically she wanted to know what my intentions were."

Darn it, Allie, you better not have messed things up, Jessie thought grimly. She'd almost done that herself this morning. If Allie were to suggest that Ben should make an honest woman of her, he would bolt for sure. "She seems to think you're some kind of hothouse flower, or something."

Jessie watched him take a huge swallow of his drink, wondering whether they were off dangerous ground yet. "Compared to her, I guess I am. With any set of twins, there's always one who's dominant. In our case, I'm the other one."

Ben eyed her curiously. "Explain 'dominant.'"

Shrugging, she said, "You know—the leader. The stronger one, the more outgoing. The more *everything,* for that matter."

Her cheeseburger was polished off in short order, and now Ben tackled the fries, dipping them into a pile of catsup three at a time. "You've hinted as much before. Why do you put yourself down like that?"

"I'm not putting myself down. At least I don't think I am. That's just the way things are."

"What a load of crap, Jess."

"Excuse me?"

He pushed his plate away and leaned forward, resting his forearms on the table. "You and Allie are different, sure, but to say she's stronger is pure hogwash. She's just more reckless. You've got far more sense than she does.''

"You *would* think that. After all, I let you push me around and she doesn't. Which only proves my point.''

Ben snorted. "Push you around? That'll be the day. You give as good as you get, princess. What I mean is, in a crisis situation like all of us are in right now, you're levelheaded enough to make the right choices, unlike your sister. That's strength, not weakness.''

"You're forgetting this afternoon,'' she reminded him.

"Even that was because of your concern for Allie, which is more consideration than she's shown you, in my opinion.''

Ben's evaluation pleased her, but Jessie protested, "Poor Allie. If only she knew what a thorough roasting you're giving her.''

"Okay, I'll stop. I just wanted you to know that you don't take a back seat to your twin or anybody else.''

"Why, Ben . . . thank you.''

"Especially not in bed,'' he added with a wink.

Jessie's bubble of pleasure burst abruptly when he reduced his compliment to sexual terms. It was hard to pretend it didn't bother her, but she wadded up her napkin and threw it at him in mock irritation.

Deftly he caught it and, smirking, tossed it back. "Come on, let's clear this stuff off and go start a fire in the living room.''

Jessie wondered what kind of fire he had in mind.

He did, in fact, light a real fire in the fireplace before joining her on the couch. Then he surprised her by stretching out on his back with his head in her lap.

"Tired?'' she asked.

"If your sister wasn't hogging my bed, I could be talked into a nap. She's not the only one who hasn't gotten much sleep lately. Not that I'm complaining. It's times like this when I wished I'd remodeled some of the upstairs bedrooms.''

Jessie smiled and idly began playing with his hair. It flowed like water through her fingers, soft and clean. Ben took the hand lying on his chest and pressed it to his lips, enfolding it in the warmth of his before returning it to the cotton of his shirt. He closed his eyes, giving a huge sigh of contentment.

She looked down at him, enjoying their quiet closeness. "This is nice, isn't it?"

For a moment as she gazed into his dear, freckled face, she was almost overcome by yearning.

His eyes opened suddenly and he looked up at her. "Jess..."

Not sure she could hide her wistful emotions, Jessie lifted her gaze to the brightly burning flames in the fireplace. "Hmm?"

He kept his eyes fixed steadily on her face. "Want to know what I said to Allie before, about my intentions toward her twin?"

She managed to keep her voice even. "What did you say?"

"I told her to butt out. What we do is our own business, right? She doesn't have anything to say about it. Right?"

"Right."

Ben seemed to relax when she gave her agreement. "Does it bother you that she knows we're sleeping together?"

"Like you said, it's none of her business."

"That's right." He closed his eyes again, but they popped open immediately. "About this morning, Jessie, when you... I don't know if I made myself clear. I mean, what's happened is only natural when two healthy people with a strong physical attraction are thrown together the way we've been. That doesn't mean... I don't want you to get hurt. If I thought you were really serious about me..."

She gave his hair a little tug. "Hey, stop worrying about me. I've given what you said this morning some thought and realize I just got a little carried away. People have affairs all the time. They don't have to be in love to enjoy each other. I appreciate your pointing that out to me."

After a moment of silence, Ben's mouth twisted into a wry smile. "Glad I could help."

"You've been good for me, Ben, and not just because you showed me how wonderful making love can be. Someday I'll find Mr. Right, I suppose, but until then, I've decided an occasional relationship won't hurt me—if I like the man and am careful of diseases and everything."

"Here's a tip, Jess," he said brusquely. "Don't plan your next affair in front of your current lover."

"Oh, sorry. I just wanted to assure you that I'm not taking this too seriously—circumstances being what they are. I know what I'm doing." *At least, I think I do,* she added silently.

"Good," Ben said.

"When all this business with Allie is over and I'm back home again, we'll probably wonder—"

"Jessie." Ben maneuvered his body to a half-sitting position over her lap and braced himself on one elbow, lifting his free hand to the back of her head. He pulled her face down close to his so their mouths were just touching. "You convinced me. Shut up."

Jessie closed her eyes and gave herself over to his kiss, hoping with all her heart she wasn't making the worst mistake of her life.

Ben drank in the honey of Jessie's mouth greedily, even while he damned his own soul to hell. He knew when it was over she would be hurt, and he wasn't going to do a thing to stop it.

There was a limit to a man's nobility.

He'd tried to tell her this morning that there could never be anything permanent between them, but she'd changed the subject. Her doing, not his. To be brutally honest, at the time he'd still been reeling from their night together. Hearing Jessie say she loved him had given him a hell of a rush. On the heels of that surge of emotion, though, had come the reality of who and what he was. He'd felt duty bound to set her straight about her expectations, all the while knowing that it probably meant the end of sleeping with her.

Could he help it if she hadn't backed away?

It wasn't until busybody Allie had challenged him that he faced his suspicion that Jessie might not have taken him seriously, and he had to admit he hadn't made a wholehearted attempt to convince her. Allie's protective streak had prodded his conscience, so he'd felt compelled to give Jessie another chance to back away. Well, he'd tried—sort of.

Ben didn't believe the rot she had just spouted any more than she meant it. But he wasn't going to call her bluff. She'd had her chance to make a break, and instead she'd elected to ride it out with him. Her choice. No reason for him to feel guilty.

He did, though. He knew she thought she could change him, and he wasn't going to try again to talk her out of hoping.

Jessie moaned and drew back, breathless from his kisses.

Ben smiled. "Why don't you stretch out here beside me, honey? With Allie in the next room, I can't do what I really want to, so we might as well try to catch a few winks before Leutzinger comes."

"Will we both fit?"

"If we snuggle up."

The next few minutes were a scramble of arms and legs while they got situated spoon-fashion on the cushions.

"There." Ben slipped his arm around her. "Are you comfortable?"

"Very," she murmured.

Heel, cad, snake in the grass—Ben deserved every disparaging epithet ever heaped on a man who led a woman on to get what he wanted. Because the fact was, he just wasn't ready to let Jessie Webster go. He had to have her sweet warmth a little longer.

Chapter 13

"Was that the famous Agent Leutzinger?" asked Allie an hour or so later. She came out of the bedroom as Ben hung up the phone, in fine form after her lengthy nap.

Jessie, on the other hand, felt bedraggled. It seemed she had just fallen asleep when the call had wakened them.

Ben, too, was looking a little worse for wear. He rubbed his bristly jaw tiredly as he accepted the steaming mug Jessie handed him. Jessie wondered if there was anything left of his stomach lining after all the coffee he'd drunk today. This had to be his seventh or eighth cup.

"Thanks, Jess." He took a worshipful sip before he turned to Allie. "Yeah, he and Ed are on their way over here now. Rory Douglas is posting bail, by the way. His lawyer will have him out in a couple of hours."

"You can't be serious!" Allie exclaimed. "Didn't they check the guy's record? If you ask me, he's a serial rapist or something, a creep who chooses old women for his victims. Sickos like that shouldn't be out on the streets."

"He's an assistant U.S. attorney," Jessie said.

"So? I hear it happens in the best of families."

"You don't understand, Allie," Jessie began.

Ben interrupted her. "You should know, Allie, that his version of what happened today is quite a bit different from the one you gave the arresting officer."

"I'm not surprised," she said disgustedly. "Lying would be the least of his sins."

"He's threatening to file charges against you for assault as soon as he's cut loose from jail himself."

"Against me." Allie's eyes flashed. "I'm the *victim!*"

Jessie laid a soothing hand on Allie's arm. "I've been dying to hear what happened ever since we got your call. Why don't we all sit down while you tell us about it?" She guided her volatile twin to a corner of the sofa and took a seat beside her.

"Here, I'll stir up those coals and get the fire going again," Ben said.

Looking bemused, Allie watched him crouch on one knee in front of the fireplace with a poker in his hand. "How could he possibly turn things around and make *me* the attacker?"

"According to Leutzinger, he says he was across the street at a convenience store," Ben explained as he worked. "He happened to glance over at the motel, and he saw an old woman about to be mugged as she entered her room. Without thinking, he ran to her aid. The mugger, he says, saw him coming and took off. Then, much to his surprise, the old lady turned on him without provocation, bloodying his nose and rendering him unconscious."

Allie was outraged. "That's not what happened. I don't care what he said, there was nobody else there, just him. He forced his way into my room as I was closing the door and grabbed me."

Jessie paled as she pictured the violent scene. "Good heavens, Allie, you must have been terrified. What did you do then?"

"I screamed bloody murder, that's what. And I fought like hell. While we were struggling, he lost his balance and fell. It was his head hitting the dresser that knocked him out, not me." This last she said defiantly, as though daring Ben and Jessie to doubt her. "I started to tie up his hands and feet with nylon stockings while he was out of it, but my hands were shaking so hard I could hardly make a knot. Then a man and his wife came in—the door was still open—and he took over and finished the job."

Ben turned to her, an arm braced on his knee. "Did either of them see Douglas attack you?"

"No, they just heard me scream and came to see what was going on. The woman called the police, and by then I had calmed down enough to call Ben. The two of them waited with me until the police came."

Playful flames leapt around the log Ben had added to the fireplace. The fire was an incongruously cozy accompaniment to Allie's harrowing story, Jessie thought, and nowhere near as romantic as she had found it earlier in the evening with Ben's head nestled in her lap.

Ben stood up and brushed his hands together. "Rory Douglas isn't a serial rapist, at least not that we know of."

"You mean you don't believe me?" Allie said incredulously. "Maybe *I* should get a lawyer."

"Of course we believe you," Jessie said. "That's not what Ben meant. Tell her, Ben."

Ben retrieved his coffee from the end table where he'd placed it earlier. "Any information we give you is off-the-record for now, agreed?"

Allie's eyes lit with sudden interest as she looked from Jessie to Ben. "For now, yes."

Taking his time, he lifted the mug and took a swallow of coffee before leveling a discerning gaze at Allie. "You weren't a random victim of some crazy off the streets, Allie. When he attacked you, Douglas was after Mai Duan's journal."

It was plain by the expression on her face that Allie was shocked by that revelation, just as Ben intended.

"Think about that until Leutzinger gets here," he said softly.

Leutzinger arrived with Ed only minutes later. Both men, Jessie noticed, looked a little wan.

"The bastard's going to walk away clean," Leutzinger told Ben disgustedly. "He wouldn't budge from that cock-and-bull story of the assault, and he refused to take a lie detector test. With that slick lawyer of his reminding us of his client's civil rights every two minutes, we didn't get a thing out of him. Too bad you or Ed couldn't tie him to Mai Duan. He swears he's never been near her place."

"I don't remember his name from Mai's list in the journal," Allie said from the couch, "though I couldn't swear it's not there."

Leutzinger turned his head sharply and looked at her. "You're the other Ms. Webster, I presume?"

Allie lifted her chin at his unfriendly tone. "And you must be Leutzinger. Finally."

"Would either of you gentlemen care for some coffee?" Jessie asked in order to diffuse the hostile currents flowing between her sister and the chief agent.

"That would be great," Ed said as he took a seat on a leather hassock near Allie.

When Jessie returned from the kitchen, Leutzinger had claimed the recliner. " . . . so I guess you're not as clever as you think," he was saying to Allie.

Uh-oh, Jessie thought. Things are not going well.

Allie snapped impatiently, "I was in disguise, I drove a rented car—*nobody* knew where I was staying. I don't know how this Douglas character knew where to find me."

Leutzinger's eyes were sharp behind his wire-rimmed glasses, and Jessie felt the cutting gaze on her as she handed him his coffee. "You can thank your twin sister for leading him to you," he said.

Startled to be the focus of his remark, Jessie exclaimed, "Me! How?"

"Oh, I don't know. Maybe he just had a hunch that an innocent-looking, respectable woman would be capable of sending a whole contingent of FBI agents to the zoo in freezing weather just to look at the animals. Being a liar himself, perhaps he recognizes the tendency in others."

Jessie uncomfortably cleared her throat.

With a last searing look, Leutzinger dismissed her like a worm and turned to Ben, who had settled in the corner of the couch opposite Allie. "Douglas begged off going with me to the zoo, saying he didn't think he was needed. Which was true."

"He probably doubled back after leaving here and staked us out from the street," Ben said.

"And I led him straight to Allie. He must have seen us to-gether at the museum and followed her back to her motel. If only I'd known." Jessie felt wretched. Douglas's attack on her twin was all her fault.

Allie patted her hand.

"Ms. Webster, I'm going to give you the benefit of the doubt," Leutzinger said, addressing Allie again.

Now that he's flattened me, Jessie thought. The man was not in a good mood.

"I'm going to assume that you haven't cooperated with us so far because you don't understand the gravity of the situation. The only possible motivation for Douglas following you today is to get his hands on Mai Duan's journal. The question is why. Do you have any idea as to the answer?"

"Well...he's a lawyer for the government," Allie said. "Maybe he's afraid his name is in the journal. That couldn't be good for his career."

"I'm afraid it's more than that, Ms. Webster. We've suspected for months that Mai Duan was tangled up with organized crime here in Chicago, and now we believe Rory Douglas is their man, too. He wasn't assigned to our investigation until after the original prosecutor had an automobile accident. A little too coincidental, don't you think? In his new position Douglas has been privy to all the information the bureau has gathered on the Duan case, right up to this afternoon, including everything we know about you and Mai's journal. And so is whoever he's working for."

Leutzinger paused, but Allie said nothing.

"The fact is," he went on, "your life isn't worth the price of one of your newspapers as long as you've got the thing, disguises and clever machinations notwithstanding. You're no match for the mob. Those people kill to get what they want."

Jessie felt the blood leave her face. Allie, too, looked shaken. Jessie was glad to see it, sure now that her sister would hand the thing over.

"All right, I'll give it to you tonight, if you promise me an exclusive interview after the arrests are made," Allie said.

"Allie. For God's sake!" Jessie blurted.

"No conditions. This is your last chance to turn it over before I slap you with an injunction and an obstruction-of-justice charge. Jail, Ms. Webster. You're not in a bargaining position."

"Why not, dammit? You wouldn't even know about the journal if it wasn't for me."

"Go and get it, Ms. Webster. If you make me waste time obtaining a search warrant, I'm not going to be inclined to leniency."

"Search warrant or no, you'll never find it without my help."

"Allie, you don't have any choice," Jessie coaxed. "Tell him."

Her plea was disregarded as Allie silently pitted her will against the obdurate FBI agent, her gaze stubbornly proud, his implacable. There was no give in either of them, as far as Jessie could see.

"Allie's got a point, Cal."

Ben's unexpected intrusion into the confrontation made him the immediate and universal focal point of attention. "I think we do owe her something. The bureau paid Donno Carr for the initial tip about the Port Mangus setup, and Donno's pond scum. Should we treat him better than a regular citizen with a clean record? Allie's not even asking for money."

"Money or favors, it all boils down to the same thing. As a 'regular citizen,' it ought to be enough for her to see these criminals put away."

Leutzinger glared at Allie and she glared right back. "That's easy for you to say. You've got a job."

"How about a compromise?" Ben suggested reasonably. "Allie, would you be satisfied with notice about the arrests in the case, say, twelve hours in advance of the official media announcement?"

Allie appeared to think it over. A hopeful sign.

"You already have an advantage over your competition because of your involvement in obtaining the journal," Ben added. "Your story would contain more in-depth information than anybody else's, even without the twelve-hour lead. With it, all the other reporters will be quoting *you*."

Allie angled a belligerent chin toward Leutzinger. "Will he agree to that?"

"I might," Leutzinger said, "if I had Ms. Webster's promise to hold the story—all of it—until I gave her such advance notice."

Allie nodded shortly. "You've got it."

"Contingent, of course, on whether the journal is a viable piece of evidence. That has yet to be verified."

"I accept your contingency."

"Very well, then," Leutzinger said. "We have a deal. Bring me the journal."

Allie got to her feet and the men politely rose with her.

"Nice going," Jessie mouthed to Ben, and he tipped his head in modest acknowledgment.

"I'll have to borrow someone's car," Allie said.

"Don't tell me," Leutzinger said. "You don't have it with you."

Neatly plucked eyebrows disappeared under the feminine fall of hair on Allie's forehead. "Of course not. I'm not a fool."

"I think that debatable point is best left unexplored for now. Where is the damned thing, if you don't mind my asking?" Leutzinger was growing increasingly sarcastic.

"In Oak Park."

"Oak Park." For a tiny moment in time, the agent raised give-me-strength eyes to heaven. "Please be more specific, Ms. Webster."

"Certainly, Mr. Leutzinger," Allie responded haughtily. "I hid it in a tree."

"Stop pacing, Jess. You're wearing a path in the carpet."

"I can't help it. Something's gone wrong, I just know it. They should have been back an hour ago."

Jessie walked to the window for what seemed like the hundredth time, her hopeful eyes straining through the postmidnight darkness outside. Just as before, nothing penetrated the blackness shrouding Ben's long driveway beyond the gate. Certainly not the awaited headlights that would herald the return of her twin and the two agents who had taken her to Oak Park over two hours ago.

Ben's arms encircled her from behind. "Don't borrow trouble, honey. They'll probably be here any minute."

"But what if they're not?" Even Ben's soothing touch could not banish her escalating anxiety. "Can't we go and see ourselves what's taking so long? I know right where they are."

"I know you do, but it's still too dangerous for you out there. It's bad enough that Allie had to go along. There's no point in risking your neck, as well."

Allie had hidden Mai's journal in the split trunk of an old tree behind the house where she and Jessie had grown up. Their mother had sold their girlhood home five years ago before moving to Florida. It was located in the neighborhood where Jessie lived now, just a couple of blocks from her garage apartment.

Though the men had not been thrilled with Allie's hiding place, Jessie thought it was brilliant. She agreed with her twin that the journal was perfectly safe in their old hidey-hole. Allie had wrapped the book in plastic to protect it from the elements, and no one would ever think to look in a tree for anything valuable.

When the others left for Oak Park, it hadn't crossed Jessie's mind that Allie might come to harm in the company of two government agents. Not until the trio was long overdue did all the frightening possibilities occur to her.

They might have had car trouble or even an accident, and those were the best prospects she could envision. The more chilling scenario was that they had somehow been discovered by some of Rory Douglas's partners in crime, who would be bent on getting the journal, no matter what the cost.

"Please, Ben. I don't care if it's dangerous. They might need us," she pleaded over her shoulder.

"Tell you what," Ben said. "If we don't hear something soon, I'll call the FBI office and see if I can find out what's going on."

"That's a good idea." Jessie turned in his arms, buoyed by the chance to take some action. "But why do we have to wait? Can't we call them now?"

He sighed. "Okay, but I can't promise anything. If the agent on duty doesn't know me, he might not be willing to give me any information."

"Just try. Please."

He let her go and walked to the phone.

Jessie turned around immediately and resumed her vigil at the window.

Ben made the call as much for himself as for Jessie. Though so far he'd downplayed his concern, his instincts for danger were humming. The trip to Oak Park shouldn't take more than forty minutes each way, and pulling a book out of a knothole in a tree trunk was a three-minute job at most. There was no good reason why Ed and Leutzinger hadn't had Allie back here by midnight.

The duty agent who answered the phone had never heard of Ben Sutton, but he was well versed in the polite runaround. Ben was getting nowhere fast with him when suddenly Jessie cried, "They're back."

She left her post and ran to push the button that opened the gate and simultaneously turned off the sensors in the yard.

Ben called, "Wait, Jess! You don't know that's Allie!" but she'd already unlocked the door—without disabling the house alarm—and was on her way outside to greet the car that had just driven up. A part of his mind registered the security system's high, insistent warning that told him in a minute and a half, all hell would break loose.

He ignored it. Without another word to the uncommunicative agent on the line, he dropped the phone into its cradle and tore out after her.

Outside he saw Jessie's shadow in surrealistic outline against the rays of approaching headlights as she hailed the vehicle coming through the gate.

A perfect target.

"Jessie!" The agonized syllables of her name were torn from his throat. He propelled himself forward and somehow reached her in an endless flying tackle that brought her down to the frozen ground. At once he shifted to cover her body with his own, half expecting any moment to feel an assassin's gunfire rip through his flesh.

Instead he heard two car doors open and close. A woman said, "What in the world—?"

Allie's voice.

"It's us, Ben," Leutzinger said right after.

Jessie struggled under him until he realized she still bore his full weight. He rose and helped her to her feet, adrenaline still beating at his temples.

She took one look at his face and said, "I've done it again, haven't I? We both could have been kil—"

Her last word was drowned out by the ear-shattering whoop of the external alarm, and suddenly they were blinded by the glare of several floodlights whose combined incandescence spilled into every corner of the yard and beyond.

Ben swore and ran back to the house. He hurried inside to the nearest code box, which was out of sight inside the coat closet. Quickly he pushed the correct numbers on the keypad and blessed silence reigned. Next he called the security station to report there was no need to send the police.

Then he sat his limp body on the couch and closed his eyes, listening to his heartbeat as it pounded in his veins.

"Ben."

His eyes opened to find Jessie standing between his wide-spread thighs, looking down at him, regret written on every feature.

"I'm sorry.... I—"

He leaned forward, grabbed her wrist and pulled her down until she knelt on the floor in front of him.

"Don't do that again," he told her through clenched teeth.

"I won't—ever, I promise."

He jerked her in and leaned forward to meet her in a hard, desperate kiss. Their lips separated with an abrupt smack.

"You little nitwit...."

"I know. I should have waited...."

"If anything had happened ..."

"You protected me...."

"Did I hurt you?"

"No, no, I'm all right. What about you?" Her fingers skimmed frantically over his face.

"I'm okay, too, but I've never..."

"I'm sorry, I'm sorry...."

Ben ran his hands up and down her arms. "God, I was so scared...."

"Ahem!"

It was Allie's congested throat that interrupted them, but Leutzinger's exasperated voice that said, "Dammit, Ben—"

Jessie scrambled to her feet, her cheeks a becoming shade of pink. Ben got up, too, and stood beside her. The rueful entreaty in the glance she arrowed up at him had his fingers twitching to grab her again and assure himself she was safe, but now he was mindful of their audience.

The FBI chief's disapproval of the intimate scene he'd witnessed was evident. Every law enforcement agency in the country discouraged romantic involvement on the job and Ben knew Leutzinger had every right to call him on it. But he hoped he wouldn't. Ben would have a hard time justifying to his superior what he couldn't justify to himself.

Allie broke the awkward silence. "That's some kind of alarm you have, Ben. I nearly jumped out of my skin." Her eyes swung from his face and shifted to Jessie. "Are you okay, sis? He tackled you like a linebacker. You must be full of bruises."

With the tension eased, Jessie visibly pulled herself together. "No, I'm fine, though if I weren't, it would be my own fault. I shouldn't have run out like that, but I was just so anxious to reassure myself that you were safe—"

"Never mind that," Leutzinger said impatiently. Apparently willing to let a breach of professionalism slide in the face of more weighty matters, he turned to Ben. "We've got trouble."

"I *knew* something was wrong," Jessie said. "You were gone so long."

Ben suddenly realized their little group was smaller than it had been. "Where's Ed?"

"Good question," Leutzinger said in a disgusted voice.

"We might as well start at the beginning." Allie walked to the couch and sat down. "The journal wasn't where I'd left it. I guess that old tree trunk wasn't such a hot idea, after all."

"Really?" the agent sneered.

"Hey, I didn't know about that kid," Allie retorted defensively. "The last I remember, a middle-aged couple with teenagers was living in our old house."

"Wait a minute," Ben cut in. "You mean a *kid* took it?"

Allie nodded. "A real cutie. The poor little guy had asthma."

"Which he demonstrated at a most inconvenient time," Leutzinger added, taking a seat on the recliner.

"That was your fault," Allie accused hotly. "He wouldn't have if you hadn't scared him!"

"The kid was lying to us. Even *you* could see that."

"Good grief." Ben was beginning to feel like a spectator at a Ping-Pong match. "Could we have the story from just *one* of you?"

"*I'll* tell it." The look Allie flung in Leutzinger's direction defied him to disagree. "I hid the journal before driving Christie back to Kansas. It was the middle of the night and the house was dark. I had no trouble slipping in and out of the yard. But tonight the man and his wife were still up."

"A good thing," Leutzinger interjected. "*Some* people may think nothing of disregarding personal property and privacy laws, but agents of the government don't have that option. We had to get permission from the owners to look for the journal, and they were very cooperative, in spite of the late hour."

His interruption netted him another dark look from Allie. "When we discovered the journal wasn't where I'd left it," she went on, "the man suggested that his son may have found it. So we all trooped into the house, and the woman got the boy out of bed. The poor kid was scared he was in trouble for taking the journal—that's why he didn't tell the truth right away. But big, brave Mr. G-man here flashed a badge under his nose and in general intimidated him into confessing."

"Quit sniping, Allie." That was Jessie. "Honestly, what's gotten into you? Just tell us what happened next."

Hear, hear, Ben seconded silently.

With ill grace, Allie said, "He ran into his room, came back with the journal, and handed it to me."

"And *you* handed it to Ed," Leutzinger said, glowering.

"Why *wouldn't* I, dammit? He's FBI, isn't he?"

"That had nothing to do with it, and you know it. You just didn't want to give it to *me*."

"Cut it out, you two." Ben's voice erupted, loud and unexpected between the nit-picking pair. He'd had enough. Once everyone's startled eyes had turned his way, he forced a more moderate tone. "Now, what's this about Ed?"

"I was getting to that," Allie said sullenly. "I did hand the journal to Ed, which was a perfectly logical thing for me to do. Ed took it and thumbed through it a little, while *Agent* Leutzinger thanked the parents for their help. Then the little boy started gasping for breath. Before long he turned blue and scared the bejeebers out of all of us. I've never seen an asthma attack before—I thought he was going to die. It seemed like it took forever before his mother found his inhaler, but once he had that, he started breathing easier. Me, too, I don't mind saying. Anyway, when it was all over and we could see he was going to be all right, we looked up and realized Ed was gone."

"Along with the journal and the government car we came in," Leutzinger said, clearly disgruntled.

"Ed Brock—a rogue agent?" This unexpected twist in the case disturbed Ben.

"We had to ask the boy's father to drive us to my place so I could pick up my own car and bring Allie back here. She's yours for the night, and you're welcome to her." Ignoring Allie's outthrust jaw, he rose from his chair and buttoned his coat.

"Hold on, I'll walk out with you." Ben grabbed his jacket from the closet. "You two stay put," he warned the women darkly with his hand on the doorknob.

Jessie's eyes swept up and connected with his. "Be careful," she said softly.

Ben saw concern for him in her gaze and something more— something he refused to acknowledge.

"Wait," Allie said. "What about my story?"

Leutzinger's lips tightened before he turned to her. "It appears we're both out of luck, Ms. Webster. Good night."

"I can't figure it," Ben said on the short walk to Leutzinger's car. "I would have sworn Ed wasn't the type to turn bad."

The agent snorted. "He's not the first good agent to jump over the fence after staring so long at the color green over there, and I doubt he'll be the last." He gestured toward the house. "At least the heat's off the women in there. I doubt Ed will waste any time handing over Mai's journal to his and Rory Douglas's mutual friends, in which case the hunt will be called off. The twins should be safe."

"You're going after Ed tonight?"

"With everything I've got." Leutzinger's voice was flat. "I want that journal, and I want Ed Brock. I hate dirty cops. I'll get him, no matter what it takes."

* * *

In spite of Leutzinger's efforts, his prey was nowhere to be found.

That news was part of the update Leutzinger provided when he called Ben in the next afternoon to officially release him from the Duan case. The government car had turned up in a small used-car lot south of Oak Park, but Ed had left no clues to his direction after ditching it. The already indistinct trail was getting colder.

Interestingly enough, Marie Brock, the wife from whom Ed had been separated for fifteen years, had taken leave from her job that morning. A family emergency, she'd told her boss, but Leutzinger's men had questioned her mother and found that the woman knew nothing about an emergency or her daughter's whereabouts. Marie, like Ed, had vanished without a trace. Which could only mean, Leutzinger told Ben, that she'd helped her estranged husband get away.

Ben had to hide his reaction when he heard about the missing Mrs. Brock. His partner hadn't mentioned his wife during their long hours of surveillance together, or even that he'd ever been married.

So much for friendship, he thought, shaking off his disillusionment. So what if the man he'd believed Ed to be didn't exist? Leutzinger hadn't guessed the agent was dirty, either, and he'd worked with the man for more than two years.

Besides, now that he was off the case, Ben had better things to think about. This morning he and Jessie had dropped off Allie at her motel. Allie had immediately loaded her bags into her rented car and headed back to Port Mangus to return the rental and assure herself that her house and belongings had come to no harm in her absence.

Which meant Ben and Jessie were alone again. It was time to see if he could finagle some vacation time out of his precinct captain.

He asked for three weeks and got one.

Chapter 14

Ben found Jessie working in the computer room when he got home.

"A vacation?" she asked. "Are you planning a trip somewhere?"

"Actually, I thought it might be nice to stay here," Ben said. "Would you care to join me?"

The hope shining in her deep blue eyes when she happily agreed was unmistakable. Obviously she read more into his invitation than he meant.

Ben didn't correct her misconception. His conscience made noises, but he silenced it by promising himself he'd take the next week from her and no more. After all, she would end up hating him, no matter when he called it quits. An additional week could hardly make things worse.

But to Ben those seven days might make a world of difference. He couldn't resist the chance to come out of the cold for a little while. And who knew? Maybe some concentrated time with Jessie would cool the fire burning in his gut for her.

Just a week—not so much to ask.

And what a week it was. Except for a single trip the first day to Jessie's apartment for some clothes and toiletries and a quick stop at a grocery store, they stayed inside and reveled in each other. Days and nights blurred together as they ate, slept and made love whenever and however the mood struck them. It was the most exhausting, absolute best week of Ben's life.

But the day inevitably came when he had to report for work again. That morning he made love to Jessie slowly and with determined thoroughness, exploring and memorizing her body as he willed his senses to hold on to the touch and taste and smell of her. When at last she begged for completion and he could prolong his own need no longer, Ben brought them both to a shuddering climax.

What a fool he'd been to think their sexual marathon might work her out of his system. He knew now he'd never have enough of her.

Jessie snuggled against him. He held her close, thinking about what she'd given him. She wanted to give more, he knew. *Ah, Jess,* he said silently. *If I was a better man, the one you think I am, I could gladly accept everything you offer and live happily ever after. Instead I have to let you go.*

How long would it take her, he wondered, to find the lucky guy who would marry her, give her those kids she wanted, and wake up beside her every day for the rest of his life? Ben hated even the thought of the nameless stranger she would someday love.

Suddenly Jessie sighed. "I guess it's back to the old grind for both of us today. I'll probably have to blow the dust off my computer, it's been so long." She gave his ribs a little squeeze and said wistfully, "But it's been lovely, hasn't it? Do you suppose the rest of the world is still out there?"

"It's there, all right," Ben said grimly.

"What time will you be getting home tonight?"

"I'm working the six to two shift." He answered absently, his mind on how to bring up the subject he dreaded.

"Two in the *morning?*" She rolled into a sitting position, tousled her curls sleepily and shrugged. "Oh, well, we can sleep in tomorrow. I'd better come here, though. You don't need the long drive to my place at that hour of the night, especially after eight hours' work."

Ben looked at her cautiously.

"It's all right, isn't it?" Uncertainty clouded her face. "I mean, I'm not going to move in, or anything. But how else are we going to see each other, with your schedule?"

There was a pillow crease on her cheek, he noticed, and her lips were still slightly swollen from his kisses. She looked vulnerable, soft and well loved.

He couldn't bring himself to say no.

"I'll give you a remote so you can get in the gate," he told her gruffly.

They settled into a routine of sorts. After spending the night, Jessie, needing solitude to write, would leave for Oak Park about midmorning to work at home. Alone and oddly restless during the hours between her departure and his late-night shift, Ben killed time by working on his house. He'd taken up renovation again, this time on the second floor, just for something to do. Even though he didn't have a clear idea what use if any the upstairs would provide, the project kept him from thinking too much and the physical labor was satisfying.

It came in a distant second, though, to having Jessie meet him at the back door after work. Her eyes would smile a welcome and her skin would be freshly bathed and soft with scented lotion under her satiny green robe. Ready for him.

He was a weak man taking advantage of a good woman. He knew it, but he didn't have the strength to stop the best thing that had ever happened to him. And, he rationalized, as long as that was the situation, he might as well indulge himself. He'd save the regrets for later.

One evening a couple of weeks after their hiatus, he came out of the precinct briefing room with a handful of other officers and looked around for an available telephone. He'd be hitting the streets in less than an hour with the narcotics task force he'd been assigned to. If he didn't settle the vague misgivings that had been distracting him since this morning, he wouldn't be worth spit out there tonight.

Spotting a vacant desk in a far corner of the large common area, Ben headed over, punched in Jessie's number and waited through a long series of rings. Finally she answered with a breathless hello that reminded him of the startled little gasp that always escaped her lips in the sweet moment before she found

·lease in his bed. He smiled and eased a hip and thigh onto the
·esk. "Did I catch you doing something unmentionable?"

"Ben." The knot of tension inside him loosened a little at the
·arm recognition in her voice. She didn't sound mad.

"I'm so glad you didn't hang up before I got here," she
·ushed on. "I was already outside, on my way to your place,
·hen I heard the phone. Is something wrong? You've never
·alled from work before."

Ben lowered his voice. "Nothing's wrong. I was just won-
·ering why I woke up alone this morning."

"Oh." Jessie's voice softened, too. "I had to come home
·arly today to call my agent, and didn't have the heart to wake
·ou just to tell you I was leaving. You get so little sleep."

"What about you?"

"Unlike some supermen I know, I nap during the day. Any-
·ay," she teased, "I knew what would happen if I woke you
·p."

Out of the corner of his eye, Ben saw a uniformed cop slip
·nto a chair at a nearby desk. "Uh-huh. So how come you
·alled your agent?"

"Oh, we're changing the subject, are we? Okay, I can take a
·int. No dirty talk at work."

The racy remark made him grin. Jessie had come a long way
·rom the scarred divorcée who hadn't known the power of her
·emininity. In his arms she'd blossomed into a desirable, pas-
·ionate woman, confident of her sensuality and comfortable
·ith her body. Ben took pleasure in knowing he'd given her
·hat, at least.

"... write a series of books with secondary characters from
Midnight Lies. My agent loved the idea, since that title was my
·op seller. What do you think?"

His wandering mind came to attention and just managed to
·atch the gist of what she was saying. Jessie often asked his
·pinion about her work, and wouldn't listen when he pro-
·ested he didn't know anything about the writing business. He'd
·iven up arguing about it, figuring her agent would keep her on
·he right career path.

She was pleased that he'd read a couple of her novels. Ben
·ad every intention of reading them all, and not just to humor
·er. She told a good story, and the loves scenes were some-

thing else. The truth was, he didn't just admire her talent, he was proud of her.

"I liked that book, too," he said. "Go for it."

"I think I will, but I have to finish this one first," she said. "Oh, Allie called this afternoon. And guess what? She said Cal Leutzinger talked her into withdrawing her complaint against Rory Douglas. She's coming back to town tomorrow."

"I know. Cal told me."

"He did?" She sounded surprised. "I thought you weren't working for him anymore."

"I'm not. It's just professional courtesy. He knows I'm still interested in the Duan investigation, so he calls me whenever something happens. Did Allie tell you she didn't agree to drop the charges until he promised her a personal interview if he breaks the case? He's gritting his teeth thinking how she must be gloating over finally getting her way."

"Those two." Jessie laughed softly. "I'm still surprised he talked her into it, the interview notwithstanding. She really wanted Rory Douglas to get what was coming to him. Me, too. I don't see why he should get away with assault. It doesn't seem right. Allie could have been seriously hurt."

"It's just another trade-off, Jess," Ben said. "It's not every day an assistant U.S. attorney is charged with assault. Allie's case would have drawn a lot of publicity, not to mention she would have had to testify in open court about Mai's journal. The FBI wants to keep that quiet, at least until Ed turns up and they know for sure what he did with it. Cal's still hoping they can salvage something out of the whole mess."

"Speaking of the journal, did he tell you whether they got any information from the men whose names Allie remembered?"

"Nothing useful. None of them would admit to anything more than having spent time at Club Duan, which was what Cal expected. They'd be stupid to confess even knowing about Mai's other services."

"You mean the FBI hasn't learned *anything* new since you've been off the case?"

"Nothing important. The real break in the case would be finding Ed Brock. The way Cal figures it, Ed's the key to ev-

rything from Mai's vanishing act to the ringleaders she was
orking for."

"I hate to think that's true. I liked Ed."

"Yeah, well, he fooled a lot of people."

"Hey, Sutton!"

Ben turned at the sound of his name and waved an acknowl-
dgment to the man signaling him. "I've got to go, Jess," he
aid. "Oh . . . and about this morning?"

"Yes?"

"Next time wake me."

"Why, that sounded suspiciously like an order," Jessie
rooned provocatively.

"Yeah," he sassed back. "I'm a real drill sergeant."

She gurgled. "You're bad, Ben."

"Just wait till tonight."

"I'll be there."

Over the next several hours Ben prowled shadowed city
treets, blending into the seething atmosphere of desperation
nd hopelessness as though he belonged there. He'd been wired
or sound, and an unmarked police van followed him dis-
reetly. They were after pushers tonight, and Ben knew how to
ind them.

Methodically he worked, by turn becoming belligerent and
oulmouthed or wary and grasping as the situation demanded.
Iis performance was flawless, perfected by experience. One by
ne he sought out the targeted dealers and bought drugs. As
oon as each recorded buy was completed, the team swooped
 for the arrest. Then they moved on to another block, an-
ther bust.

For the limited type of operation they were running, it was a
ood night. In all, Ben and the task force got four small-time
ope peddlers off the streets, at least one of whom appeared to
e willing to sell out his supplier for clemency.

At a little before two in the morning, while the rest of the
roup hung around the station to congratulate themselves and
ne another on their night's work, Ben filled out his paper-
ork and dropped it off at the sergeant's desk.

I'll be there, Jessie had said. Not wanting to take time for his
sual shower, he changed out of his grubby and tattered work-

ing clothes and walked quickly to his car, barely able to repress his simmering impatience.

The Trans Am rumbled to life. A messy drizzle started to fall, and Ben turned on the intermittent wipers as he guided the car onto the expressway. If the weather turned a few degrees colder, he thought, they might have snow for Christmas, which was only a little over a week away. Jessie would like that.

Christmas was a big deal to her. She'd talked him into putting up a tree in the living room, his first Christmas tree ever in all the years since he'd left his parents' home. The afternoon they'd spent buying the ornaments and decorating the tree had filled him with a kind of excited pleasure he hadn't felt since he was a child.

It had grown dark by the time the last shiny foil icicle had been hung. Jessie had turned off all the lights but those on the tree, and they'd made love on the floor among the discarded ornament boxes. Ben would never forget how she had looked stretched out under him, the soft multicolored lights reflecting off her naked body like transparent paint on an artist's palette of warm skin. He cherished that memory, hoarding it along with a multitude of others he'd gathered over the past weeks like a miser. After Christmas, they would be all he'd have left of her. Last week he'd made sure of it.

I'll be there.

On a night like this, she would probably have a fire burning in the fireplace when he got home. She always fussed over him, making him sit down, worrying if he was hungry or tired, bringing him a drink so he could relax. When he was settled on the couch, she'd cuddle up next to him while he unwound. Then she'd want to talk.

Ben frowned. He'd have to head her off tonight before she asked the usual questions about his work. It was obvious she didn't like his unwillingness to discuss what he did every day. Last night, in fact, she'd been more dogged than usual and had gone all quiet for a while when, feeling backed into a corner, he'd flatly told her to drop it.

He had his reasons for avoiding the topic. For one thing, he knew only too well there was strong justification why so many women found it too stressful to live with cops, and undercover work was the worst. He hadn't forgotten that Becky hadn' been able to cope, not with the hazards of his job or the deception. No way in hell was he going to present Jessie with that reality.

He had resented Becky's unfair judgment of what he'd chosen to do, but now he realized she'd done him and herself a favor. Their marriage would never have worked, even if they'd really loved each other.

He wouldn't put Jessie through that kind of choice. He was no good for her, no good for anything anymore but lifting up rocks and smashing the bad guys who scurried out. He couldn't even make himself tell her she was better off without him.

That was why he'd agreed last week to take the job after Christmas. It would force him to leave her, and by the time he got back, he'd wouldn't have to say anything. He'd just stay away.

He hadn't told her about the new assignment yet. Ultimately he'd have to, but he would put it off as long as possible.

I'll be there.

Ben's foot pressed a little harder on the accelerator. Soon he'd be with her, reveling in how easily her robe's slippery sash came apart in his fingers, feeling the warmth of her naked curves, watching her go wild under the touch of his hands.

Which reminded him—his supply of condoms was low again. Jessie took birth control pills now, but her doctor had warned she couldn't rely on them exclusively for another few weeks. She didn't know yet she wouldn't need to.

Regretting the delay, Ben turned off the expressway at the next exit.

He'd made his purchase and was leaving the convenience store when he heard the pickup peel out from the curb across the street. He caught a glimpse of the driver, a pointy-faced man who looked oddly familiar, as the truck squealed away. He stared after it for a moment, trying to place the face, then shook his head. He didn't know anyone in this part of town, and he didn't recognize the pickup, either.

The incident was easily forgotten as he climbed back into his car.

Jessie was waiting for him.

* * *

"Jess?"

Here we go, Jessie thought from her seat on the recliner. She squared her shoulders for the coming confrontation and called out, "In here."

Ben's eyes found her immediately. He probably wondered why she hadn't been at her post, ready to open the door for him and cater to his every whim.

But there was no censure in his gaze. He smiled. "There you are."

She couldn't stop her body's thrumming reaction as he skirted the couch and came to her. Already she could feel her body softening, preparing itself for him.

With his hands braced on the arms of the chair, he zeroed in for a controlled but thorough taste of her mouth. Jessie submitted to the kiss, lifting her hand to caress his stubbled jaw as she struggled to keep her defenses in place.

Ben straightened, taking in the slacks and long-sleeved blouse she wore and the pages of her manuscript resting in her lap. "Working late, I see. The book must be going well."

"Not really. I've written less than three pages all day. My hero isn't cooperating."

He walked to the closet and removed a small sack from his pocket before putting away his cap and jacket. "You probably need a break. Take tomorrow off and go shopping or something."

Jessie smiled and shook her head. "That's not the problem. I just have other things on my mind."

"What other things?" He looked at her speculatively as he closed the closet door. "Is something wrong? Are my crazy hours getting to you?"

"Of course not. You know I'm a night person."

He flashed his teeth in an engaging grin. "A middle-of-the-night person, too, as I recall from pleasurable experience. And—" his voice lowered and the smile tipped slightly off center "—an inspired morning person."

Jessie knew which morning he referred to. At dawn a few days ago, the murmur of Ben's voice had awakened her. She'd opened her eyes and seen the faint smile and the flicker of his eyelids as he slept. When his hand moved down his body t brush over his groin under the covers, she realized he was having an erotic dream. Her imagination was fired. What was his dream lover doing to him?

Fascinated and unable to help herself, Jessie lifted the sheet and found him magnificently aroused. A wave of mischievous sensuality swept over her. Wickedly, slowly, she moved over him, being careful not to disturb his sleep. Delicious anticipation heightened her passion while she straddled him and poised over his erection like a moist, waiting sheath. She watched his face, eager to see his reaction as she lowered herself onto him.

It was not to be the slow joining she'd envisioned. His head tossed once on the pillow when the tip of his manhood made entrance, then he grabbed her thighs and arched his hips upward, impaling her on his thick hardness to its very root. Jessie's eyes closed at the depth of his possession. When she opened them, he was awake, his gaze hot and hungry, consuming her.

"Surprise," she whispered.

He cursed, but it was a tender expletive. Taking control, his strong fingers jerked at her hips while he bucked under her. A moaning climax shook him after only a few deep, frenzied thrusts.

"Baby, you are a fantasy come to life," he'd breathed while she rested on his pounding chest afterward.

Then he'd taken an exquisitely long time to reward her for waking him.

"We didn't use protection the first time that morning," Ben said now, proving his thoughts were in sync with hers.

"I know, but I was taking the pill by then. It'll probably be all right."

She waited for him to say more about the possibility of their having created a child, but he said, "You know, that was the single most fantastic thing that's ever happened to me. I'll never forget it."

Eyes charged with golden promises, he advanced on her, set her manuscript pages on the table beside her and growled next to her ear, "Let's take a shower together."

Jessie's determination to have it out with him wavered. If only he wouldn't use that voice. Hastily she shored up her resolve. "You go ahead. When you're finished, I'd like to talk to you."

"We can talk in the shower."

She had to smile. "Ha! You know very well we'll do precious little talking."

"Even better. Does it matter whether we talk before, during, or after?" He nuzzled her neck. "I need you."

Dangerously close to giving in, Jessie pushed him away. "No, Ben. Let's talk."

He straightened. "This sounds serious."

"To me, it is," she informed him firmly as she pointed to the couch. "Sit over there."

Ben didn't move. "What's this all about, Jess?"

Suddenly she was apprehensive about the outcome of the next few minutes. She wished she could predict how he would react. Unbidden, a sigh escaped her lips.

"You're tired, honey." He smoothed a hand over her hair. "You don't have to come over every night, you know."

"It's not that." She raised her eyes and found him staring broodingly down at her.

"No, I've been selfish, lapping up all your TLC like it was my right," he said. "Tonight it's your turn. Let me take care of *you*, for a change."

Disarmed, Jessie stopped him in the middle of reaching to help her up from the couch. "I'm not tired. Really."

His eyes, more green now than gold, wrinkled at the corners as he smiled. "Come on, give me a chance to baby you a little. A cup of tea, maybe, before I feed you grapes in your bubble bath. Then an all-over body massage to relax you. Soft music to lull you to sleep."

She eyed him suspiciously. "You'll go to any lengths to avoid talking about this, won't you?"

The smile evaporated. "What do you mean? I made an honest offer."

"I'm sorry," she said, regretting she had offended him. "I'm tempted to take you up on it, but this is more important."

"What the hell is *this*, I'd like to know." He shoved his fingers through his hair and turned away.

"Our relationship."

He sat down in the chair opposite her, his features guarded. "What about it?"

This was it. Time to stop waffling around. Jessie leaned forward earnestly. "Every time I try to talk to you about what you do when you're away from here, Ben, you turn me off. I want to know why."

"So you *are* carrying a grudge about last night. Jessie, why do we have to talk about my job in order to have . . . a relationship?"

It was Jessie's turn to be offended. "Sex, you mean. And we have more than that, at least I think we do. Ben, you have a whole other life that you're keeping from me. At least acknowledge that our *relationship* is worth discussion."

Ben sighed heavily. "You're right. I apologize."

Soothed by his contrite words, Jessie said, "That's all right. It's hardly surprising, given how quickly everything has happened between us, that there are some rough spots we need to work out."

"You don't hear *me* complaining."

"Come on, Ben. This isn't about leaving your socks on the floor."

He took a long time to answer. "I don't think I should talk about my work. You'd only worry."

"I can handle it."

"You may think so. . . ."

"I know so. What I can't handle is being shut out of a part of your life that's important to you. It feels like I'm being compartmentalized."

Ben looked away. "Yeah, I can see how you'd feel that way."

"I guess I'm still good at covering up and pretending nothing's wrong. I did that with Antonio all the time. But I'm not going to do it with you. I won't let myself fall back into those old ways—I can't live like that again. It wouldn't be good for either of us. I don't want what we have together to be spoiled."

"I can't do it, Jess." He looked truly sorry.

Jessie panicked. "Why not? I'm not asking for much. It's not like I have to hear the gory details of what you do. Surely there are people you work with you could tell me about, or ordinary day-to-day activities. You're not in danger every minute, are you?"

"Most of the time I work alone," he said somberly. "And you wouldn't like the person you'd see if I played out my day-to-day activities for you. Hell, *I* don't like him. I told you before—this is the place I come to get away from all that."

"I see." She *did* see, better than Ben himself, Jessie thought. For the first time she put together his refusal to talk about his work with the things he had told her about himself. She realized she had misunderstood completely what he was doing and the reasons for it. He hadn't compartmentalized her, he had compartmentalized his life, and had been doing so long before they'd met. It was his way of dealing with a career for which he was temperamentally unsuited.

He sat forward, letting his hands hang limply between his knees. "So where does that leave us, Jess?"

"How have you stood it for eleven years?"

"Stood what?"

"The strain of doing a job you despise?"

His head jerked up. "What are you talking about? I'm a damned good cop."

"That's not the point. The real issue is your happiness and well-being. Police work isn't right for you, at least not working undercover. Don't you see that?"

"How did you reach that brilliant conclusion?"

She winced at the sudden derision in his voice but continued doggedly. He needed to understand what he was doing to himself.

"It's the way you live, almost like you're two different people who hate each other so much they won't have anything to do with each other. Here, in this house with me you're a wonderful, kind, loving man. But out there, on the streets, you're—what? Who do you become, Ben? What do you do that makes you—"

"I do what I have to do to get the job done," he said through gritted teeth. "I am not a schizoid crazy person with multiple personalities."

"That's not what I'm saying."

"Close."

There were two spots of color on Ben's cheekbones. In spite of his obvious anger, his voice remained quietly level.

"Don't try to make me over, Jessie. I managed to stumble along okay before you came into my life. Some people even appreciate what I've done."

"I know that." Jessie could see she shouldn't have started this. A little desperately she said, "I just meant that... Ben, you said yourself the only reason you became a policeman was because of your sister, Maddie. I'm sure she wouldn't want you to sacrifice your whole life to her memory."

"I'm not sacrificing anything. Just where do you get off, anyway, dammit?" His hands curled into fists on his knees.

At that moment, Jessie could have sworn he actually disliked her. She recoiled from his narrow-eyed gaze. "I—"

"Listen, you don't know me from horse manure. I can count the number of days since we met on my fingers and toes and have digits left over. So how can you think you have the inside dope on what makes me tick? Hell, I should have known better than to think this would work. It never does."

Every muscle in Jessie's body went absolutely still. "What are you saying, exactly? That it's over?"

The color faded from Ben's cheeks and she saw his nostrils flare. "It's up to you—I don't care. Just don't psychoanalyze me."

"You'd let me go so easily?"

He didn't answer.

"Ben?"

"I didn't say it was over." He stood and walked to the window, his steps rigid, at odds with his usual fluid movements. As though he'd said all he was going to, he stared out into the night.

"You're sure as hell not telling me to stick around."

Without turning to face her, he said, "It's your choice. It has been from the beginning."

"That's it?" she asked his back. "It doesn't make any difference to you whether we're together or not?"

She couldn't believe that was true. How had everything gone so wrong so fast? Frantically she tried to regain some lost ground. "Ben, this isn't like you. I've got to have something I can hang on to. I thought we were building something here—something that would last. We can work this out if you're willing—"

"I never thought it would last. I told you that when we started—you even agreed with me, remember?"

His words cut through her entreaty like a sharp knife, clean and lethal. Jessie felt the pain of it deep in her heart. "Yes, but I thought..."

"I know what you thought."

Ben turned around, and she saw in his eyes he'd withdrawn from her totally. "I told you, Jess—cops don't make good husbands. Sooner or later the job gets in the way."

"This isn't about your job," she protested. "It's about you."

He shrugged as though he couldn't care less. "Same thing. Law enforcement is not just what I do—it's what I am, like it or lump it."

Jessie knew as surely as she knew her name that he was wrong, but his cold voice took the fight out of her. "All right, then. I'll go."

With leaden feet she walked to the closet and got her coat and purse.

"You're leaving now? It's the middle of the night."

"I don't want to burden you with my presence any longer than necessary."

She pressed the gate button and stepped halfway into the closet to turn off the nighttime alarm, which Ben had reengaged from the rear door code box when he'd come in from work. It reminded her that he would probably change the codes now, as he had when he realized Ed Brock still had one of the spare remotes.

"Please don't change the security codes until after tomorrow." She slipped into her coat. "I'll come back while you're at work to get the clothes and things I've left here."

"I'm not going to change the damned codes. I know you're not going to do anything."

Surprisingly, Ben's irritation gave her a lift. She even managed a smile. "Then . . . I guess this is goodbye."

As she unlocked the door, Ben said in a sudden rush, "Give it another week, Jess."

She froze. "What?"

"Look, we've got a good thing going, don't we? We understand each other now, so why cut it short before we have to?

Don't call it quits until Christmas. I'll be gone after that, anyway."

"Gone? Where?"

"I've been assigned to a survivalist camp about forty miles south of here, and I'll be staying there for an indefinite period—it could be six months to a year."

"Six months to... a year?"

"These things take time. The local cops think the camp is manufacturing methamphetamine and maybe LSD and distributing them to school kids. They need a stranger to infiltrate the operation, so I volunteered. It's what I do, Jess."

Jessie ignored the faint note of entreaty in his last words. "You volunteered."

"Well, yeah. These people have to be stopped."

The fragile hope his last-minute offer had stirred in her breast splintered, and she opened the door.

"No, thanks," she told him. "It's pretty clear where my position is on your list of priorities. I deserve better than that."

Angry tears gathered in her throat. She left quickly before Ben could see them fall.

"Dammit," Ben whispered when the door closed behind her. He heard her footsteps cross the porch and the muted clicking noises of the outside door latch. Then nothing. "Goddammit to hell."

What the hell had happened? An hour ago he'd been looking forward to getting naked and watching Jessie hang on to him as if she never wanted to let him go. Instead she was gone, believing he didn't care about her.

Well, wasn't this what he'd been after? Better that she think him a self-serving bastard than the truth.

It was just that it had happened before he expected. He hadn't prepared himself.

He needed a drink, maybe two, to make the yawning emptiness inside his chest go away. He was in the kitchen pouring whiskey into a tall water glass when he heard her.

"Ben?"

She was back! He hurried to the living room, only to stop short at the sight that greeted him.

Jessie stood inside the door with Ed Brock's arm around her neck in a choke hold, his other hand pointing a .45 semiautomatic pistol at her head. Ed's clothes were rumpled and stained, and it looked as though he hadn't shaved since he'd made off with the journal. But his hand was steady, his voice calm as he nodded and said, "Hello, Ben."

Ben's blood congealed in his veins. "I'm surprised to see you, Ed." He kept his tone cordial. "Leutzinger figured your friends had probably spirited you out of the country by now."

"What friends? I'll take care of myself," Ed said. "But first you and Jessie are going to come with me."

"What do you want with us?"

"It's you I want out of the picture for a while. Jessie just happened to get in the way. Though I guess I have her to thank for letting me in here without bells going off."

"Let her go if it's me you want."

"No. Something tells me you'll be a lot easier to handle with this gun pointed right where it is. Do what I tell you and she won't get hurt." He nudged Jessie's temple with his pistol. Her eyes closed tightly.

"You all right, Jess?" Ben asked her softly.

"Yes," she whispered, opening her eyes. There was fear there, and her face looked pinched, but she appeared to be composed.

Good, Ben thought. Maybe he stood a chance to get her out of this.

Those were the last words their captor allowed either of them for a long time. With the gun never wavering from its point-blank target, he told Ben to get a jacket.

Ben kept watching for an opening, a letdown in Ed's guard, but not for an instant was the deadly hold on Jessie relaxed. He couldn't try anything while she was a split second away from getting her head blown off.

With Ed half pushing, half dragging Jessie in front of him, they all piled into the front of Ben's car. Ed forced Jessie to sit with him in the passenger seat while Ben drove them to a desolate section of town. The deserted, mostly empty warehouses here were homes for vagrants and the occasional drug deal. On Ed's instructions, Ben guided the Trans Am to a ramp behind one of the larger buildings where a wide, wavy aluminum door stood open.

"Park it in there, and don't turn off the lights," Ed ordered him. When the car was inside the warehouse, he said, "Now get out and close the big door. There's a catch on the inside."

"What—"

"No talking."

Frustration gnawed at Ben as he did what he was told. Their situation was growing worse and worse, and he was powerless to do anything about it. One after another of his ideas had been abandoned as Ed had foreseen a possible move on his part. His ex-partner was too smart, too experienced to make stupid mistakes.

But Ben had been a cop for a long time, and his brains and experience counted for something, too. Ed was human; sooner or later he was bound to slip up. Ben would keep watching and be ready to do whatever he had to do. Jessie's life depended on it.

He had time to turn slightly at the sound of footsteps behind him as he latched the door, time to hear Ed's voice say, "Sorry, pal." Time to realize he'd been second-guessed again.

But he was too late to deflect the blow that swallowed up the glow from his car's headlights and rendered him unconscious.

Chapter 15

He came to with the mother of all headaches.

Ben opened his eyes to slits and saw a dirty expanse of drywall. Through the throbbing pain in his skull, he took stock warily. He lay on his stomach, his cheek resting on a cold floor, shoulders pressed forward awkwardly. Someone had tied his hands behind his back.

"I think he's coming around. See? I told you he'd be okay."

"No thanks to you."

He knew those voices. The first was masculine and reassuring, the second, feminine and accusing. Ben remembered everything in a sudden rush.

He tried rolling to his side to face Ed and Jessie, but the nucleus of pain behind his ear shot sharp blades of agony into his brain. He groaned and squeezed his eyes shut until the worst of it passed.

"Ben? Are you all right? Ben. Help him, damn you."

"Ease off, Jessie. He's got a headache, that's all."

Ben's torment settled to an aching tom-tom keeping time with his pulse.

"How do you know? You're not a doctor. He could have a concussion, or pressure on his brain. He needs a hospital—emergency care."

"I didn't hit him that hard."

"You shouldn't have hit him at all. Look, he's not moving anymore. Ben? . . . Ben!"

Jessie's frantic summons gave him the strength to speak. "I'm not dead yet, Jess."

He heard her sigh of relief. "Oh, thank God! Are you in pain? Don't try to move. Can't you do something, Ed?"

He needed to see where he was, Ben thought, and whether there was any way to get him and Jessie out of this mess. That wouldn't be easy. He knew now his feet were bound as tightly as his hands.

"You want to sit up, Ben?"

"I'm not sure," he said sardonically.

He heard Ed's feet approach and stop close to his left shoulder. Strong fingers closed over the biceps of one arm, lifting and turning him onto his side.

"Bend your legs and ease your back up along the wall," Ed said, adding in a warning voice, "and don't try anything dumb."

Sitting up was an ordeal that caused Ben's throat muscles to strain against the demon percussionist in his head, but with Ed's help he managed it. The first thing he saw when he was upright was the dull gleam of a well-tended handgun aimed right at his kneecap.

"For heaven's sake, put that thing away," Jessie protested. "Do you think an injured man with his hands tied behind his back is going to jump you? Two minutes ago he was unconscious."

Her gibe came from Ben's right, but he didn't look over. His gaze was locked with Ed's, probing to find whether his former partner had murder in mind. Ed's eyes were carefully blank.

"I won't shoot to kill," he said as though Ben had asked the question, "but I can slow you down for a long time to come."

Ben heard Jessie draw in a sharp breath.

After making his point, Ed lowered his gun and walked to the other side of the room. There he laid his weapon on one of two wooden crates positioned close together. He sat down on the other one.

The immediate threat over, Ben checked on Jessie. She sat on the floor, knees up, leaning against the bare wall adjacent to his. Her feet were tied with rags wrapped securely from ankle to midcalf; her arms, like Ben's, were cocked behind her back. Otherwise she seemed to be unharmed.

Her worried eyes met his. "How's your head?"

It was still pounding like a son of a bitch. "Not bad. Did he hurt you?"

"No, I didn't," Ed said with a trace of impatience. "I didn't want her involved at all. How was I to know she'd still be at your place after all this time? Since she was, I had no choice but to bring her along. Believe me, if it had been just you, I wouldn't have knocked you out."

"Oh, so it's *her* fault I have this lump on my head."

"There was no other way to get you both from the car into this room in the dark. One of you had to be put out of commission for a while, and being a man, you were the obvious candidate."

"How chivalrous," Jessie muttered.

"To tell you the truth," said Ben, "I'm having trouble making sense out of your bringing either one of us here. Just what are you trying to accomplish?"

"Maybe it's for nothing, but I had to be sure."

"Sure about what?"

"Donno told me you saw him and Rory Douglas in his truck tonight."

"Donno...?" Ben's puzzled voice trailed off. Eyes glaring at him from a ferretlike face hunched over a steering wheel flashed in his memory. The face clicked into place. No wonder the man he'd seen speeding away outside the convenience store had looked familiar. He was Ed's snitch Donno Carr, the guy who'd given Ed the first hints about Mai's operation in Port Mangus. Ben hadn't recognized the informant immediately because they'd never met. Donno was a petty criminal, and Ben's only introduction to him had been via a mug shot Ed had once pointed out.

"So? I still don't—wait, did you say he was with Rory Douglas?" Ben had been vaguely aware of a passenger in the ruck, but only as a shadowy figure in the background.

"You didn't know. Dammit." Ed breathed a resigned sigh. 'Well, what's done is done. I'm going to play this thing out ow, regardless."

"I don't understand," Jessie said.

Ben didn't understand, either, exactly, but he was getting ome ideas. There had to be good reason why a man like Douglas, who prided himself on his class, would fraternize with street slug like Donno.

Ed turned his head Jessie's way, his worn-out face looking ld by the light of the camp lantern sharing space with his gun n the makeshift table. Automatically Ben's mind recorded the attery-operated lamp and Ed's close position to the pistol. He lso made a mental note of the keys to his Trans Am resting ear the base of the lantern. He'd have to grab those if they nanaged to escape.

The room itself was small and relatively barren. A portable erosene heater with tiny yellow ventilator holes near the top vas placed close to a rumpled pallet in the corner to Ed's right. A gasoline can took up another corner and presumably held uel for the heater. There were no windows in the room, and the ingle door was closed and padlocked from the inside. Their rison was obviously Ed's hideout, probably an old office in he warehouse he'd brought them to.

"I guess it doesn't matter if I tell you," Ed said to Jessie. 'You can't do anything about it until I'm long gone, anyway. Donno's been working for me ever since the night I took the ournal. I ran into him by chance while looking for a spot to ose myself for a while. He found me this place to stay."

"Isn't it nice to have friends?" Ben said snidely.

Ed barked a short, humorless laugh. "You know, I under-stimated that little weasel, Ben. He's been slipping me tiny rumbs of information for years, and I was proud of the way 'd played him into a solid source for the bureau. If I'd had any lea of the things and people he knows . . . well, let's just say hings are different now that I'm on this side of the fence."

He shook his head, whether in wonder or regret, Ben ouldn't tell.

"'Course, with Donno, you don't get chicken crap unless there's something in it for him. He's helping me because he figures he's on to a real windfall."

"How so?"

Ben was less concerned about Donno than in keeping Ed talking. He needed time. He'd come to the conclusion that their only hope of escape was to overpower the ex-agent. He couldn't do that with his hands tied, and so far he couldn't see a damned thing in the whole room, let alone within his reach, that he could use to cut through the restricting rags around his wrists. Somehow he had to find a way. . . .

"He has inside information, what else?" Ed answered. "He knows I'm coming into some money shortly. Matter of fact, since I have to keep a low profile these days, he's acting as a kind of broker for the deal."

"Let me guess. He's dealing with Rory Douglas."

"Yup. Douglas's people want that journal real bad."

"I'm surprised you'd trust Donno. He's not exactly a candidate for sainthood."

"Yeah, well, I can hardly be choosy, can I? But I'm no fool, either. I don't trust him any more than I trust the mob. I've told Donno only what he needs to know to be my messenger, and bought his loyalty with the promise of a hefty bonus when all this is over. As for Douglas and his bunch, they're aware that if they're stupid enough to do away with me, Leutzinger himself will be reading Mai's journal before my body gets cold."

"But what about when you turn the journal over to them? What's to stop them from leaving you with a bullet between the eyes instead of a satchel of money?"

"I thought of that," Ed said grimly. "That's why I didn't set up the exchange that way. There *is* no satchel of money—just a nice, discreet deposit wired into a numbered bank account in the Caymans that the feds can't get access to. When I meet with Douglas in a few hours, he'll give me a faxed copy of that deposit, and I'll take him to get the journal. He and his gang will have what they want, and since they won't have any way to get back their payoff, they'll have no reason to kill me. It'll be a straightforward business deal, and we can all go our merry ways."

Ben had to admit it was a reasonable plan that had a good chance of succeeding. The banking system in the Caymans, a small group of islands in the Caribbean, was well known for its unquestioning acceptance of funds and rigorous confidentiality, much like the system in Switzerland.

"And you'll just fade into the sunset, right?" he said. "With never a second thought about aiding and abetting crooks like the ones you spent almost a whole lifetime trying to bring down."

His derision had little effect on the ex-agent. Ed lifted his shoulders in a dismissive shrug. "I had it all worked out to a tee, until you came along tonight. Just my bad luck—and yours—that you were in that neighborhood. When Donno told me you'd seen him and Douglas together, I had to make sure you couldn't get to Leutzinger before my meeting with Douglas. After that it won't matter—I'll be outta here."

"What are you going to do with us?" Jessie asked.

Ben heard an edge of anger in her voice. He didn't blame her. She hadn't asked for any of this.

A pang of emotions—part regret, part guilt, part need—bolted through his heart as he remembered the moment she had walked out of his house. Talk about bad luck. If Ed had waited just fifteen minutes before making his move, she would have been safely away—forever.

Somehow I'll get you out of this, Jess, he vowed silently.

"Nothing'll happen to you—or Ben—as long as you don't give me any trouble," Ed told her. "I'm just gonna leave you here. Then after I'm too far away for Leutzinger's watchdogs to find me, which shouldn't take more than a day, I'll make an anonymous phone call to the newspapers to let someone know you're here. In the meantime, you two may get hungry and uncomfortable, but otherwise you'll be okay."

"You know you won't get away with this, Ed," Ben said. "Why don't you let us go now, give me the journal and put yourself in my custody? Jessie and I'll put in a good word for you, and it won't go too hard on you."

"Forget it. You and I both know I've come too far for it to go easy on me. If I have to face prison, I'm going to make damned sure I get something out of it. And dirty money spends just as easy as the other kind. For a change *I'll* be the one flashing the bucks."

Ben turned his head away in disgust.

"Don't be so damned righteous!" Ed snapped. "Do you know how old I am? Fifty-four years old. And I gave twenty-five of those years to the bureau. For twenty-five long years I told myself working for the government was a high calling, a noble cause—that patriotic duty came before anything or anybody else. And what did I get out of those years of dedication? Alimony payments. Fifteen years of alimony payments, and no wife to come home to."

The anger seemed to drain out of his face, and he leaned forward earnestly. "Zilch, Ben, a big *z-e-r-o*, that's what I got. If I could look back and see I've made the world a better place, it might be worth it, but you and I both know not a damned thing I did in all that time made a rat's ass bit of difference in the long run."

"You're breaking my heart," Ben said unsympathetically.

"Ah, what the hell. Why am I trying to explain? I can't expect a young man like you to understand what it's like. I don't even care. Understanding won't make up for all those wasted years. Money will, though, and the only way I'm going to get it is to sell that journal."

"You're taking a big chance, dealing with the mob," Ben reminded him.

"I told you, I've covered all my bases. Nobody knows where the journal is but me and Marie, and if Douglas tries any funny business, Marie fixed it with a lawyer so the FBI will get it instead of the mob."

"You involved your *wife?*"

"Don't worry, she knows even less than Donno about what's going on. I needed somebody I could trust to help me, and now that I'm through with the bureau and soon to be a rich man, she's decided to come back to me. Finally I'll be able to give her all the things she always wanted."

"And something she *doesn't* want," Ben said. "A long inside look at a federal penitentiary."

"Uh-uh," Ed said. "Nothing I had her do was illegal, so Leutzinger can't get her as an accessory if I'm caught. Which I don't intend to be."

Jessie angled her bound legs to the floor, heels to hips, and leaned toward Ed intently. "But you can't be sure—"

Ed cut her off. "I don't feel like talking about it anymore, okay? Don't . . . I just don't want to talk about it."

"Well . . . all right, but I think you're making a big mistake. If you love Marie, and I think you do—"

"Drop it, Jessie."

Jessie sighed and sank back against the wall. Ben gave her points for a damned good try, but it was clear Ed wasn't willing to be deterred.

Even so, things were looking up. The gun was still a threat that couldn't be ignored, but Ben was confident now that Ed meant them no harm. If nothing got screwed up, he would be gone before long. Then Ben and Jessie could scoot together and work on untying each other's bonds. Ben didn't put much stock in Ed saying he'd notify someone to rescue them. Even if he meant it, too much could go wrong in the meantime.

The sudden loud knock on the door made them all jump. It came in a burst of three rapid thumps, followed by three more, even and slow. Obviously a prearranged signal.

"There's your payoff now," Ben said to Ed.

Ed got up, looking puzzled. "No, it's not. I'm meeting Douglas later at an all-night grocery store."

The coded knock came again, accompanied this time by a muffled, "Open up, man. It's me—Donno."

Ed approached the padlocked door, but made no move to open it. He raised his voice enough to be heard on the other side. "What're you doing here, Donno?"

"We got a glitch in the plans," came the disembodied voice. "Douglas is with me. He's nervous about seeing that cop tonight. He thinks you might be setting him up for a fall and made me bring him here. He's . . . he's got a gun on me, man."

Ben mentally echoed the heartfelt curse that exploded from Ed's lips. Here was a wrinkle Ed obviously hadn't counted on. The throbbing in Ben's head made itself felt again as he considered what this could mean for him and Jessie.

"You there, Douglas?" Ed called.

"Yes, I am." Even through the door, it was easy to recognize the raised voice belonging to the suave attorney. It was ominously pleasant.

"What's your problem?"

"Like Donno said, I'm nervous. It's time for a change in the rules."

"There's no need for that. I give you my word, I'm not working any double cross."

"I'm glad to hear it. Let me in, then, and we'll take care of business right now."

Ed glanced at Ben, then Jessie. "I'd rather stick to the original plan," he said to the door.

"Look, Agent Brock, I'm short of patience tonight, and your friend here is going to reap the consequences."

"You mean Donno? I wouldn't exactly call him a friend."

"Then I guess you won't mind if my finger slips on this trigger and his brains get splattered all over the wall, will you?"

"Do what he says, man," Donno whined. "I don't wanna die."

Ed closed his eyes and muttered a foul expletive under his breath. "Did you bring the fax?"

"You'll have to open the door to find out," Douglas answered.

"First put your gun away and let Donno go."

There was a brief silence. "You don't give me much credit, Agent Brock. I know when I'm holding the high cards."

"Then I guess we're at a standoff. If you want to blow our arrangement, go ahead. I told you, Donno's no friend of mine. And I've still got the journal."

"Hey, man, wha—whaddaya mean? I been helpin' you out all this time, ain't I?" Donno sounded desperate.

"Sorry, Donno," Ed said unrepentantly. "How about it, Douglas? You want a murder rap on your head, or do you still want to deal?"

Ed turned his head and met Ben's gaze. He didn't try to hide his anxiety. Ben knew in that moment the ex-agent was bluffing for Donno Carr's life.

Maybe for Ben's and Jessie's, too, if Douglas found out Ed had brought them here.

"So cold-blooded. You surprise me, Brock," Douglas said. "Do you put as low a premium on your ex-wife's well-being as you do Mr. Carr's?"

Ben could see Ed's sudden pallor, even in the dim yellow glow of the lantern.

Douglas's voice continued evilly. "Her name's Marie, isn't it?"

"What about her, you son of a bitch?"

"Ah, so you do care. Tell me, do you know where she is at the moment?"

Fear and rage etched themselves into the prominent lines on Ed's face. "Somewhere safe from bastards like you," he growled.

"You think so? I admit it took us awhile to find her. She led us quite a chase until we remembered that someone had to go to the Caribbean to set up that numbered bank account for you."

A fine sheen of perspiration glowed on Ed's skin. For a moment, his mouth moved soundlessly. "What have you done with her?" he finally managed.

"Nothing, really. Our men are just keeping her company right where they found her. She's—how shall I put it?—*un-damaged* for now. And as long as you cooperate, she'll stay that way."

"How do I know you're not bluffing? I want to talk to her."

"I'm surprised at you, Agent Brock. You of all people should realize there's no need to bluff. You know very well what the resources of my organization are." Douglas's voice grew suddenly hard, as though he'd tired of the game. "Your request is denied. Now, are you going to open this door, or do I leave to make a phone call to the men holding your wife in the Cayman Islands?"

Ed seemed to collapse in on himself for a second, then slowly he straightened, his features grim and set. "You didn't wire the money, did you?"

"Finally you're beginning to understand. Now I'm getting tired of talking, Brock. I didn't hesitate to kill Mai Duan, and I can just as easily pull the trigger on Donno right here to show you I mean business. One more body won't make a damned bit of difference to me. And the next one will be your wife."

"Wait!" Ed cried. "You know I don't have the journal here."

In a flurry of silent motion, he hurried to the other side of the room and picked up his pistol.

"I'd like to check that out for myself," Douglas said. "You have ten seconds to open this door."

Ed rushed back to the door and shouted, "No. Give me a little time to think."

"Ten seconds." Douglas started counting.

The next thing Ben knew, Ed was kneeling beside him and cutting the rags at his wrists with a pocketknife. "I'm giving you the gun," he whispered.

Ben stared at him. "Why?"

"Kidnapping is one thing, but I got a feeling Douglas has murder on his mind. It's going to take both of us to stop him. Now, I don't have time to load this thing, so you'll have to fake it."

"It's not *loaded?*" Ben whispered back incredulously.

"I didn't want to accidentally shoot you. Pretend your hands are still tied and wait for an opening. Douglas'll be distracted when he sees you and Jessie. I'll try to take advantage of that."

"See if you can cut the light," Ben rasped. "Leave me the knife, too. A gun without bullets isn't going to do me a hell of a lot of good."

"Here. Good luck."

The knife handle pressed against Ben's palm, and he grasped it. It felt small, inadequate to the danger of their situation.

Good luck. A precious commodity, Ben thought. What they really needed was a miracle. Douglas had freely admitted his crimes, which could mean only one thing. He intended to leave no survivors.

Ed rushed back to the door, his hand in his pocket. He fished out a key as Douglas intoned "nine," and fit it into the padlock.

"Okay, you win," he said as he turned the key. "I'm letting you in."

He turned and looked at Ben then, and for a moment they were two cops again, pitting their wits against a common adversary.

Jessie observed the unfolding drama without feeling like an actual participant. It was more like having a center seat in a movie theater, watching the protagonists in a suspense film move toward certain disaster. She saw that Ed had left the gun with Ben, but had been unable to hear their furtive whispers.

Something terrible was going to happen, she just knew. The sense of impending doom increased when she pulled her eyes from Ed and found Ben, tense and alert, his attention focused on the door.

She blamed herself that he was in danger yet again. It was her fault that they had quarreled, her fault that Ed had been able to take them by surprise. What had been so important to her just a couple of hours ago now seemed insignificant in light of their current peril. She wished she could tell Ben she was sorry, that she loved him, that if somehow they got out of this hopeless situation, she wanted to try again.

But now wasn't the time for such revelations. She could only hope and pray there would be a time somewhere in the uncertain future.

Ed turned the knob and opened the door only a crack, moving away immediately to a position in front of the two wooden crates. Pretty smart, Jessie thought. Douglas would have a hard time watching everybody at once, when the three of them were spaced in a triangle at least ten feet from each other.

A man poked his stocking-capped head warily around the door. His eyes shifted in jerks about the room, then widened in surprise, darting to Ben, to Jessie, to Ed, and back to Ben. The infamous Donno Carr, Jessie presumed.

"Hey, man." Donno's pointy chin aimed his slightly nasal voice over his shoulder to Rory Douglas, who had not yet come in. "The cop's here, and some babe, all trussed up like turkeys for the kill."

The door flew back on its hinges and struck the wall with a bang that echoed through the warehouse.

"Well, well, an unexpected pleasure. Struttin' Sutton at my mercy." Douglas stepped in behind Donno, his height dwarfing the smaller man. "And Ms. Webster, too. Things are getting somewhat complicated. But then, I've always been one to rise to a challenge."

The deadly looking pistol he held competently in his manicured hand swept the room and stopped, its barrel pointed steadily at Ed's stomach. Ed lifted his hands slowly, palms out, his eye on the gun.

"Frisk him, Donno."

Once again Jessie had the unreal impression that she was watching a movie—a second-rate one, with clichéd dialogue.

"All *right!*" Donno approached Ed with a gleeful smirk. "I always wanted to do this. Put your hands behind your head, man, and spread your legs."

At this unmistakable evidence of his hireling's collusion with Douglas, Ed spat, "Bastard!"

"Sorry, man," Donno replied with a shrug of his narrow shoulders. "Looked to me like things was getting flaky. I had to hedge my bets. Besides, Mr. Douglas pays better than you."

He took his time patting Ed down, then stepped back. "He's clean, man."

"Search the blankets and under the mattress. He may have stashed his gun there. Look for a blue cloth-bound book without a title, too."

"Let Jessie go, Rory," Ben said to Douglas's back. "She's an innocent victim in all this."

Douglas kept his eyes on Ed, obviously considering him to be the greater threat, since Ben was tied up. Shaking his head slowly, he said over his shoulder, "What an idealist you are, Ben. Still championing women and underdogs, just like you did back in high school. It never occurs to you that some people might not want your help."

"In your case, I got the message," Ben said.

"God, how I hated you and your goody-goody parents. I was making it just fine until you butted in."

Ben's vigilant gaze never left Douglas's eyes, which were still on Ed. "That's not the way it looked to me."

As he spoke, Jessie saw his right hand slowly move from behind his back and ease its way under the bridge of his knees, holding an open pocketknife. Quickly she averted her eyes so she wouldn't give him away. Hope surged in her breast.

"You hold a grudge for a long time, Douglas," Ed said.

"Some things a person never forgets." Bitterness tinged Douglas's words.

"Like what?" Ed asked. "What did Ben do to you, anyway?"

"He interfered in my life when it was none of his business!" Douglas snapped. "He saw some bruises on my ribs once while we were playing basketball—*old* bruises that were almost gone. I told him it was nothing, but good old Ben couldn't let it go. The next thing I knew, his father and mother were at my place with the county children's welfare department, and my sister and brother and I were all farmed out to foster homes."

"Hell, it seems to me he did you a favor, if your old man was beating you," Ed said. "Most kids would *want* to get away."

"The beatings weren't so bad I couldn't take it. I was fourteen, and big enough that I had already started to fight back."

Jessie sensed a change in Douglas's mood. He was no less tense than he'd been when he first entered the room, and the gun in his hand remained level and unmoving. Still, as he spoke to Ed, his eyes seemed less focused, as though he were looking inward, remembering. Donno, too, was distracted by the conversation, occasionally stopping to listen as he searched the bedclothes and pallet on his hands and knees. A quick glance out of the corner of Jessie's eye showed the bonds on Ben's legs were loosening as he severed the cloth from the underside.

Keep talking, she mentally urged Douglas.

"I was the only one who stood between that drunken sadist and my mother," he went on. "When they took us away, I begged her to leave him, but she wouldn't go. Without me there to protect her, it took him less than a year to beat her to death."

"Damn, that's tough," Ed said with what sounded like genuine sympathy. "But you can't blame Ben for that."

"Oh, but I do. If he hadn't interfered, I could have killed the old man sooner, and my mother would still be alive. As it was, I had to wait to avenge her, and I never got to tell her how I made him suffer. On my eighteenth birthday I drove him to Indiana, to an isolated woods over two hundred miles from here where he'd be a nameless bum. He was drunk as usual, but I waited until he was good and sober before I did anything. I wanted him to feel every punch, every kick."

He spoke almost fondly of the memory, and Jessie shuddered in revulsion.

"It was my birthday present to myself. There was no finer way to celebrate my coming of age than to pound the life out of that stinking excuse for a father with my bare hands."

"Damn," Donno breathed reverently.

"That day I learned revenge is very sweet. And now, thanks to you, Agent Brock, tonight I can have vengeance on my old childhood enemy, too, at the same time as I take care of the problems you've caused me. Very convenient."

"Yeah, I'm a real accommodating guy," Ed said.

"Accommodating, but not very clever. You'll be glad to know nobody in my organization knows about this deal we cooked up. It was in my best interest to keep it to myself, since the man at the top is already upset with me for getting arrested, not to mention making Mai disappear and bringing the law swarming all over the Port Mangus operation. I have to do something to redeem myself. Presenting him with this journal will go a long way to securing my future. So, Agent Brock, my threat about your wife involved a good piece of guesswork. You should have called my bluff."

The single syllable Ed uttered was fervent and obscene.

"Now, now, there's a lady present. Did you find the gun, Donno? Or the journal?"

Donno scurried to his feet, the spell broken. "No, man, there's nothin' here."

"You might as well stop looking," Ed said. "I lost my gun somewhere while I was getting away from Leutzinger, and the journal is in a bus locker in Detroit. The key is with a lawyer, by the way, and he won't release it to anyone but me."

"Not so convenient, after all," Douglas mused aloud. Then he appeared to come to a decision. "I guess I'll have to take you with me, then. Donno, take that gas can in the corner and soak the other two down. Save a little for the bedding, if you can."

"You wanna *burn* 'em? Hey, man, I didn't sign on for no murder."

"Do it." The order was calmly stated and allowed for no argument.

"Not so fast, Douglas," Ben said.

All eyes turned to his side of the room.

"He's got a gun!" Donno shouted.

Everything happened at once then. Douglas aimed and fired just as Ben flung himself to the side, no longer hampered by the restricting bonds. Jessie screamed, afraid he'd been hit. The light suddenly went out. Scuffling sounds and masculine grunts filled Jessie's ears, but she could see nothing. Suddenly another shot rang out, and a searing pain tore through her thigh.

Stunned, Jessie clumsily lay down on the floor and pulled her knees to her chest, hoping to make herself a smaller target. Her injured leg felt hot from her knee to her groin. Amazingly, she felt only a little soreness lingering from the first powerful sting of impact. It was curious that the ache in her tied arms caused her greater discomfort than the more serious wound. How could that be?

There were two more shots. They made brief, horizontal candle flames in the darkness, the flashes spewing out of the end of the gun barrel close to the floor. Jessie realized a struggle for possession of the gun was in progress, and she could very likely be hit again. She drew her legs up tighter and closed her eyes, praying that Ben was all right, that they all would come out of this alive.

Another shot. Sudden weakness assailed her. Odd. She was already lying down; she shouldn't be feeling dizzy. And when had her head started pounding? A swirling black hole in her mind beckoned, promising oblivion.

From a long distance, like a voice in a dream, somebody said, "This is the FBI. Put down your weapons and come out with your hands up."

A bad movie, Jessie thought again. Then she gave in to the seductive pull of the dark whirlpool and knew no more.

Chapter 16

Ben wasn't allowed into the ambulance that carried Jessie away, so he chased it in his car, recklessly running every red light and stop sign right behind the wailing vehicle. At the hospital, he cursed and veered off to visitor parking when he saw the Ambulance Only sign at the emergency entrance. By the time he raced into the trauma center reception area, Jessie was already out of sight in a treatment room.

Forced to wait and wonder what was going on behind the closed double doors, he paced the hallways and badgered the staff for news until an exasperated nurse behind the desk took him to a small private waiting room to get him out of the flow of traffic.

At some point a harried doctor took just enough time to rush in and tell him Jessie was still not out of danger, and no, Ben couldn't see her yet. A few minutes later, the nurse returned with a message for him to call Leutzinger at the county jail. Making sure first that she would come to get him if there was any word on Jessie, Ben found a pay phone in the lobby.

"I thought you'd like to know what a coup we pulled today," Leutzinger said. "Donno and Brock are singing like Pavarotti to save their scrawny necks. They both heard Rory

Douglas say he killed Mai Duan, and Donno gave us some good information tying Douglas to the Port Mangus operation, too, so we've got him on drug running, prostitution and murder one. Plus Brock told us where to find the journal. From all the trouble it's caused, it ought to be pretty juicy. With all that ammunition, we offered Douglas immunity to testify in court against the top guys in his organization, and he went for it. I've already put the wheels in motion to get him out of town to a safe house. We're getting the big boys on this one, Ben."

"Congratulations," Ben said without enthusiasm. The last thing he wanted was to see Rory Douglas get off scot-free after what he'd done to Jessie. But he knew as well as Leutzinger how the game was played.

"How's Ms. Webster doing?" the agent finally remembered to ask.

Ben relayed the discouraging report the doctor had just given him.

"I was hoping for better news," Leutzinger said compassionately. "But at least she's still alive."

"Yeah, there's hope," Ben replied with an optimism he didn't really feel. He couldn't bear to think of the alternative. Could anyone lose as much blood as Jessie had and survive?

"It's too bad we didn't get to that warehouse sooner," Leutzinger said.

Ben shook off his morbid thoughts and gave the conversation his attention. "I was surprised that you showed up at all. How did you know we were there?"

"We didn't. Actually, we didn't know what to expect when we got inside. The agent who's been tailing Douglas ever since he was released on bail acted on a hunch when he called for backup. He'd seen Douglas and Donno together plenty of times, but they'd always met in some out-of-the-way place, talked for a while, then gone their separate ways. They never went anywhere *together,* until last night. That break in the pattern made our man suspect something important was going down, so he radioed headquarters. I headed over as soon as I got the word, and the backup was inside already when I got here. They moved in as soon as they heard gunfire."

"They did a good job," Ben said.

"A few minutes sooner and we could have kept Ms. Webster from getting shot. It was a tough break and I'm sorry, Ben. I know you two are . . . Well, this must be tough on you."

At this expression of support Ben swallowed, unable to answer. Leutzinger broke the heavy silence with forced cheer. "Oh, I meant to tell you. I called her sister in Port Mangus as soon as I could get to a phone. It'll take her a few hours to drive down here, but she's on her way."

"Oh, hell," Ben said. "I should have thought of that. Thanks, Cal. I know Jessie would want Allie to be here."

"No problem. There's just one other thing and then I'll let you go. I hate to bother you with this right now, but I'll need your statement about the kidnapping whenever you can get over here. Ms. Webster's, too, if she, uh . . . when she feels up to it."

"I'll give you a call," Ben said.

Allie arrived a couple of hours later. She rushed into the waiting room, calm but obviously anxious, her long, unbuttoned coat billowing like a cape behind her. Without ceremony, she said, "Ben. How is she? They wouldn't tell me anything at the desk."

For the barest instant, Ben thought she was Jessie. She'd put her hair up and wisps of it were escaping from the careless knot in crinkled ringlets around her face. The resemblance to her twin was so strong, it hurt to look at her.

He rubbed the back of his neck wearily. "She's okay, I think. I'm not sure. They're still working on her."

Something about his answer caused Allie's eyes to sharpen. She gave him a critical once-over. "You look terrible."

Ben didn't doubt it. He needed a shave, a shower, a shirt and a solid eight hours' sleep.

Allie slipped off her coat as she moved farther into the room. "Come on. You'd better sit down before you *fall* down."

She folded her coat in front of her and perched on the edge of a cushioned chair with metal arms, obviously too tense to relax, in spite of her composure. Ben took the matching chair next to her.

"Aren't you too warm?" she asked distractedly, glancing at his zipped-up jacket as he sat down.

For a terrible moment his mind flashed back to the grue-ome scene in the warehouse and the reason he was bare chested nder the concealing leather. He answered evasively, "I'm ine."

But Allie's attention was already back on her sister. The orried look returned to her face. "Have you been able to talk o a doctor yet?"

"Yeah, about half an hour ago. Dr. Panelli."

"Is it bad?"

There was no easy way to put it. "Bad enough. She took two ullets and lost a lot of blood by the time the ambulance came. he doctor told me she started to go into shock and was in and ut of consciousness for a while. But they finally managed to tabilize her, and now she's in surgery."

Allie's eyes widened in alarm and she sat up straighter. ursing himself for his bluntness, Ben said quickly, "It's not fe threatening, as long as no complications set in. Panelli's just igging the bullet out of her leg and fixing the artery that was it. He couldn't do it sooner because she wasn't stable. Now hat she is, it's a routine procedure, he said, with minimum risk. he other wound is nothing to worry about—only a gash about n inch long above her ear where the second bullet grazed her kull."

The color had left Allie's cheeks during his recitation of Jes-ie's injuries. "Is she going to be all right?"

"According to the doc, in a few days she should be fine."

"What do you think about Dr. Panelli? Is he competent?"

"He's a trauma specialist, Allie," Ben said gently. "He deals with gunshot victims every day. He knows what he's doing."

"Oh, a specialist. That's good." With a relieved sigh, Allie lumped and propped her elbows on the arms of the chair. "Who would believe it? My sister, who wouldn't hurt a fly, etting shot."

"I know," Ben said grimly. "Out of all of us in that room, nobody was hit but her, and she was the only one of the whole unch who didn't deserve it. It was just a damned good thing eutzinger was there to radio for an ambulance right away, or he might've . . . Well, it could have been a lot worse."

Not until he'd knelt over Jessie's unconscious body while waiting for the paramedics had Ben realized how lost he would be if the life drained out of her. He was sure the pain of those long minutes would never be erased from his memory. In the midst of all the chaos created as Leutzinger and his men subdued, cuffed and Mirandized the three bastards who had caused all the trouble, Ben had sat on the floor beside Jessie, pressing his shirt against the hole in her leg, willing the blood to stay in her body. Over and over he whispered to her around the lump in his throat, *Don't die, don't die.* And inside his head, he threatened, cajoled and pleaded with the God of heaven, the God he hadn't turned to in eleven long years, to spare her.

The world without Jessie would have no light, no joy.

Allie asked, "Where did it happen? How?"

"It was my fault," he said. Then he looked at her and added derisively, "Some bodyguard, huh?"

Ignoring his self-condemnation, she said, "Tell me."

He sketched out the night's events for her without sparing himself—his argument with Jessie, Ed's abduction, the subsequent struggle in the dark warehouse with his old enemy, the terrible moment when he'd called out Jessie's name and she hadn't answered.

"Did you get them all?" Allie demanded fiercely when he was finished. "Douglas, Ed Brock and that other guy, Donne what's-his-name? Did anybody get away?"

"No. Leutzinger has them all in custody." Ben decided not to mention that Douglas planned to trade his freedom for somebody else's.

"Good." The vengeful light in Allie's eyes glimmered with satisfaction.

She leaned back with a sigh, apparently content to wait in silence now that Ben had answered her questions. After a while she said, "I knew Jessie needed me, even before Cal called. I don't know how I knew, I just did. I was already dressed and ready to go when the phone rang. God, the miles between here and Port Mangus have never seemed so long. All the way I kept telling myself that she was still alive, that surely I'd know—I'd *feel* it if she . . . didn't make it."

Ben nodded. "She told me once that you two have that kind of connection."

Suddenly Allie jumped from her chair and took several long steps across the carpet. She did a quick about-face when she reached the small sofa on the other side of the room. "I hate waiting like this. How long can it take to cut a bullet out of... somebody's leg?"

She choked on the last words and her face sort of crumpled. But she held out an arresting palm when Ben rose to go to her. A strangled sound halfway between a laugh and a sob came from her throat. "No, don't you dare comfort me, or I'll fly to pieces."

"Do you want some coffee or a soft drink? There are vending machines just down the hall."

"Yes, please, a cola. Diet, if they have it."

When Ben came back with her drink, she had regained her composure and returned to her chair. He popped the top on her cola and handed it to her.

"Thanks," she said. The previous shakiness was gone from her voice. Ben admired her control.

"Aren't you having anything?" she asked him.

"Uh-uh." He sat down again, slouching so he could stretch out his legs. A huge, audible yawn caught him.

"It looks like you could use a nap." Allie's smile was her first since dashing into the room. "Why don't you lie down on that couch over there and try to sleep?"

"Not till I know Jessie's okay. I'll be all right."

She studied him for a moment. "You shouldn't blame yourself, you know. It was a whole combination of people and events that led to her getting hurt, not just one. For that matter, *I* contributed. If I hadn't taken Mai's journal—and now I wish I hadn't—Jessie wouldn't have been involved in any of this."

"Yeah, but you didn't practically kick her out of your house in the middle of the night. You didn't get yourself knocked out and tied up like an untrained *civilian*, for God's sake, so you were of no earthly use to her whatever." Ben shook his head in self-recrimination, remembering the frustrating helplessness.

"You're right. You're beyond the pale, you dirty bird. Let'
string 'im up," Allie declared with rousing fervor.

He whipped his head around and saw her watching him witl
an ingenuous expression on her face.

"Well," she said, shrugging, "if you're determined to bea
yourself up about it, I'm not going to stop you." In a softe
voice, she added, "You love her, don't you?"

Ben didn't answer.

"She loves *you*."

He swallowed. "I know. God knows why. Look what
brought her to. She deserves better."

Allie clucked her tongue impatiently. "Honestly, Ben. Wil
you listen to yourself?"

Ben replayed his self-pitying words in his head, grimaced an
then smiled ruefully at Allie's knowing look. He was startin,
to like this difficult woman.

"Mr. Sutton?"

A tall, dark-haired man appeared in the doorway dressed i
surgical scrubs. Ben shot to his feet.

"Relax. Your fiancée is fine," Dr. Panelli said with a sligh
smile. "We got the bullet out and repaired the severed artery."
The surgeon's gaze shifted to Allie for a second. "There'll b
some scarring, of course, and she may have a good bit of pai
for a few days, but that leg should heal up nicely now."

Ben felt a wide grin of relief split his face. He took the doc
tor's hand in both of his and shook it warmly. "Thank you."

"You're welcome. I want her to stay off her feet for a fev
days. If she has someone at home to fetch and carry for her, I'l
release her after twenty-four hours. Otherwise, we'll keep he
a little longer."

From behind Ben, Allie said, "I'll take care of her." Ben sho
her a dark look over his shoulder.

Panelli's look, however, was more cordial. "Do I detect
resemblance to my patient?"

"You do." Allie stepped forward. "I'm Alicia Webster, Jes
sie's twin. May we see my sister now, Doctor?"

"She'll be in ICU until the anesthesia wears off in a coupl
of hours or so," the doctor said. "You can see her for a fev

minutes after she's moved upstairs. Just ask the staff—one of them will tell you the room number."

He was gone as quickly as he'd appeared.

Allie raised her eyebrows at Ben. "Fiancée?"

He shrugged. "I had to tell them that, or they wouldn't have given me any information."

She held his eyes steadily for so long he began to feel as if they were in a staring contest. Finally she said, "You're good for her, you know, and you can't persuade me otherwise. She's been happy with you, happier than I've ever seen her."

After that remarkable statement, she asked Ben to excuse her and went to find the ladies' room.

But her words stayed with him for a long time.

"How's the view?"

At the sound of the dry, familiar voice of her sister, Jessie's eyes swung with pleasure from the overcast sky outside the window to the door of her hospital room. She should have known Allie would come.

Wrinkling her nose, she said, "Boring. I'd rather watch the squirrels chase each other around the trees in Ben's backyard. How did you get here, Allie?"

Allie approached the bed. "I might ask you the same question, sister dear. I thought *I* was the twin who didn't know how to stay out of trouble. Is it safe to hug you?"

"You'd better." Jessie held out the arm that wasn't connected to the IV. "I'm so glad you're here," she whispered as Allie embraced her.

Allie drew back but stayed close to the bed. "Cal Leutzinger called me. I tell you, Jessie, if I hadn't already been planning to move back to Chicago, this morning would have settled it. Every mile I drove to get here seemed like a hundred. I was never so scared in my life. But, hey, at least that interview Leutzinger promised me will be a doozy, won't it? I'm sure to get a job now."

She smiled, but the worried look didn't leave her eyes as she grabbed Jessie's hand and held on tight. "I can only stay for five minutes, so tell me how you're feeling. Does your leg hurt?"

"Not too badly, but I'm pumped full of painkillers. Why can't you stay longer, Allie?"

"I will, this evening during regular visiting hours. Right now, though, there's a dragon of a nurse at the nurses' station who says you need rest so soon after your ordeal."

"That's ridiculous. I'm a little tired, but otherwise I don't feel bad. Even if I did, having you here gives me a lift."

"That's nice to hear, sis, but I want you to do what you're told. Let's not take any chances."

Jessie couldn't hide her disappointment. "I suppose you're right."

Allie patted her arm sympathetically. "Dr. Panelli said we can get you out of here tomorrow, so hang in there, kiddo."

"Allie, have you seen Ben? Do you know if he's all right?"

"Are you kidding? I practically had to wrestle him to the floor to get first dibs to see you. If I go a second over my time, he'll probably haul me out of here bodily. I don't think he'll completely convinced you're okay until he sees you for himself."

"He's here? Now?" Jessie jerked her hand out of Allie's and touched the bandage on her head. "How do I look, Allie? Is there a mirror somewhere around here? I know they shaved my hair around this gash on my head. Does it look too awful?"

"Vanity, thy name is Jessie. Do you think Ben is going to care about that?" Allie rolled her eyes but leaned over and examined the bandage, anyway. "I don't think they shaved too much, though it's hard to tell. In any case, it's covered up for now. By the way, you're going to get your wish."

"What wish?"

"The one about watching the squirrels in Ben's yard. You're going to recuperate at his house."

Though she had heard every word Allie had said about how anxious Ben was to see her, this announcement caused Jessie some trepidation. "Whose idea was that?"

Allie looked at her quizzically. "His, of course. The only way the doctor would let you go tomorrow was if you had somebody at home to wait on you hand and foot, and Ben volunteered for the privilege."

"But...what about his job?"

With a maddening lack of concern, Allie shrugged. "He said he'd make arrangements."

"What arrangements? He told me he'd be leaving town the day after Christmas."

Allie exhaled impatiently. "For Pete's sake, Jessie! Ask the man himself, why don't you? *I* don't know what his plans are."

Jessie remembered Ben's harshness after she'd pushed him into a confrontation the night before. He'd been willing enough then to be rid of her. Knowing how his overblown conscience worked, he must be thinking he owed it to her to nurse her through her convalescence. Which would come first, she wondered, the discharge of his self-imposed obligation, or his new assignment? Either way, she'd be alone. Jessie wasn't sure she could face the pain of separating again.

"Why can't *you* help me, Allie? You're between jobs right now."

Allie put her hands on her hips. "It's not that I can't or don't want to. Look, I was perfectly willing to take care of you at your apartment for as long as you needed me, and I said so. But Ben overruled me, okay? I fought the law, and the law won. End of story."

"Please, Allie. He just feels responsible that I got shot. I don't want to be in his house just because he feels guilty. He doesn't want me there, not really."

"That's not the way it looks to me. Why are you fighting this, Jessie? Do you think he's still mad at you over that disagreement you had? I can tell you without a shadow of a doubt, he's not."

Jessie gaped at her sister. "How did you know we'd quarreled?"

"*Ben* told me, how do you think?"

"*Ben* told you?"

Glancing around, Allie wondered aloud, "Is there an echo in here?"

"What did he say?"

Exasperated, Allie threw up her hands. "You two are the limit. Ben's crawling in the dirt because he thinks he's not good enough for you, and you're running away because you're afraid he doesn't want you. Why don't you just sit down and *talk* to each other?''

"Talking is what got me into trouble in the first place," Jessie muttered morosely.

"Then you didn't say the right things," said her twin in her matter-of-fact way, glancing at her watch. "And since my time is up, you'll have a chance to do better any minute now. I need to get in touch with Mom, anyway, and let her know what happened. I haven't called before now, because I wanted to be able to tell her definitely how you're doing. Do you have a message for her?"

"Tell her I love her and that she doesn't need to come flying up here. I'll be fine."

"Got it. I'll send in you-know-who now."

Allie kissed Jessie on the cheek, promised to come back that evening and sailed out the door.

Ben appeared almost immediately. Jessie's smile felt wobbly as she watched him walk into the room. He found her eyes and held them until he reached her bedside. Only then did he speak. "Hi."

She was so glad to see him, tears threatened, and she had to swallow to hold them back. "Hi, yourself."

"Are you doing okay?"

"Yes, I'm fine."

"How about your injuries? Are you in much pain?"

"Not much. Actually, I've got a buzz on from whatever's in this bag here."

Ben smiled crookedly and looked at the IV hanging from its stand. He followed the path of the dripping solution to the needle taped flat against the back of Jessie's hand. Then he sobered. "I want to say I'm sorry, Jess—sorry for everything."

He kept his eyes on her hand, as polite and distant as a stranger. Suddenly Jessie remembered that dark moment in the warehouse when she wished for a chance to start over. Well, here it was, and she'd be darned if she'd waste it.

"I'm sorry, too," she said.

His head came up. "About what?"

"Mostly because you're so far away." She held out her arm the way she had to Allie.

Ben's eyes lightened and his set expression relaxed. He started to reach for her, then paused. "I don't want to hurt you."

"You won't. Come here, Ben."

Carefully he leaned over the side of the bed and snaked his arms loosely around her. "Okay?"

"Closer. I won't break, honest."

She wrapped her arm around his neck and pulled him down until she could rest her head on his shoulder. He sighed, and Jessie felt the tension leave his big body as he held her gently to his chest.

"God, Jess, this feels so good." He burrowed his face in the hair on top of her head. "I've been going crazy, thinking I'd never hold you again."

"I'm here," she said. "I'm fine." She clutched him fiercely with her free arm and basked in the enveloping warmth of his strong, masculine embrace.

Ben shifted his weight. His elbow dug into the mattress. He shifted again. Unexpectedly he chuckled. "I hate to say this, sweetheart, but this metal railing is digging into my legs, and my back is killing me."

Jessie loosened her grip on his shoulders and lay back, amused. "At least I didn't clip you in the chin this time."

Ben straightened and studied the bed. "Let's try something else. This is your good leg, right?" While Jessie nodded, Ben untied his sneakers and slipped them off. "Move over and make room for me on this side of the mattress. The old battle-ax out at the desk will probably have my head for it, but what the hell—let's make the most of my five minutes."

"It's more like three now," Jessie said, delighted. She lifted the covers so they wouldn't rub the large bandage on her thigh and gingerly scooted her bottom closer to the edge of the mattress.

"If we're lucky, she isn't counting."

"Watch out for the IV," Jessie warned.

"I've got it. Here, put your arm around me so you don't pull the damned thing out." With caution, Ben eased onto the bed and lay down on top of the covers. "Now, where's the controller that operates—here it is."

After a couple of misses, he found the right button and raised the head of the automatic bed to a near-sitting position. Then he turned to Jessie, slipped his arm under her shoulders and settled back.

"That's better," he murmured. "Is your leg okay?"

"Every part of me is humming." She smiled up at him. For the first time she noticed his unshaven jaw and bloodshot eyes. "Have you had any sleep lately?"

"Not since nine o'clock yesterday morning, when I woke up alone in my bed and realized you'd sneaked off to call your agent without saying goodbye."

"Was that only yesterday? It seems like a lifetime ago, now."

"It almost was. I was so sure I would be poison to you, I made it a self-fulfilling prophesy."

Jessie frowned and put her hand over her lips. "Don't. It wasn't your fault that I opened the gate last night and practically walked into Ed Brock's gun muzzle so he had a convenient hostage to use against you. None of what happened afterward was your fault, either, any more than..." She bit her lip and finished lamely, "I just don't want you to blame yourself."

"Any more than what?" Ben prompted. "Go ahead—finish your thought."

"I'd better not. Last night I spouted off, and we saw how that turned out."

He laughed softly. "Don't look now, but you're making a good case for my blaming *you* for all of it."

Jessie blinked. He was right. Chagrined, she said, "There, you see how ridiculous it sounds?"

"Allie felt responsible, too—did she tell you? She said if she hadn't stolen the journal, you wouldn't have taken those bullets."

"Oh, brother," she said disgustedly.

"Do you see a pattern here? Allie, me, even you—all of us are trying to take the blame for what a bunch of criminals did to you."

"I'm glad you see that."

"You were going to say that last night wasn't my fault, any more than what happened to Maddie was my fault, weren't you?"

Sighing, Jessie gave in. "All right, yes. You think you should have been there to stop it, but there's no guarantee you could have changed anything, even if you had come home the weekend she was killed. *Presidents* have been shot, for goodness' sake, while they were surrounded by Secret Service men. And don't you dare get up and walk out of here just because I can't control my runaway mouth!"

She tightened her arm around him and pressed her head against his hard shoulder, though she knew very well if he wanted to leave, she couldn't stop him. "I don't care if you feel responsible for what happened to Maddie or me or anybody else, Ben. I don't care if you won't talk about your job or bare your soul to me. I don't even care if you take more undercover assignments, as long as you come back to me. I don't care about *anything* as much as I care about being with you."

Ben put his hand on her neck and caressed her jaw with his thumb. "I'm prepared to make adjustments."

She tilted her head back. "What?"

He looked into her eyes, his gaze intent and searching. "Allie told me I make you happy, Jess. I admit it's hard to believe that after what you've been through, but with that twin ESP thing the two of you have, she should know, right?"

His voice sent chills through her. "You do make me happy— happier than any woman has a right to be."

"The thing is," he said, "I want you back. You were right when you said I didn't give us a chance to work things out. I want to give it another shot, honey, if you're game."

Jessie's eyes filled with happy tears and his face blurred. "I'm game," she said softly.

Somehow, in spite of their positions, Ben found her lips in a brief, sweet kiss, then lay his head back down against the elevated mattress. "I talked to Leutzinger this morning while the doctors were working on you. He was all excited about recovering the journal and maybe getting Rory Douglas to testify against some major crime figures. And you know what? I couldn't have cared less. There was no sense of accomplishment, no feeling of triumph that we got the bastards. I just felt sick of the whole business. I've decided I'm not going to work undercover anymore, Jess. I'm going to back out of that assignment after Christmas."

"Oh, Ben, I'm so glad. I know somebody has to do it, but it was destroying you."

"If I have to, I'll quit the force altogether. But first I thought I would lobby the city council to put my neighborhood program into effect citywide. If they go for it, maybe they'll let me head it up. If not, I can always go back to school. I could get a masters in psychology or sociology and do social work of some kind. What would you think of that?"

"You're asking me?" Jessie asked cautiously.

Ben squeezed her. "I guess I'm getting ahead of myself. Do you . . . still love me, Jess?"

Her heart took wing at the direction of the conversation. "More than anything," she said fervently. "Can you live with that?"

"Honey, I can't live *without* it. That was another thing I realized this morning. I always believed I was destined to be a loner forever, but life looked pretty grim when I thought you weren't going to be in it anymore. The thing is, I love you, too."

Jessie shrieked. Somehow she managed to push herself higher and pull his head closer. She scattered messy kisses all over his face. The wound in her leg protested, but not unbearably, so she ignored it.

"Hey." He laughed. "Watch it, you're going to pull that IV loose."

"I don't care," she said happily.

"What's going on in here?" a strident voice demanded. "What are you doing on that bed? That's against hospital regulations."

Ben and Jessie turned to see the battle-ax, plump arms akimbo, glaring at both of them.

"Sorry, guys." Allie peeked out from behind the nurse's broad figure. "I couldn't keep her away any longer."

Ben beamed his most winning smile across the room. "Please don't make me leave yet, Nurse. I'm in the middle of a proposal."

"You told me you were already engaged to her," she said with a suspicious frown.

"Not quite, but if you'll give me a minute, I'll take care of it," Ben coaxed charmingly.

Apparently the woman's crusty exterior hid a romantic soul. Her face softened briefly before she stiffened her spine, tightened her lips and said gruffly, "Get on with it then. You have three minutes."

She herded Allie out in front of her and closed the door.

As soon as they were gone, Ben turned to Jessie and stopped the laugh that threatened by the simple expedient of covering her mouth with his. It was a wonderful kiss, one that soon touched the core of passion inside her. She opened her lips to tempt his tongue, and he accepted her lure. Their lips slid together deliciously, Ben's stroking tongue rough and agile in her mouth. Jessie moved against him in pleasure.

He drew back, cupped her tenderly through her hospital gown and whispered, "These wonderful breasts. They almost make me forget myself."

He kissed her again, but in Jessie's mind, he ended it too soon, lifting his mouth away and drawing her face to his chest. His breath had quickened, and she could feel the strong, rapid beat of his heart under her ear.

"Marry me, Jess," he rasped into her hair. "Let's fill those bedrooms upstairs in our house with our sons and daughters, make a family, and grow old together."

"That sounded more like an order than a proposal," Jessie sassed, happiness filling her heart to bursting.

He put his hand under her chin and tipped it up. She saw the playful warning in his eyes and heard it in his voice. "Are you suggesting I'm pushing you around again, woman?"

"Well . . ." she drawled.

"I've got about thirty seconds left before that old war-horse comes in here and throws me out," he growled. "Say yes, dammit."

She pretended to consider, then sighed in resignation. "Oh, very well. Yes, dammit."

When the war-horse returned, she found them laughing in each other's arms.

*   *   *   *   *

MIRA™

The brightest star in women's fiction!

This October, reach for the stars and watch all your dreams come true with **MIRA BOOKS**.

HEATHER GRAHAM POZZESSERE
Slow Burn in October
An enthralling tale of murder and passion set against the dark and glittering world of Miami.

SANDRA BROWN
The Devil's Own in November
She made a deal with the devil...but she didn't bargain on losing her heart.

BARBARA BRETTON
Tomorrow & Always in November
Unlikely lovers from very different worlds... They had to cross time to find one another.

PENNY JORDAN
For Better For Worse in December
Three couples, three dreams—can they rekindle the love and passion that first brought them together?

The sky has no limit with **MIRA BOOKS**.

Silhouette Books
is proud to present
our best authors, their best books...
and the best in your reading pleasure!

Throughout 1994, look for exciting books
by these top names in contemporary
romance:

DIANA PALMER
Enamored in August

HEATHER GRAHAM POZZESSERE
The Game of Love in August

FERN MICHAELS
Beyond Tomorrow in August

NORA ROBERTS
The Last Honest Woman in September

LINDA LAEL MILLER
Snowflakes on the Sea in September

*When it comes to passion,
we wrote the book.*

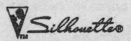

Jilted!

Left at the altar, but not for long.

Why are these six couples
who have sworn off love
suddenly hearing wedding bells?

Find out in these scintillating books
by your favorite authors,
coming this November!

#889 **THE ACCIDENTAL BRIDEGROOM**
by Ann Major
(Man of the Month)

#890 **TWO HEARTS, SLIGHTLY USED**
by Dixie Browning

#891 **THE BRIDE SAYS NO**
by Cait London

#892 **SORRY, THE BRIDE HAS ESCAPED**
by Raye Morgan

#893 **A GROOM FOR RED RIDING HOOD**
by Jennifer Greene

#894 **BRIDAL BLUES**
by Cathie Linz

Come join the festivities when six handsome
hunks finally walk down the aisle...

only from

SILHOUETTE® Desire®

JILT

INTIMATE MOMENTS
Silhouette.

NIGHT SHIFT, NIGHT SHADOW, NIGHTSHADE...
Now Nora Roberts brings you the latest
in her *Night Tales* series

NIGHT SMOKE
Intimate Moments #595

The fire was under control when American Hero
Ryan Piasecki got there. But he was an arson
inspector, so the end of the fire was the
beginning of his job. He scanned the crowd,
looking for that one face that might give him a
clue, a lead. Then he saw her.

She was beautiful, elegant, cool—an exotic
flower amid the ashes. She was an unlikely
candidate as an arsonist, but as a woman...

As a woman she probably wouldn't even give
him the time of day.

**Look for Ryan Piasecki and Natalie Fletcher's
story in NIGHT SMOKE, coming in October to
your favorite retail outlet. It's hot!**

**And now Silhouette offers you
something completely different....**

SPELLBOUND
ROMANCE

**In September, look for
SOMEWHERE IN TIME (IM #593)
by Merline Lovelace**

Commander Lucius Antonius was intrigued
by his newest prisoner. Although spirited
Aurora Durant didn't behave like any woman
he knew, he found her captivating. But why did
she wear such strange clothing, speak Rome's
language so haltingly and claim to fly in a silver
chariot? Lucius needed to uncover *all* Aurora's
secrets—including what "an air force pilot lost
in time" meant—before he succumbed to her
tempting lures and lost his head, as well as
his heart....

SILHOUETTE... Where Passion Lives

Don't miss these Silhouette favorites by some of our most
distinguished authors! And now you can receive a discount by
ordering two or more titles!

SD#05750	BLUE SKY GUY by Carole Buck	$2.89	☐
SD#05820	KEEGAN'S HUNT by Dixie Browning	$2.99	☐
SD#05833	PRIVATE REASONS by Justine Davis	$2.99	☐
IM#07536	BEYOND ALL REASON by Judith Duncan	$3.50	☐
IM#07544	MIDNIGHT MAN by Barbara Faith	$3.50	☐
IM#07547	A WANTED MAN by Kathleen Creighton	$3.50	☐
SSE#09761	THE OLDER MAN by Laurey Bright	$3.39	☐
SSE#09809	MAN OF THE FAMILY by Andrea Edwards	$3.39	☐
SSE#09867	WHEN STARS COLLIDE by Patricia Coughlin	$3.50	☐
SR#08849	EVERY NIGHT AT EIGHT		
	by Marion Smith Collins	$2.59	☐
SR#08897	WAKE UP LITTLE SUSIE by Pepper Adams	$2.69	☐
SR#08941	SOMETHING OLD by Toni Collins	$2.75	☐
	(limited quantities available on certain titles)		

TOTAL AMOUNT	$_____
DEDUCT: 10% DISCOUNT FOR 2+ BOOKS	$_____
POSTAGE & HANDLING	$_____
($1.00 for one book, 50¢ for each additional)	
APPLICABLE TAXES*	$_____
TOTAL PAYABLE	$_____
(check or money order—please do not send cash)	

To order, complete this form and send it, along with a check or money order
for the total above, payable to Silhouette Books, to: **In the U.S.:** 3010 Walden
Avenue, P.O. Box 9077, Buffalo, NY 14269-9077; **In Canada:** P.O. Box 636,
Fort Erie, Ontario, L2A 5X3.

Name:_____

Address:_____ City:_____

State/Prov.:_____ Zip/Postal Code:_____

*New York residents remit applicable sales taxes.
 Canadian residents remit applicable GST and provincial taxes.

SBACK-SN

Silhouette®
™